Also by Mira Lyn Kelly

The Wedding Date

May the Best Man Win

The Wedding Date Bargain

Back to You

Hard Crush

Dirty Player

Hot Friction

just this
once

MIRA LYN KELLY

sourcebooks
casablanca

Copyright © 2018 by Mira Lyn Kelly
Cover and internal design © 2018 by Sourcebooks, Inc.
Cover design by Dawn Adams
Cover image © Shirley Green Photography

Sourcebooks and the colophon are registered trademarks of Sourcebooks, Inc.

All rights reserved. No part of this book may be reproduced in any form or by any electronic or mechanical means including information storage and retrieval systems—except in the case of brief quotations embodied in critical articles or reviews—without permission in writing from its publisher, Sourcebooks, Inc.

The characters and events portrayed in this book are fictitious or are used fictitiously. Any similarity to real persons, living or dead, is purely coincidental and not intended by the author.

All brand names and product names used in this book are trademarks, registered trademarks, or trade names of their respective holders. Sourcebooks, Inc., is not associated with any product or vendor in this book.

Published by Sourcebooks Casablanca, an imprint of Sourcebooks, Inc.
P.O. Box 4410, Naperville, Illinois 60567-4410
(630) 961-3900
Fax: (630) 961-2168
sourcebooks.com

Printed and bound in Canada.
MBP 10 9 8 7 6 5 4 3 2 1

To Sheila Thompson

Chapter 1

FUCKING SHOW-OFF.

Sean stood at the front of the Chicago Wyse Hotel circle drive and watched Max rev his engine and pull his bike to a stop. The pair of shapely legs—a fair observation, not some pervy, inappropriate last-minute play on his part—bracketing Max's shifted, and then Sarah was stepping off the bike, somehow managing the frothy pile of white dress enough to keep herself decent in the process. The girl had skills.

Max crawled off the bike himself, and despite the guy's inexplicable refusal to tux up for the big day, the off-white suit and open shirt collar looked damned good. And Sarah… Well, shit, she was a knockout. Total boner material—or she would be if she wasn't marrying one of his best friends.

"Sarah, you're breathtaking. Absolutely radiant," Sean offered, the filter between his brain and mouth fully engaged on Wyse Hotel grounds.

"So awesome!" Molly squealed, bouncing over to her brother and future sister-in-law. "How was it getting over here?"

Her feet were bare, and there was a bruise the size of a quarter next to her shin. Sean felt a grin tugging at the corner of his mouth. How the hell had she gotten that? With Molly, it could be anything. As with that shock of hair in the front. When he'd seen her at eleven the night before, it had been purple, but now it was the hottest pink he could imagine.

"The ride of my life." Sarah beamed, toeing off the clunky motorcycle boots that had served as her "something borrowed" and exchanging them for the pair of strappy heels dangling from Molly's fingers.

"You ready to do this, Big Brother?" Molly asked, sticking her feet into her boots.

"Like eight years ago." Max grinned, then checking his watch, he looked back to Sarah. "Why'd we have to get here so early again?"

Sean knew why. Molly had clued him in the night before while making that little squick face of hers. Turns out Sarah was all about too-much-informationing Molly into sticking to a set of boundaries no one had managed with his girl before. So any time Molly even edged into inappropriate-question territory, Sarah gave her an answer sure to scar her for life. This time, the answer had to do with how hot it had made her to remember Max pulling up to CJ's wedding in a tux, and that actually *being* the bride on the back of Max's bike might mean a little "alone time" was in order before the ceremony.

Hence the additional room booked for the pre-wedding activities. Definitely information Sean didn't need about his very fucking favorite employee. But since Molly had to bear it, he did too.

Sarah tugged Max down to whisper in his ear, and Molly grimaced beside Sean.

Max's brows rose. His expression darkened. And then Molly wasn't the only one uncomfortable with the way the heat had just cranked up there on the sidewalk.

Without taking his eyes off his bride, Max tossed his

keys to Sean. "Yeah, so we're gonna go get cleaned up some before the ceremony. See you in about an hour."

Sarah had her finger hooked into a button on Max's shirt and was walking backward, leading him into the hotel.

Damn, Max had found his perfect match in that girl.

One of these days, Sean would find his own perfect match. He'd been looking. Even thought he might have found her once or twice. But despite everything on paper being *right*—the right name, the right school, the right looks and connections—he hadn't been able to pull the trigger. Then again, after the shit storm between his parents these past months, that was probably a good thing.

"It's not the infidelity," his mother had spat out that day in their Manhattan Wyse apartment. *"It's your lack of tact I take issue with, Warren. We've both had our indiscretions...but at least I had enough respect for you and what we've built together to make sure they didn't follow me home. You humiliated me."*

His father had straightened his tie where he stood, his voice as calm as if he'd been ordering room service. *"I thought it was enough. A million dollars, Beverly. It's not like I could force them—"*

Talk about pulling the curtain back.

And ever since, Sean had been looking at things... differently.

Reevaluating the plans he'd had in place forever.

Questioning exactly what he wanted his life to look like, and the only solid answer he'd come up with so far was...*not like that*.

But he'd figure all that shit out another day. *Today*

he was Max Brandt's best man, and he had one last gift for the groom.

"Hey, Moll," he said, catching her hand in his before she could dart off. "Hang back a sec."

"Yeah?" She peered up at him with those vast blue-sky eyes and that open, excellent smile.

Dropping her hand, he took a step back, giving her a jut of his chin. "You get the rent from your roommate yet?"

The big blues cut away, and her smile firmed into a flat line. "I said I'd take care of it."

She had said so. Six months ago, when the dick cheese holed up in her spare room stopped paying rent on time, sometimes skipping a whole month before giving half of what he owed. Why did she have to be so stubborn? If she'd let him, Sean would've had the rent paid in full and the guy out within a week. But no. Not little Miss Independent-to-a-Fucking-Fault.

That tightening sensation across his chest warned he needed to rein it in. Because as pissed as he was that this bullshit was still an issue—that Molly wouldn't let him help her—going nuclear beneath the awning of his hotel wasn't going to happen.

But he knew what would.

"You remember *what I told you*, Moll?"

She didn't answer, but the subtle tensing of her shoulders told him she remembered just fine.

"If *you* didn't take care of it, *I* would." He'd warned her, but she hadn't listened.

Turning abruptly, that sheer, creamy skirt twirling around her pretty knees, she glared up at him. Her arms crossed, turning her into a miniature version of her brother. Well, a miniature hot and cute and not-quite-as-tough-as-she-wished-she-was version.

"Don't you even think about getting Max involved in this." She sucked a breath through her nose and narrowed her eyes at him.

Damn, she was fun when she was fired up. But he had to stay tough—he was fired up too.

"Sean, just stay out of it. This is my problem. My apartment. My life. My situation to handle. If I wanted your interference, I'd ask for it. Understand?"

He nodded once, watching as she started inside for the wedding that would be held on the garden terrace.

He understood exactly. Molly had too much damned pride, and there was no fucking way he was going to stand by and let this *wad* screw her over for even one more day. Pulling his phone from his pocket, Sean hit Dial and waited for the call to connect. "Yeah, go ahead and load it up. Use the keys I left on the coffee table at my place to get in to hers… Yep, good."

Then, with a twirl of Max's keys around his finger and the perfect combination of testosterone and righteous indignation thundering through his veins, he hopped on Max's bike, revved the engine, and took off for Molly's place.

Get ready to meet your new roommate, Moll.

———

Three hours later, Sean stood at the edge of the dance floor in the Wyse Villa Ballroom watching Max dance with his brand-new bride to Ray LaMontagne's "You Are the Best Thing." Max was smiling down at her, looking like the happiest man alive.

They deserved this. The dance, the day, the future. The happily ever after. All of it.

A smooth hip bumped his, and Sean turned to find Molly beside him, swaying in time to the soulful love song. Slinging his arm around her shoulders, he pulled her in so she was tucked close to his side. His hand rested over her bare shoulder, his thumb playing with that silky braided strap in a back-and-forth rub, until... Shit, right—this was *Molly*.

Slip-ups happened.

She grinned up at him, completely oblivious to the mental lapse on his part. "They look so damn good together. Seriously, can you believe that's my brother out there? Commitment-phobe of the century?"

Sean shrugged. "Guess when you know, you know."

Letting out the kind of dreamy sigh Molly would skin him for noticing, she nodded. "I guess."

At the next chorus, the dance floor opened up to the wedding party.

Oh yeah. About time.

Without missing a beat, Sean had her hand in his. "Here we go, Moll. Let's show 'em how it's done."

He spun her out before reeling her back in, held her against his chest for a beat, and then laughed as they mirrored each other, advancing and retreating into the shared space. He didn't know how she did it, but even in those clunky boots, every move was fluid and free.

Pulling her in again, he sang along for a few lines, getting a kick out of his girl's absolute delight. He meant every damn word.

Molly was the best thing. The best friend he had.

And he was going to soak up all her laughter and

sweet smiles while he had them, because she was going to be *pissed* once they got back to her place.

"What's with that face?" Molly asked, moving easily in time with him.

"What are you talking about?" he replied, giving her his polished best, the practiced society-page-ready smile he'd perfected too many years ago to count. The one she hated.

She fake gagged, giving him a disgusted look. Definitely not photo ready. But that was Molly, and hell, it was probably what Sean loved about her most. She didn't care what anyone thought.

He'd caught a snap of her making that face about a year ago—with her lip curled, one lid a little lower than the other as she rolled her eyes at something he'd said— and instead of crawling all over him trying to steal his phone to delete it, she'd blown it up and posted it over the Belfast bar with a caption that read: *Don't Drink and Drive.*

Just thinking about it had the more genuine smile she never failed to score breaking through his professional one.

"There we go," she said, her head rocking to the beat of the music just a little. "That's more like it. But seriously, what's got your manties in a twist?" She scanned the ballroom around them. "Everything looks perfect. Your guys are bringing their A game tonight for sure. The food was tasty, the servers are rocking their jobs…and you know, being in the industry, I'm picky about that stuff."

She was. And the event team was working like a well-oiled machine. But then they'd be nuts not to, considering Sean signed their paychecks and the bride headed sales and marketing for Wyse Hotels' Midwest territory. Still, he liked hearing it.

Molly cleared her throat, waiting. Right, because she didn't bother with questions she wasn't fully expecting an honest answer to.

He shrugged. "Little jealous, maybe."

Her big, blue eyes went wide with alarm as she grabbed his lapel, jerking him close to her face. *Subtle*.

"Over Sarah?" Molly sounded likc she was going to puke, and who could blame her if she thought he was pining over her brother's new bride? Okay, and sure, Sarah was the one who got away, though technically speaking, she'd been Max's one who got away before she'd been Sean's, and ix-nay on the pining, because he'd seriously only begun to register the assortment of desirable traits that might have qualified her as a potential Mrs. Wyse when Max started beating his chest and tripping over his damn feet because of her.

No way Sean was getting in the way of that. His real friendships were too few and far too important to risk over a *maybe, possibly* kind of interest. So after Max's first chest thump, Sean had shut down the maybes and possibilities altogether. A skill he'd perfected over the years. And aside from the occasional clinically dispassionate observation that, under different circumstances, yeah, Sarah would have fit in with his former plans pretty damn well, he hadn't thought about her like that again.

"Nah, not Sarah," he assured Molly with a curt shake of his head. "But the nailing-down-their-forever, yeah, some."

Molly's smile went full-on imp. "Always a best man…never landing your bride?"

Sean coughed out a laugh. Because *this girl*. "Something like that," he acknowledged.

Then more seriously, she added, "Must be nice to have someone love you like that." Cutting him a sidelong look, her eyes narrowed. "Not that I'm interested."

Right. She didn't like people to know what a softy she was underneath her tough outer shell, but he knew the truth. Molly was all marshmallow inside. Sweet and gooey and his favorite platonic treat.

He tugged her close. "*Liar*. But it's okay, Moll. Your secret's safe with me. You want *lurve*," he joked.

A motorcycle boot on his toes was her answer, but the way she was fighting that grin, her cheeks turning a pretty shade of pink, was reward enough. "Yeah, right."

"You know you do," he added, all singsong just above her ear. More of the blush filled her cheeks, hitting him like a drug and giving him everything he wanted.

Teasing Molly had been his favorite pastime since she'd basically moved into the quad he was sharing with Max, Jase, and Brody the second week of their freshman year in college. She'd been fifteen, still in high school, but so desperate to escape the war zone at home that she'd been willing to make the hour commute each day. It still killed him to think about that girl who'd been as lost and displaced as they came. Sullen and isolated. Shut off from everyone, even her brother.

It got to him. Seeing a kid like that with eyes so sad.

His family wasn't anything like the Brandts', but he knew what it was like to feel alone, so he'd made Molly his pet project. Chatting her up as if they were long-lost friends. Carrying on conversations between them where he'd ask her a question and then—because even pulling a single-word response from her could be damned near impossible—answer for her, making up outrageous claims. Clowning around and making faces at her every time he caught her sneaking a look from beneath the too-long fall of white-blond hair that was always in her eyes. Until finally, one day about three months into school, he did it. He teased that first smile out of her, and—*Christ*—he'd never gotten over it. Even eleven years later, Molly's smile still topped his list of favorite things.

"Whatever. I'm not the one who's been taking applicants for a wife for the past five years. Looking at every spoken-for female, like *there's another one who got away*. You're the one desperate for love."

He barked out a laugh, knowing she was only half joking. He'd been serious about settling down, but not like that. "Love wasn't really the objective."

"Even worse." She snorted. "But I know. You wanted the partner. The *pedigree*."

"Come on," he groaned, though why he gave her the satisfaction, he had no idea.

"The right *school*, the right *name*, the right *connections*. The right *breeding*."

"Jesus, you make it sound like I was looking for a dog." He hadn't said half of that stuff, and the truth was, none of that really mattered to him. But it did matter to his parents. And he'd been going along.

Blindly.

Looking at Max and Sarah, who had that blissed-out, eye-staring thing happening, he couldn't help but wonder if he'd already blown his chance at that kind of love. There had been a lot of women over the years. Women he'd shared a night with but refused to give a chance beyond that because they hadn't fit the vision of what his future was supposed to look like.

Molly followed his stare and then stopped dancing.

"What?" he asked.

"I see you ogling their happily ever after." She crossed her arms in that mini-Max stance that always put a smile on Sean's face. "Just so we're clear, I'm not making any deals with you about five years from now, if both of us are still single. No matter how many fancy hotels you have under your belt."

Sean coughed a laugh into his hand, scanning the room out of habit to see who might be watching.

"Have it your way," he replied. Then giving her a devilish grin, he pulled her back into the dance. They'd been to enough weddings over the years that she fell into step without a thought. "But you're missing out. The hotels under my belt are really, *really* big. Awe inspiring. *Life changing* even. You should be so lucky to get your hands on one of my hotels."

A disgusted grunt. She loved him.

"I see someone's trying to compensate again." Her pitying look hit all his sweet spots.

As to compensating…not really. But what he *was* trying to do was make the most of Molly's good spirits before she found out what he'd done.

There were times when he kind of got off on her temper. But generally, it wasn't directed at him. This time, it would be. And with that spine-deep stubborn streak she had going, there was no telling how long

it would be before she let him off the hook. But he
wouldn't back down. And even if he wanted to, it was
too late. The roommate was gone. Sean had gotten the
text from the movers he'd hired to pull the guy's stuff
from the apartment, and Gary was out.

Molly would thank him. Eventually.

After she'd tortured him for a while, but whatever.
He'd had enough of the asshole taking advantage of her.

The next song that came on was one of those older
classic indies, with a slow beat and a dark, lulling melody
Molly couldn't get enough of. Wrapping an arm around
her waist, Sean pulled her close. Her arms linked around
his neck, her head falling back as she let him lead, one of
those gorgeous contented smiles on her face.

Maybe she wouldn't be mad for too long.

He hoped not.

Leaning over her so she bowed back while the singer
held a note and the bass pumped, he drew a breath close
to her neck. Damn, she smelled good.

"What is that, coconut?" he asked when he pulled
her back up.

"Yeah, I just got it. Smells good, right?" Her hips
following his, she cocked her head to the side, offering
him another whiff of her neck.

Going back in for a second hit, he nodded. "It smells
like one of those candy cocktails we were drinking down
in Mexico."

Molly's eyes squinted, and he had the feeling he was
witnessing her attempt at a sexy look. "I'm *intoxicating*."

Yep. Supposed to be sexy. "Watch out, men. She
comes across sweet, but she'll knock you on your ass if
you aren't looking."

Her answering nod was pure delight. "Hells to the yeah."

Damn, she was cute.

But now he was thinking about the guys who were always sniffing around her, and he mentally added: Even if Molly *wasn't* strong enough to knock them out, Sean and her brother sure as hell were.

"Sean, you are *such* a cock blocker," Molly hissed, elbowing her favorite partner in crime in the ribs. The guy would not leave her alone. "Seriously, you're cramping my style. People are going to think we're together."

"Cock blocking?" Sean snorted from behind her at the south bar, not showing any signs of stepping back. Not that she'd thought he would. Sean tended to do what he wanted. And in all honesty, when he wanted to hang out with her, she didn't mind. Even if it was costing her the hottie bartender who'd been giving her his A game all night. Clingy Sean was her favorite Sean. He didn't show up too often, but when he did, he was full of hugs and private jokes and the dirty, crass comments she'd loved since way back when he was just another college kid. Back before he'd become the face of the Chicago Wyse and tucked all his awesomely bad behavior behind the facade of his proper public image. "Moll, you know I love it when you talk like you have a pair, but I'm pretty sure there's nothing for me to block."

She rolled her eyes. "Obviously, the blockage would take place from the other side. I don't need you getting in the way of… Gah, never mind."

Sean craned his neck and searched the crowd. "One

of these guys? I thought you had a thing about not dating cops. And so far as I can tell, they're the only single guys here."

"Hmm," she replied noncommittally, because no way was she going to give up the identity of her flirty bartender. Too much fun watching Sean try to weasel it out of her.

He didn't like that. Suddenly, everyone was a suspect, earning that overprotective, narrow-eyed look that if she really let her imagination stretch, she could almost pretend was a distant cousin—*a very distant cousin*—to jealousy. It wasn't. Sean didn't think of her like that. He thought of her as the little sister he'd never had. Which made her lucky, and she was totally good with that.

The wild crush of her youth was almost completely tamed these days—and had been for years. Sure, there was the occasional flare-up, but she knew better than to give it too much room to breathe, and usually, she had those rogue emotions back to heel within a couple of days, if not hours.

She was *that good*.

"Tell me it's not that guy Jimmy," Sean grumbled. "The one who's always getting carried out of the bathroom."

This time, *her* eyes were narrowing. "A little credit, please." Like she would be waiting on a notorious puker? Not likely. Besides, Sean was right. She didn't date cops. Ever. In fact, she worked tremendously hard to make sure she didn't date anyone within her brother's immediate circle. She liked her privacy and independence, which were easier to maintain with a little distance. Sure, if she was with a guy for any extended period, eventually Max and everyone got to know him…but she generally tried to cast her reel into distant ponds. More convenient when stuff went south, and safer for the guy if he turned out to be not so cool to her.

"I know, I know," Sean assured, though he wouldn't have brought it up if he wasn't at least slightly concerned. Annoying, but this was too great a day to hold much of a grudge.

"Come on," he cajoled. "Give me a hint."

"I don't think so."

"A baby hint. Like, which side of the room is he on?"

For a second, Molly pretended she was ready to give him that much, but then she closed her mouth and shook her head. "A lady doesn't kiss and tell."

She knew it was wrong to get off on that stunned scowl, but come on, Sean's slack-jawed reaction was priceless. "You were kissing?"

"Wouldn't you like to know?" she said, giving him her most mysterious look. Which might have been a smidge too much, because then Sean was shaking his head and laughing into his fist.

"As a matter of fact, Molly, I would. And if you don't tell me, mark my words, I'll ruin your shot at picking up anyone at this wedding."

Brows rising, she grinned. "And just how do you plan to do that?"

Sean smoothed his already-perfect golden-brown hair, scanning the ballroom. "You were worried about people thinking we're together…and that was just from me hanging around. You don't think I can do better?"

Molly gulped, because she didn't doubt he could do

way better. But he wouldn't. Because he was Sean and she was Molly. Period.

"I'm not going to leave your side, Moll," he warned, rolling up to the balls of his feet. "Where you go, I go. Feel like taking a load off? I'll join you for a drink at the table. Want to dance? Hello, partner. Some fresh air sound about right—?"

"And what if I feel like taking a tee-tee break? You gonna join me in the little girls' room, Sean?"

The smirk dropped from his lips, but his eyes held steady. "Pass. But I'll be happy to wait outside the door."

Molly shook her head and laughed. "I guess there are worse things than having you as my shadow for a few hours. But just so you know…I'm still not talking."

Sean's expression was every kind of victorious—and then it wasn't. He tugged at his collar and leaned closer. Looking almost nervous.

"Hey, Moll, the reason you don't care about me cramping your style at the wedding isn't because you already made plans to meet up with this guy later, is it?"

"Umm…no plans."

This was weird. Sean was a chatty guy, and when it came to deets about the men she'd broken up with, he couldn't get enough. But as a rule, when it came to her sex life *in the now*, Sean tended to steer clear. That whole residual big-brother thing, she figured. So having him ask about the night to come was unusual.

But not as much as the look of relief on his face at hearing she didn't have plans.

"What's up with you?" she demanded.

His brows rose, and he took a step back. "Me? Nothing." Then reaching for the tie that wasn't there—because neatening his look was sort of like snuggling with a security blanket for Sean—he shrugged. "I was just thinking I'd crash at your place after the reception and didn't want to get in your way."

Now things were really getting weird. "My place. Sean, we're literally seven floors beneath *your* place. In the *hotel* you own. What gives?"

"I'm having some work done, actually. And you know how I hate to stay in hotel rooms."

She grinned, because that was one of her favorite quirks about Sean. Wyse was one of the most successful luxury hotel chains in the world...but Sean had a thing about staying in the rooms. Whatever.

"It's fine. But this better not be some ploy to muscle my roommate."

The corners of Sean's mouth pulled down into an exaggerated frown as he shook his head. "Promise. I won't give your roommate a hard time at all."

"And you're staying on the couch. Last time you crashed in my bed, you took up the whole thing, and I couldn't sleep at all." He was big. Not quite as tall as her brother or the other guys, but still, six feet was a lot of man. Especially when said man was off-limits and keeping a solid twelve inches of space between them was the only way she could ensure she didn't wake up with her legs tangled with his or her mouth against his chest.

"I'll stay out of your bed."

She eyed him a minute longer just to make sure he knew she was serious and then gave up her grin. "Okay, deal."

Chapter 2

Sean had known it would be rough when Molly realized what he'd done. But stepping into her Southport apartment at 1:43 a.m. and seeing that the douche who'd been taking advantage of her for months was finally gone was totally worth Molly shoving futilely at his chest as she put all her weight into trying to push him out the door he'd just walked in.

"You rotten…low-down…stinking…jerk!"

Patting the back of her hand, Sean grinned and sidestepped her to walk farther into the apartment. "Settle down, Moll. I get that you're pissed, and I'm sorry. But it's been months, and you still hadn't done anything."

"So you did?" she screeched, storming around him with her fists balled tight at her sides. "After I told you I would handle it. After I explained in no uncertain terms that I didn't need your help."

"Yeah. After all that. Because you didn't handle it. And you really did need my help. That piece of garbage wasn't going anywhere. You should have seen him when I showed up here this afternoon."

Gary had been stretched out on her sofa with a skillet of burned eggs that looked hours old half spilled out on the cushion beside him.

"Oh my God. Before the wedding," she said accusingly. "You took Max's bike and came over here."

A nod. That's what he'd done, and he'd do it again.

Gary was a total pig with zero respect for Molly or her space, as evidenced by his regular habit of bringing company home with him at 4:00 a.m. after the late-night bars kicked them out and then firing up the Xbox at full volume. Molly worked three jobs and paid half Gary's rent, so the least he could do was let her sleep, but no. He ate her food and drank her beer, even when she asked him not to.

As if that wasn't enough, she kept finding little things broken around the apartment. A mug, a tiny blown-glass motorcycle Sean had found for her in Prague a few years back, a chair, and a dozen other things he didn't even want to think about. And it wasn't like Gary even came clean about it. Molly would just stumble across the toaster oven with the door hanging off the front or the fresh dent in the plaster next to the bathroom.

She'd mention it, but Gary didn't have the money for rent, so he sure as hell wasn't kicking in extra to cover the damage. And Molly just let him get away with it again and again because the guy had this down-on-his-luck thing she couldn't turn her back on.

But Sean was through letting the weasel whine his way out of the offenses. It had been time for him to go, so Sean made Gary an offer he couldn't refuse.

One that involved a handful of bills, a new job, and a week's stay at a hotel. Not the Wysc. And not of the guy's choosing. Anything he didn't want to take with him was at a storage locker. It was all very up and up. Because Molly was convinced the guy was helpless, some tragic victim of circumstance. And she had that thing about people—even shitty people—worrying about whether they'd be able to keep a roof over their head or be out on the street.

She'd known that worry for too many years herself, thanks to her epically asshole-ish dad. Not her biological father, who she'd never met, but Vic Brandt, the bastard married to her mom when she got pregnant with another man's kid. Something Vic had never let any of them forget and had held over their heads like a threat for fifteen years.

Blowing a slow stream of breath through his nose, Sean unclenched his fists and reminded himself that Vic was dead. And Molly had Sean and all the guys looking out for her these days.

Meeting her eyes, he nodded. "That's right. I handled it before the wedding, and now he's out of your hair."

"What did you do to him? You know what a hard time he's been having since he lost his last job. Where's he going to stay? What's—"

"I got him a place to stay and a job." Sean didn't mention the money or the threats. "He's good." Better than he should be.

"And I'm out his rent!" Molly exclaimed, her arms flying to her sides.

Now this was getting frustrating. "*He wasn't even paying you all of it*."

"But he was paying me *most of it*, which was better than the *none* I'll have until I find someone else." She leaned in to him. "That was money I needed, Sean."

He knew. Because Molly was all about building her security. And part of that involved a plan to buy the building she was living in. She'd been saving for the down payment but more slowly than she should have.

"Well, good thing I already found you another roommate." He'd had enough of this. "It's late, Moll. Let's talk about it tomorrow."

"What?" Molly coughed out, indignation written all over her too-proud, too-pretty face. "We're not done here. I don't know who you *think* you've lined up for me, but the only person who decides who comes or goes in *this* apartment is me, mister."

"Yeah?" He ducked, catching Molly at the waist with his shoulder. Ignoring her squeal of protest and the two fists banging their way down his back, he hoisted her up and started toward her room. "You want me to get the freeloader back in here?"

Silence and then a low growl.

"That's what I thought."

"Don't you *that's what I thought* me, Sean. You had no right, and no way am I letting you pick who moves in here."

"Moved," he corrected, grabbing the loop of keys she'd thrown on the table when she walked in.

"What?" she asked, stilling where she hung over his shoulder.

Walking to her bedroom—and its door with the dead bolt she'd installed four roommates ago and locked from the inside at night—he flipped through the keys. He'd about lost his mind when she'd put in the dead bolt, because what did that say about how safe she felt in her own apartment?

"*Moved* in. Past tense. Your roommate's already here."

"What the *eff*, Sean," she hissed, starting to struggle anew. "There's someone here already?" She craned, pushing her palm into his face as she tried to get a look at the other bedroom. "Who is it?"

And the fact that she'd started whispering now was one of the best things about his girl. Because he knew why she was doing it. She wouldn't want someone with the shit luck of ending up as her new roomie to know they weren't wanted. She wouldn't want to make them uncomfortable.

Little did she know, but the way she was squirming over his shoulder and gripping his belt about two inches above his ass was making her new roomie very uncomfortable.

Enough of that. Flipping her forward, Sean dropped Molly onto the bed with a bounce that sent her flowy skirt billowing high around her thighs as he followed her down. She gave one futile shove at his chest and then gave up the fight, her scowl firmly in place.

And that was the opening he'd been waiting for. "It's me, Molly."

All that hot challenge cleared from her eyes, and a searching confusion took its place. "What did you say?"

"I'm your new roommate."

She blinked a few times, looking away before meeting his eyes again.

And without all that feisty defiance coming back at him full strength, Sean was suddenly aware of the position he'd put them in. The way he'd braced on his arms above her with one knee planted between her legs and the other outside her thigh. The rise and fall of her chest too close to his and the open vulnerability in those big, blue eyes peering up at him.

Shit.

The lines with Molly were clear, and sure, he had fun

nudging at them from time to time. But this friendship was too important for him to ever risk actually crossing one of those lines. So what the fuck was he still doing on top of her, still staring into her eyes? *In her bed?*

Especially when he'd just signed on to share this space for the next however many months.

Clearing his throat, he backed off the bed, doing his damnedest not to look at how much of her bare thigh was on display.

"Wait, Sean," she said, sitting up. "You can't just drop this on me and walk out."

He could, and he would, and it would be a hell of a lot better if he didn't explain why. "Night, roomie. We'll talk more in the morning."

Drumming her fingers over the kitchen butcher block, Molly stared at the front door, her temper rising with every second that passed. This was one of those moments when she wished she were the kind of woman who could manage a full set of nails. The satisfaction of each click had to be greater than what she was getting with her fingertips silently padding against the wood. And while she was wishing, it would have been nice to be an early riser. This lying-in-wait would probably have been more effective if she'd been glaring at Sean's bedroom door when he stumbled out at five or whatever insane hour he'd gotten up that morning. Instead, here she was, waiting for him to get back from the gym at nearly eleven, a half-eaten bowl of cereal beside her.

Finally, the door opened, and she shored up her scowl, preparing to lay into him.

"Hey, Moll, how'd you sleep?" he asked, breezing into the apartment with that sun-god smile going full tilt. Like he'd had an awesome morning already and wasn't taking the threat of her impending wrath seriously at all.

"Terribly," she stated flatly, ready to set him straight. "I guess my best friend betraying me, totally disregarding my wishes, and having no respect for my feelings about my own home just got in the way of those perfect z's."

One neat sandy-blond brow pushed up, tugging the corner of his mouth with it. "That so? 'Cause I was feeling pretty shitty about stalking off after springing the news on you last night. Came back about fifteen minutes later, and you were out cold." Dropping his gym bag inside his room, he turned back to her and ran his fingers through his sweat-dried hair.

Molly tried not to notice the way his gray Bears T-shirt hugged his shoulders and chest or how it rode up, skimming the low waist of his white basketball shorts.

Post-workout Sean was undeniably hot, but this was important.

"I was fake sleeping," she lied. She didn't even remember her head hitting the pillow. "I heard you coming and didn't want to talk to you again."

Nodding amiably, he walked past her and grabbed a bowl and a spoon. "Moll, you know you never need to *fake it* with me."

She snorted, because of course he couldn't resist.

Then sliding onto the open stool across from her, he started to fill his bowl with Count Chocula. "Pass the milk."

She handed it over and watched as he poured half the amount she liked in her bowl. He wouldn't even drink the milk after. So weird.

s

"Sean, I'm mad."

"Yeah, I know."

"It wasn't your place."

His eyes met hers, and she squirmed a little, because maybe that wasn't a totally fair or accurate statement. She and Sean looked out for each other. They had for years.

He blew out a slow breath. "You're right. It wasn't my place. I just can't stand seeing guys like Gary take advantage of you. And I guess I lost it. I'm sorry, Moll."

Molly bit her lip and nodded. It was hard to stay mad at Sean when his heart was in the right place. And the truth was that Gary had needed to go, but the guy had been so down on his luck. She just hadn't been willing to pull the rug from under him, especially since she hadn't found a better prospect yet. And while he hadn't been paying everything he owed, the money he had given her mattered.

Mr. Razul had told her he'd wait, but he wouldn't wait forever. If she wanted this building, and she did, she needed the cash. Which brought her to the stack of bills tucked beneath her napkin dispenser. It looked like pity money, which Sean really ought to know better than to try to give her.

"Look, fine, I get why you wanted Gary out. I wanted him out too, though I would have preferred his exit to be on my terms. But that aside, what are *you* doing here?"

Spooning a bite into his mouth, Sean chewed around his words. "I live here. Rent's on the counter. First and last."

She shook her head, not wanting to laugh again, but *this* Sean—this slightly disheveled, imperfectly mannered, borderline belligerent Sean, with the mischievous eyes and good intentions—got to her in a way she couldn't always resist.

"You don't live here. You live at the Wyse. In an apartment probably four times the size of this place, with a view that's to die for."

He shrugged, shoveling another giant spoonful into his mouth. "A view to die for and an interior in serious need of modernization. I wasn't lying to you last night. I'm getting some work done on the place. Though in the name of full disclosure, renovations don't start until tomorrow." He pointed his spoon at her. "But now that I think about it, the movers were there getting my stuff out while we were at the wedding. So I really was having work done yesterday, and without my bedroom stuff, it really wasn't livable."

So he hadn't actually lied. "Wow, and that teaspoon of inadvertent honesty sprinkled on this mountain of deceit is actually supposed to make me feel better?"

Sean stood and carried his bowl to the sink, where he washed it out and dropped it into the drying rack before turning back to her. Hands hooked on the sink edge behind him, he crossed one ankle over the other. "No. But being able to sleep without your bedroom dead bolt should. Or just helping out a friend in need?"

Her mouth fell open. "And now with the guilt?"

Amusement lit his eyes. "Whatever it takes."

Standing up, she propped a fist on her hip. "Too bad I don't guilt easy. Not when my so-called friend in need has another apartment available to him just a few floors away."

The half smile said she'd nailed him. His hands came up in front of him. "My parents' place?"

"Yeah. Aren't they heading back to New York this week? It'll be empty and—"

"Hell no. You've been there. It's a museum. The furniture is uncomfortable as fuck, and I can't put my feet on anything. I've got a meeting with them tonight before they head back, and I'm already uncomfortable."

"A meeting? You're having Sunday dinner with them."

"Tomato, tomahto. Besides, I can't move out. Not yet. The minute I vacate, Gary is going to be back at your door with another sob story, and you're going to be right back where you started. Stuck with the most pathetic freeloader of all time. Both of you need to move on, and I'm the guy who's going to help you do it. Like it or not."

Her brows shot high, because that sounded suspiciously like the gauntlet being thrown.

"I don't think so, Wyse." Sean really had done her a favor, since she hadn't had the heart to kick Gary out herself. And even more so by letting the guy think that Sean would be moving in himself, because Gary was the epitome of the three *P*s. Pushy, persistent, and pathetic. If he knew the second room was available, he'd have been working her over to let him back in already.

But still, no way was Sean going to tell her how *it* was. *She told him* how it was. Just maybe not tonight.

He walked over to the couch and dropped into the deep cushions. "You want to watch *Bob's Burgers* or *Dark*?"

"We're caught up on *Bob's Burgers*," she said, taking the far side of the couch and pulling her legs up so she was sitting cross-legged. "And don't get too comfortable. I want to see what happens next, but this conversation isn't over."

He slumped comfortably, kicking up his legs. That damn half smile on his lips. "Fair enough."

She was glad they'd shifted into a more agreeable place, but Sean was definitely going to have to go. Not today or maybe not even tomorrow. But soon. He'd have to. Because she remembered what it had been like the last time they lived together, and no way could she go back to that.

Sure, she was older now, and it had been years since that unfortunate, misplaced crush had flared up…but still, having Sean on the other side of her wall every night was very different from indulging in the occasional crushy moment at her place or once-every-blue-moon post-shower, low-slung-towel sighting. Every day though? A girl could get ideas when she had too much quality Sean time on her hands. A girl could get feelings. And she knew firsthand just how hard it was to wrestle those tenacious emotions back to the friendly side of the fence. So no. No way was Sean spending a month sharing a wall with her.

But for now? "We saw that one… Yeah, there we go. Perfect."

Chapter 3

"BUT *LIVING WITH HER*?" BEVERLY WYSE TSKED WITH THE kind of long-suffering sigh only a mother could muster. She offered her flawlessly smooth cheek for her husband's kiss as he pressed a glass of wine into her hand and then claimed the wingback chair beside her in their Wyse apartment a few floors up from where Sean's place was being worked on. There hadn't been mention of the "embarrassment" since his father "handled it," and the ease with which his parents had slid so seamlessly back into their roles of perfect parents and doting spouses was freaky. But nothing compared to the discovery that, after a lifetime of wishing for siblings to help fill the empty apartments his parents would leave him in on rotation around the country and world, he had two brothers. Frank Lemoy, born five years after Sean, and Derek Greggory, born two months before.

"Darling, you know we *adore* Molly. She's like family. But you have to think about what it *looks* like."

Sean grimaced, forcing himself not to shift on the stiff love seat. Even after everything that had happened, he didn't like seeing disapproval in his parents' eyes. But where did they get off, judging anything he did? Especially when it came to Molly.

"It's temporary. A month. Two at the most," he assured them smoothly. "And it's not like I'm on anyone's radar these days."

He had Derek to thank for that. His older brother had
been the one to come to Sean about Frank. And what
a fucking shit show that had been. The asshole from
boarding school who'd made Sean's life a living hell for
four years showing up at his office a few months back
with not just the news they were actually brothers, but
that they had another brother, and Frank had been about
to come after their dad with a blackmail scheme. So
yeah, Derek had really come through. Which had been
about as easy for Sean to swallow as a pint of nails, but
at least it meant Sean was only making the papers when
he worked the society circuit.

"Don't be naive, Sean," his father stated flatly.
"You're always on someone's radar."

Pursing her lips, his mother agreed with a regal nod.
"Think about Valerie. I know you haven't made your
mind up on that front, but she deserves your respect and
discretion." Her stare hardened. "You will not embarrass her, or us."

The warning rubbed.

He and Valerie were compatible in many ways, and
Sean knew both families were expecting a union. But
there was something missing. They'd gone out several
times over the past couple of years—they got along,
and he'd even go so far as to say they were friends—
but it had been all too easy to let their relationship
slide. As things stood, he and Valerie were very much
on hold and had been for some time. Both were in
agreement that if they found someone else, wonderful. If not, perhaps they would revisit the subject at
a later date.

Not exactly the stuff of fairy tales.

"What if I cut ties with Valerie?" he asked, more curious how his parents would respond than anything.

Lips pursed, his mother studied the crystal glass in her hand as she addressed him. "That would be disappointing, to say the least. Honestly, I expect better judgment from you, Sean. Valerie is such a lovely girl, and her *connections…*" She sighed almost wistfully. "She would be such an asset to you if you would just let her."

"We've seen you together," his father added gruffly. "You get on well, that's clear enough. But that said, if you truly object to Valerie, we'll simply find another suitable match." Then after a pause. "Perhaps Gretchen and Miles's girl?"

The words shouldn't have surprised Sean, but actually hearing them made him bristle.

"Jesus, do I even have a choice?"

"Don't be ridiculous," his mother chided. "Of course you have a choice. It's not as if we'd force you to marry someone you didn't find agreeable. We want you to be happy, Sean. And part of being happy means finding a partner equipped to handle the position and responsibilities of being your wife. Of being a Wyse."

Being a Wyse. He wasn't even sure what that meant anymore. Knowing how to hide who you truly were, even from those you were supposed to trust most? Using the business as a justification for living a lie?

It didn't feel right to him.

His father cleared his throat. "You understand as well as anyone the importance of finding someone suitable… appropriate, if you will."

His parents weren't saying anything new, but Sean's body and mind rebelled at the words.

"What if that wasn't the way it turned out?" he challenged.

The temperature in the room dropped, and both his parents grew eerily still. Then his father asked, "What are you suggesting?"

"I'm just asking… What if I fell in love? Hypothetically, of course, what if I fell in love with someone like Molly… and I wanted to marry her?"

It wouldn't happen. That's not how it was between them. But if it was… Molly was beautiful, intelligent, funny, and driven, and she respected hard work. She was his best friend, and suddenly he wanted to know how his parents would handle it. Because it was one thing to settle for a mutually advantageous marriage when he'd never been in love. When it seemed a practical solution at no emotional cost.

But what if things were different with him?

How would his parents react if he was lucky enough to find that elusive connection he'd only witnessed in his friends' lives?

"Sean, you're being difficult," his mother said dismissively as she checked her jewelry.

He'd been serious, but the warning look in his father's eyes told him he'd pushed far enough. For the life of him, he couldn't figure out why he'd asked at all.

"Thanks, Carson," Sean offered, stepping aside as his assistant for the past three years wheeled in a gleaming luggage cart laden with the bags Sean had taken to Molly's place Saturday.

"She dropped them with the concierge this afternoon. Said you'd be expecting them."

Sean grinned. He'd been expecting something.

Hell, Sean had never known a woman to get her back up more over unsolicited rescues. And yeah, he had a pretty good idea where that chronic case of independence had originated. No one could grow up the way Molly had without it leaving a mark. But her shitty upbringing was only part of the problem. There'd also been those years when they'd lived together at school.

She'd been young, and even when she wasn't young anymore, she'd been younger than they were. He and Max might have been a smidge overprotective, which apparently Molly hadn't entirely appreciated. So he got it. These days, she preferred him to stay out of her business…and he hadn't.

"Appreciate you seeing to this stuff."

"Not a problem. And if you're good, I'll take off for the night."

"Thanks, Carson. See you tomorrow."

Standing at his desk, his back to the floor-to-ceiling view of Lake Shore Drive and the lakefront, Sean dug through one of the bags. Molly had collected the clothing and toiletries he'd brought to her place, packed them as neat as a pin, and tucked a note scrawled on Wyse stationery within.

Looks like you forgot a few things when you left this morning. Wouldn't want you to miss them tonight at your parents' place.

Cute. But not a chance.

—◆◆◆—

Walking up the dark sidewalk from the L, Molly noted the shifting glow from the TV in the windows of her apartment. A smile tugged at her lips. She'd known he'd be back. No way would Sean let her off that easily. And while there was no way *she'd be backing down that easily either*, a part of her wasn't complaining about getting to spend a few minutes together before she kicked it for the night. Sean might be driving her nuts right now, but the guy was still her best friend.

Letting herself in through the security door, she started up the stairs. She'd hassle him a little first, just so he didn't get the wrong idea. And then she'd see if he wanted to split a frozen pizza with her, because cripes, her shift at Belfast had taken it out of her tonight. But at the top of the stairs, she realized it was close to two in the morning, and Sean had been up since five.

Forget pizza. The guy had probably fallen asleep on her couch after working one of his fourteen-hour days.

As quietly as she could, she eased the key into the lock and slipped into the dimly lit apartment. Closing the door with a quiet snick, she turned toward the couch and cocked her head at the sight of him sprawled across the cushions. *Wearing the clothes she'd packed that afternoon*.

Her eyes narrowed. Maybe quiet was the wrong approach.

With a flick of the lights, she bellowed her greeting, "Hey, did I wake you?"

"What the…?" Sean jerked upright, his usually perfect hair sticking in every direction at once.

One chunky motorcycle boot hit the wall with a satisfying thud and then the other. "*Wow*, long night at Belfast," she said, strolling over to the couch where she allowed herself a single tousle of Sean's hair before bouncing onto the cushion beside him. "Somehow, one of our cases of Ketel One got stocked in the wrong area, and I ended up having to go through the whole last delivery to double-check our inventory. Two waitresses called in last minute, a bartender cut his hand open, and Brody was off at some dinner meeting with one of his vendors. One of the pretty ones, so I didn't want to call him, no matter how late it got. How was your day?"

The fog was clearing from Sean's eyes as he rubbed a palm over the golden stubble of his jaw. "Mine?" He shook his head again and looked at her, that bleary look almost gone.

"Yeah." She grinned, bouncing again and giving him a jostling shoulder bump. "What did you do today?"

With a shake of his head, he cleared his throat and met her cranked-up grin with one of those half smiles responsible for panties dropping around the world. "Meetings. A shit ton of them. We've got second-quarter numbers back for the Midwest territory, my dad was traveling so I had to handle the teleconference with Milan—"

"Busy," she agreed, then cocked her head and asked, "Hey, you don't still have that thing where you can't go back to sleep if you wake up in the middle of the night, do you?"

The sleepy smile dropped off Sean's face. "What time is it?"

Yawning into her hand, she stood. "'Bout two thirty. Which reminds me… I'm whipped." He was still scowling at the empty space in front of him when she paused at the door to her room. "Kind of fun having you here to chat with for a few minutes when I got home. I could get used to this. Night, roomie."

With her threat left hanging in the air, she slipped into her room.

Suck on that, Wyse.

Four hours later, Molly woke to the ringing of her phone. No one called her this early unless it was an emergency. Fumbling the phone in a haze of confusion, she managed to answer. "Hello?"

"Oh, *darn it*. Did I wake you?" Sean asked, his voice pouring through the line like sugar-free syrup. "Sorry, Moll. Just wanted to tell you I really enjoyed our chat last night too. And it means a lot to know that we're the kind of good friends who aren't afraid to wake each other up from time to time."

Eyes closed, she flopped back on the bed and pictured the cocky Eastwood-esque smile on the other end of the line. He wasn't giving up. Yet.

"Me too, Sean." Neither was she. "See you tonight." After she closed Belfast again.

"Can't wait."

Yeah, she just bet he couldn't. Returning the phone to her nightstand, she curled into her light comforter. Good thing she didn't have Sean's problem and could fall back to sleep on a dime.

—⁓—

Molly shocked awake, her limbs quaking as a series of hard knocks ripped her from the sleep she'd returned to—she glanced at the clock—not even thirty minutes ago. Which meant she only had ninety minutes left to sleep before she had to get moving for her 9:00 a.m. Tuesday gig, cleaning the Stratton condo. Too soon. Following the persistent thuds, she stumbled through the apartment and opened the door to a bouquet of flowers.

"Delivery for Ms. Brandt."

"I didn't think you delivered this early," Molly said, yawning.

"Special request."

Yeah, she bet.

It was one of those artfully decorated vases with the flowers arranged in a perfect tight ball. Gorgeous. Accepting the bouquet, she walked it over to the butcher block table. The card was from Sean, written in his neat handwriting.

Sorry to wake you earlier. Sleep tight.

SEAN

She wanted to be pissed, but she had to give the guy credit. He was good. Really good. Pulling out her phone, she snapped a picture and texted it over.

Molly: Nicely played.

A minute later, she had his response.

Sean: You didn't really think I was going to let you run me out without a fight.

No, she knew him too well to think he wouldn't take this as a challenge.

Molly: Doesn't matter. You're still going.
Sean: Sure. When you find a new roommate.

Ass. Grinning, she headed for the shower. No way she'd get any more sleep today, but she could use the extra hour to work on the Dawson website. She was on track to meet her projected delivery date, but getting ahead was always a good thing.

———

"Okay, you know I like to win," Emily Foster said, sighing after Sean dropped back onto his stool at their table for their regular Wednesday night game. She slapped her darts on the polished high top and glowered first at him and then at Molly. "But throwing the game? Come on."

Elbows resting on the table, fatigue sitting heavy on his shoulders, Sean raised a staying hand. "We're not throwing the game."

Emily's eyes narrowed. "You missed *the board*. And Molly here has zero points for the game so far. What's going on? Is it me? Do you just not want to play with me anymore because I keep mopping the floor with you?"

Jase returned to the table with a fresh beer for his wife and two steaming mugs of coffee. "It's not you, Em," he reassured her, pressing a kiss atop her head of strawberry-blond waves before sliding back onto his stool. "Frick and Frack here are roommates again. They've probably been staying up half the night watching raunchy movies and trying to out-belch each other. They're not throwing the game. They just suck because they're exhausted." Jase handed Sean one of the mugs, which he took with near-tearful gratitude. "Am I right?"

Not exactly, though Sean had certainly been looking forward to a scenario very similar to what Jase had described when he'd moved in.

"Close enough," he replied, passing the other mug to Molly, who stared down at it while biting her lip in indecision. Probably afraid it would keep her up, and after two nights of roommate wars, he got why she'd be concerned. They were both barely making it through. "Just drink it. You'll feel better."

Big, blue eyes swept up to his, vulnerable and weary. "I'm dying."

The girl had all but begged for exactly what she'd been getting by staging yet another wee-hours wake-up and then adding insult to injury by locking the coffee maker in her room, but still Sean didn't like to see her eyes like that. He didn't like the feeling deep in his gut that came from knowing he was responsible.

"Yeah, me too," he conceded, certain it would brighten her spirits to know she was giving as good as she got.

"Thanks." She smiled, but it was small and apparently took too much effort, because then she just dropped her forehead into her hands.

Leaning in so their shoulders touched, he angled his head so his words were only for her. "Look, we're both beyond wasted. How about we call a truce tonight and catch up on some sleep?" She wasn't working, so they could just go home and crash.

Peeking out from the cradle of her hands, she looked him over. "You wish."

He sighed, wondering why he'd even asked. This was Molly, and she was stubborn with a capital *S*. "Yeah, I kinda do."

A set of darts tapped an impatient staccato across the table, bringing their attention back to Emily, who was giving Sean a no-nonsense look. "You're up. Take a hit of the coffee, and snap out of it. This is no fun at all."

Sean stood, rolled a dart between his fingers, and grimaced. He'd tapped the last of his reserves to stay sharp during the marketing meeting, and now…damn, he had nothing.

A solid hand clapped his shoulder as Jase stepped up beside him and took the darts from his hand. "Friends don't let friends throw sharp objects dead tired. Take Molly, and get out of here."

Sean ran a hand through his hair. "Brody hasn't even made it out of his office yet, and I'm pretty sure he wanted to talk about camping next month."

"Trust me, he'll get over it. Besides"—Jase glanced back at Emily—"someone's got to give my wife a little competition."

It was an out he couldn't refuse, and fifteen minutes later, Sean was thanking the Uber driver outside Molly's place while she quietly snored into his shoulder. With the hard time she'd been giving him, he ought to slam the door and make as much racket as he could, but having her tucked in against him like this… Yeah, he ought to wake her up with an air horn, but instead, he gathered her in his arms as gently as he could and carried her up to her apartment.

Inside, he laid her back on her bed and paused before pulling away to detach her fingers from where they'd hooked between the buttons of his shirt. Grabbing the throw from the overstuffed chair in the corner—the one they'd found together that day it rained so hard, they'd had to run for cover, taking shelter in the cool second-hand shop down in Wicker Park—he pulled it over her and brushed a few strands of corn silk and hot pink from her brow. Those dark-blond lashes fluttered, and then she was looking up at him with eyes that weren't quite awake and a smile that made him feel—

Knock it off, man.

—a way he didn't let himself feel around Molly. Shit, he *was* tired. "Go back to sleep, Moll. You need it."

"Mmm…you," she murmured groggily. Her eyes closed again, and her head lolled to the side as she fell back to sleep. He watched her a moment longer, wondering what kind of sweet dream made that hint of a smile flicker across her lips.

Chapter 4

NOT GOOD.

That was Molly's first coherent thought when she woke to the sound of the front door closing and Sean's keys landing on the table as he walked into the apartment. The issue wasn't that she'd been woken before she was ready—it was already after ten—or that she'd slept in her clothes, or even that she had no memory of anything past leaving Belfast the night before. No, it was *Sean*. And more specifically, the dream she'd had about him. And her. Together.

The *dirty*, dirty sex dream.

Which was very bad, because it had been years since she'd suffered anything more than the occasional stray below-the-buckle thought about the guy who was without question her best friend in the world and just happened to think of her as the little sister he'd never had.

And this infraction wasn't just some wayward thought either. It wasn't lingering in one of his big bear hugs a second too long because it felt right for all the wrong reasons. It wasn't a fleeting pinch of jealousy when she was flipping through the paper and happened across a photo of him with Valerie on his arm. That stuff was harmless and didn't take more than a second to shake loose from her head. It wasn't even the XXX rating her nocturnal wanderings had scored.

No. The real trouble had been all the non-porny stuff

that had been there too. The quiet moment before that
dirty business in the shower. The way his hand lingered
at the small of her back when they walked, the press of
his kiss at the top of her head, how she'd felt when Sean
was above her, his dark-brown eyes searching hers.

The thing of it was, those moments were already hers—
only in this dream, every touch and look and whisper had
been infused with that essential *something* her real-life
interactions with Sean had always lacked. The dream had
breathed new life into the ideas she'd finally managed
to put down more than five years ago, and now she was
stuck with this heart-pounding, butterfly-belly sensation
as she caught her first glimpse of him.

Hovering at her bedroom doorway, she watched as
he walked over to the sink. His T-shirt was damp with
sweat and clung to his powerful back. Reaching over his
shoulder, he grabbed a handful of the fabric and yanked
it overhead in one swift motion.

Oh no.

He was standing there shirtless as he filled a glass
with water from the tap, all those muscles flexing and
bunching with every movement. Eyes closed, he turned
around and leaned back into the counter as he drank. A
bead of sweat trickled slowly down his neck, leaving a
wet path that was making her mouth water in a way Sean
wasn't supposed to.

No way could she go back to the years she'd spent
silently pining for him while he knuckle-rubbed her
head and then brought every other damn girl on campus
back to his room to bang. It had been grueling, and it
had taken her years to get past. Years for her to get to
a point where she didn't feel like she was lying to him

every time they hung out and dying inside every time they didn't. She wouldn't go back to that.

She couldn't.

"You have to move out," she croaked, her eyes still fixed on that rolling droplet as it ventured over the packed layers of his right pec.

Sean's eyes opened. He set his glass down on the counter behind him. "Morning, Moll. I slept great. Thanks for asking. Even pushed my schedule back to after lunch so I could catch up a little extra and get a workout in."

"I'm not kidding."

He wiped his face with the T-shirt he'd just whipped off, and a sinking feeling came over her. She knew what she'd be dreaming about tonight.

"Seriously, Moll, I don't get it."

And she hoped he never did.

"We lived together for five years, and it was awesome. You always say you love it when I crash here. Hell, you try to talk me into it every other weekend. You want—no, *need*—a roommate who actually pays rent. So what's the problem?"

She swallowed hard, trying to keep her eyes on his face. The problem was that glistening expanse of muscled chest and banded abs, shifting and flexing with his every movement. The problem was that fine trail of golden hair bisecting all of it and leading south into those too-low basketball shorts—red this time, and silky enough to hint at the contours beneath. The problem was the utterly untamed mess of dark-blond hair making her fingers itch with the need to touch it.

Pretty valid problems, to her mind anyway, but not

exactly something she was ready to share with Sean. Not if she wanted to hang on to the most important relationship in her life. She needed to look away and come up with an answer quick.

"Molly?" he asked again, sounding uncommonly stern as he crossed his arms over his chest. Which was so not helping...because *his arms* and oh God, that crazy V thing happening with the muscles above his shorts when he—

"Uhh...Molly... What...uhh... Why are you looking at me like that?"

Molly's heart stalled in her chest, and her eyes squinted shut. He'd seen it. Years she'd ached and pined and prayed for him to notice that she wasn't his little sister, that she wanted him, and he wanted her too. That they'd be perfect for each other if he'd only give up the idea of the perfect pedigreed wife. But in all that time, he'd never seen a thing. And now, after five years of walking the straight and narrow, she falls out of line for five damn seconds and he catches on?

What the hell, man?

"Okay, Moll, if you're trying to make me uncomfortable looking at me like that, uncool. I know you're just trying to find a new angle to get to me, but no matter how bad you want me out of here, that's the line you don't cross."

Huh?

One eye squinted open and then the other. Sean was standing straight now, nothing casual in his demeanor at all. In fact, he looked as freaked out as he had the day he'd been propositioned by one of his mother's friends.

He thought she'd been...*faking* that look?

Whoa, this could work.

Squaring her shoulders, Molly drew on every ounce of false confidence she could muster. "There's no line I won't cross to win, Sean. You don't want me looking at you like…like the incredibly hot piece of man-candy you are," she stated, letting her eyes run over him from head to toe and then back up again. "Well, then, I think we both know what you can do to stop it."

Her pulse was racing. Her skin hot. She had no idea if he was buying this or not, but please, oh, please let him. Not only would it serve as the perfect cover for that look he'd just busted her taking, but it would have him out of her apartment before lunch.

Sean's jaw shifted to the side as he gave her a narrow look. "No way. Look at you. You're red as a beet, and your hands are shaking."

He didn't believe her.

She was going to have to own up to the truth. She was going to have to tell him about the dream and maybe about five years ago, and even though it was going to be weird for a while and possibly never totally the same again, they'd get past it.

"No way you can keep this up," he said, suddenly a whole lot more confident than he'd been a moment ago. "Good effort, sure, but save us both the brain bleach and just give it up."

The brain bleach?

Even if it was exactly the response she ought to be hoping for, it stung. It really did.

"Give up? Not happening, Sean. And I wouldn't get too confident either, because"—she swallowed and, jutting her hip to one side, tried to channel some smolder—"I could look at you all day."

The forced words hung in the air between them, awkward and unnatural. So very not sexy at all.

Finally, Sean shook his head, giving in to a short laugh that left her dying inside.

"Okay, Moll. If that's the way you want to play it. Go ahead." Walking past, he ruffled her hair. "Give it your all."

She gulped. What had she just gotten herself into?

That had been fucking unreal. Disconcerting as hell. And just plain wrong.

And based on how they'd left the conversation… possibly just the beginning.

Sean tossed his T-shirt into the bathroom corner and cranked the water for the shower.

That look. The first one, which thank fuck she hadn't been able to re-create. He'd never seen her look at him like that before. If he had Shit, he didn't want to think about it. Because even knowing what she was up to, that look could put ideas in a guy's head. Ideas he wouldn't have a second's hesitation following through on if they'd been about anyone other than Molly Brandt.

But it had been Molly behind those few seconds of temptation and sin, and the fact that he was about to step into the shower sporting a semi because of her was making him feel like the lowest of the lows. Lower, because even the shame wasn't enough to take the hard off.

The shower had just started to steam, but no way was he getting in there like that. Reaching in, he turned off the hot and stepped under the icy spray.

"Aghgh!" This scrub was going to be all business. Lightning fast and void of any and all funny business regarding the demon in the next room.

A quiet knock sounded at the bathroom door. "Sean, you okay?"

Lathering faster, he gritted out the single word he could manage. "Yep."

Fine. Totally good. Not thinking about Molly's eyes on him. Definitely not letting his dirty fucking mind take it a step further and imagining the tip of her tongue wetting her lip or—

"Because if you need any help in there…you know… with all those muscles, I wouldn't mind getting all wet to help you out."

He froze where he was, the edges of his vision blurring in time with his pulse.

She hadn't. She wouldn't.

"No thanks, Moll," he called back, hoping like hell his years of maintaining a cool professional exterior no matter what was going through his mind would pay off. If Molly figured out she was getting to him, she'd never stop. "I got it handled—er—under control."

Shit. At least he would.

———

"You're shitting me," Brody said, staring at Sean across the mostly deserted bar. Belfast didn't open for lunch for another half hour, and while Sean needed to get back to the office, he needed someone to talk to first. And with Molly out of the running for obvious reasons and Max a no-go thanks to the honeymoon as well as being Molly's extremely overprotective older brother, Brody was the obvious choice. The guy was a world-class listener and in touch with everyone's feelings on a level deeper than they were. So after taking the world's fastest shower, Sean had darted into his room like a grade-A wuss, praying Molly wouldn't be lying in wait outside the door.

Fortunately, she'd shut herself in her bedroom, and he'd been able to dress and duck out of the apartment in record time.

"I only wish I was," Sean lamented, bracing his elbows on the bar in front of him. Brody passed him a cup of coffee, bringing one for himself as he rounded the bar and took the open stool next to Sean.

"So did it work?" he asked, the oversize mug dwarfed by the guy's meaty hands.

Sean's brow furrowed. "What do you mean?"

Brody shrugged. "She driving you out of the place? 'Cause you know that kid Gary. He's going to be back the minute he figures out you're gone."

He knew. The *dickwad* only had a few days left at the hotel. And already there'd been some problems with the job Sean had lined up for him.

"I'm not going anywhere," Sean answered.

"Glad to hear it, man." Brody nodded past Sean as one of the day staff arrived. "It's not affecting you, then?"

"Molly pretending to come on to me?" He shook his head, suddenly fascinated by the black depths of his coffee. "Give me a break, man. No way."

When he looked up, Brody was watching him with that all-too-knowing look on his face. "You ever think of something more with her?"

Sean coughed, looking around the bar as though he was afraid someone might hear them. Not totally unjustified, considering Molly managed this place part-time, so any staff who happened to be within earshot would probably report back to her before her shift even started the next day. But the girl who'd come in had gone straight to the back, so it was just Brody leaning a burly arm on the bar as he waited for Sean's answer.

"Fuck no. Come on."

"Come on, what? She's hot." And now that Sean *was thinking about it*, he remembered how a few years back, Brody had had a thing for her. A thing that had kind of bugged him but never saw the word *go*. "And if we're being totally honest here, she's not that far off from some of the girls I've seen you with."

Sean balked, and Brody held up a hand. "Yeah, she's nothing like the applicants you take for the future Mrs. Wyse position…but recreationally speaking, you seem to like a little edge, right? And hell, that Jenn McGuire you took home before you and Valerie were on again this last time… She could have been Molly's cousin, with that hair and those eyes. And Robin Whatshername, she looked like she shopped in Molly's closet with those boots and the—"

"Yeah, yeah, I see where you're going with this. Superficially, a few of the women I've hooked up with might share a passing resemblance to Molly. But that's it. I like a little variety is all. That doesn't mean Molly's my type."

She wasn't. Though now that Brody had him thinking about it, Donna Stoltz had those saucer-big blue eyes too… No.

"But even if she was. You know I'd never act on it. Those girls aren't…"

Brody waited, and Sean shoved his coffee away as if it were responsible for the turn in the conversation.

"They know it's not serious. They know before anything happens that I'm not looking for more than a night."

"Yeah. They know the score," Brody agreed calmly, making Sean wonder if he sounded defensive or something.

"I wouldn't want that with Molly." He swore and shook his head again, meeting Brody's eyes. "I wouldn't want that *for* Molly."

Brody tossed back the rest of his coffee and pushed off the stool, walking around to the business side of the bar without a word. "She deserves better than some guy killing time before he finds *the one*."

Sean nodded his agreement.

She was too special for that. And that was all a guy like him had to offer. Or it had been. Until this stuff with his family, Sean hadn't really questioned his parents' plans. They were such a shining example of a successful marriage, so why would he? But now?

Hell, Molly was a free spirit, passionate and exciting. Unpredictable. A force of nature. All the things that made her one of his best friends and favorite people. She'd never want the kind of restrained life he had to offer.

Besides, she was *Molly*. End of story.

Sean rapped his knuckles on the bar as he stood to go. "I gotta get to work. Thanks for the coffee."

"Any time. And Sean," Brody called after him, pointing a stern finger his way. "Stay strong, man."

"Not a problem."

Chapter 5

WHEN MOLLY HAD STUFF GOING ON—HEAVY-ON-THE-BRAIN stuff—there were a number of people she could turn to. Sean, Brody, Sarah, Emily…and her go-to girl for the stuff she didn't need the entire group to know about within five seconds flat.

Janice.

"Molly, what are you doing here?" Jase asked, walking out of his office with a perplexed expression on his face. "Everything okay?"

She opened her mouth to answer when Janice took care of it for her. "She's fine, everything's fine, Jase. Just keep walking. They're waiting for you up on twenty-three, and those updated reports are on the shared drive." When he didn't seem to move fast enough, she let out an exasperated breath. "Do you need something else, Jase?"

His brows shot high, his mouth dropping open. "You're here for *Janice*?"

The guy had the weirdest thing about his assistant. Like no one was allowed to have her but him. Okay, it was the middle of the workday, and they were sitting five feet from his office, but for crying out loud, the guy needed to learn to share. "Girl talk," Molly announced, expecting one of those hands-up, backing-away-slowly retreats.

Janice hissed out a breath, looking away as Jase's face lit up. "Yeah? What's going on?" he asked, a little too much excitement in his hushed tone as he hauled one of the reception chairs over next to Molly. "We could go in my office. I have some water and raisins in my drawer."

"Very generous." Molly knew what this was about and gave his hand a comforting pat. "It's not dishy gossip, Jase." Fine, it was, but she needed someone to talk to…not someone she was going to have to explain every subtle nuance to. And Janice *knew* things.

Janice had less patience and waved him away irritably. "And even if it was, we wouldn't share it with you. Go to your meeting."

He huffed and grudgingly got up. "Fine. See you around, Moll."

He looked like he was about to say something to Janice too but then wisely thought better of it and left without another word.

Janice reached into her drawer and offered Molly a Hershey's Miniature. "Okay, so let me get this straight. He caught you staring…like tongue-hanging-out, a-little-bit-of-drool-going-on staring…and thought you were just trying to scare him out of the apartment?"

Molly unfolded the foil wrapper and nodded.

"So by some miracle, he bought this, and now you're planning on just *going with it*…coming on to him over and over…because you think it's going to drive him away." At Molly's nod, Janice let out a lengthy sigh and picked up a framed picture of her year-old son, speaking to it. "I know. Crazy."

"Come on. It's not crazy," Molly countered around a melty bite of heaven. "He thinks of me as a little sister, Janice. If you'd seen how uncomfortable he was, you'd know this is a solid plan."

"Mmm-hmm. I'm just wondering how you think

waving around all those feelings you've been ignoring in hopes they'd go away for the past dozen years is going to help you. I mean, the reason you wanted him out in the first place was because you were worried spending that kind of time with him might stir them up."

Okay, so Janice was pretty wise about stuff like this. And Molly saw her point. Except… "That's the beauty of it, Janice. This is the perfect opportunity to vent some steam. And it's total BS that he thinks he gets to decide how things are with my apartment."

Pursing her lips, Janice drew a slow breath. "Agreed. But that Gary guy had to go, and you weren't doing anything about it."

Molly slumped back in her chair. "I know."

"So what's next?" Janice folded her arms neatly on her desk. "You going to put on something slinky for when he walks in the door?"

Molly laughed. "Sean's seen me in everything from my sexiest bra and panties—don't ask—to a one-piece snowsuit, and the reaction has never varied. He doesn't see me as sexy. No matter what." At Janice's skeptical look, she shrugged. "It is what it is. So I think I'm going to have to rely on words and possibly actions."

One dark brow arched high. "Come again?"

Heat infused her cheeks. "I mean, it probably won't come to that. But if the flirt alone isn't enough to freak Sean out the door, then I may have to up my game…a little…maybe."

"Molly."

"Cripes, Janice, I'm not going to grab his junk," Molly whispered indignantly. "But some handsy stuff with his arms. Or shoulders." She thought of that moment when he'd whipped off his T-shirt that morning and swallowed. "His stomach." Leaning forward so she was gripping the edge of the desk in front of her, sitting on the edge of her seat, she blurted out, "Janice, I know you don't have a lot of love to spare for Sean, but if you'd seen his stomach when he leaned back into the counter—"

"Uh-uh-uh." Janice cut her off with a wave of her hands and flipped the picture of her son so he was facing the desk. "I don't want to hear about his washboard abs or happy trail or the magic V that makes smart women stupid on that guy."

Molly closed her eyes with a sigh. "The magic V, Janice."

Fingers snapped in front of her, and then Janice was waving her away. "Congratulations, Molly, I just threw up in my mouth."

Gathering her bag, Molly leaned around the desk and tossed her candy wrapper. Looked like Janice had met her quota of sweetness for the day. "Okay, I'm going."

"How's the website stuff going? Did Dave ever call you?"

Molly grinned. "He did, and we just signed a contract Monday. Thanks for putting him in touch. I've got a lot of ideas for the site."

"I bet you do. Loved what you did for Lorie with the salon. It was so original, clean, and simple. You've got a nice eye."

Molly could feel the heat in her cheeks again, the praise—while she was right there!—making her squirm. "Thank you."

Janice laughed and adjusted her keyboard, obviously ready to get back to work. "Have fun getting Sean out of your space, hon, but be careful. You've got a tender heart, and it makes me sad to think how much of it you've given to this man already, whether he knows it or not."

Molly nodded and dropped a kiss on Janice's cheek before heading out.

———~~~———

This was stupid.

Sean hesitated outside the apartment door, his key in the lock. Molly had the night off from Belfast, and it was after eight. He was pretty sure she didn't do cleaning this late. So she might be home. Who was he kidding? The gauntlet had been thrown that morning. She was going to be there. Waiting.

Waiting for him to cry uncle and move out.

She was probably armed with an arsenal of innuendo and the kind of feigned advances that, if he were a better man, wouldn't get to him at all.

Time to sac up, Wyse.

Letting himself into the apartment, he braced—for what, he didn't even know.

"Evening, lover," Molly purred from the couch, her laptop balanced on her long, outstretched legs, a spiral notebook open on the couch beside her. "Here to get your things…or am I getting lucky?"

"Molly," he acknowledged with a tight smile, ignoring her question. "You have dinner yet?"

He normally would have had something sent up from the restaurant to his office, but his head had been full of this shit with Molly all day, and he'd barely been able to focus on work, let alone remembering to eat. So now he was ravenous.

"Uh…actually no. I was kind of caught up with this site and…no." She set the laptop aside and swung her legs over the edge of the couch to stand.

Great, and she was wearing those cutoff jean shorts that showed exactly how toned and strong her thighs were. White tank top. Pink bra that matched her hair. Pink was his fucking favorite. She had to be wearing it today.

Padding back to the kitchen in her bare feet, she opened the cabinet and pulled out a box of mac and cheese. "I've only got one. Think that will be enough?"

He crossed to the kitchen and took the box out of her hand, leaning over her to put it back on the shelf. "You don't have any butter, and I threw away whatever unholy thing your milk had become this morning."

"Oh yeah?" she said quietly…too quietly, bringing Sean's focus down to where he'd inadvertently pinned her between the counter and his body. Shit, she was blinking up at him with those big, blue eyes that were wide and soft and—Jesus, the way she was looking at him

The lover talk and sexy outfit were nothing compared to *that look*.

He stepped back a couple paces, pissed with himself for giving her another opening to screw with him, and pissed with her for taking a crowbar to the easy physical comfort that had been a part of their relationship for as long as he could remember. He didn't want to watch his step with Molly or have to think about where his hands were or anything else with her. It hadn't ever been like that between them. He didn't want it to start now.

"Grab a sweatshirt or something. I'm taking you out for dinner," he snapped more harshly than he should have.

Putting as much distance as he could between them,

he walked to his room and shrugged out of his jacket before tossing it on his bed. Jerking his tie loose, he looked through the open door to find Molly in the middle of the apartment, one blond brow, a few shades darker than her hair, arched. "You really want to go out?" she said, pulling her lip through her teeth in a scary way that made him want to reach for some lip balm for her. "Pretty sure we could find *something* here."

She was working some kind of swivel thing with her hips while she stood, her arms going to her stomach and then behind her, as if she wasn't sure where to put them. A wave of relief washed over him as he realized that look from the counter had been an anomaly. Something Molly had stumbled on by accident. Hell, it was probably a trick of the light. Whatever, the important thing was that she wasn't going to nail it every time.

More comfortable, he grinned at her. "You ready to risk the quarter box of chicken-flavored crackers that have been open in your cabinet for the last two years? 'Cause I'm not. How about Italian?"

Tossing his tie on top of his jacket, he rolled his sleeves and then grabbed his keys. "Let's go."

After a beat, the pretense fell away, and Molly shrugged. "Fine." She followed him to the door and stopped, her nose scrunching up as she pulled a bit of stretchy fabric from her tank top away from her belly. "This okay for where we're going?"

His jaw firmed, and he gave her a curt nod before looking away. Because yeah, score one for Molly. She'd gotten to him again. "You're fine."

Dinner was fantastic. Not surprising, considering Sean picked the place. Any cuisine, price range, or vibe, he always knew the best places around the city and the little hole in the wall with rustic decor, low lighting, and Puccini playing in the background was no exception. Molly had a heaping plate of the best lasagna this side of the Atlantic, and Sean had gotten the cioppino—because he hadn't tried theirs before—and based on the low, guttural moan after the first bite, followed by one of those deep meaningful looks over the top of his spoon, she was pretty sure he liked it.

"One of these days, I'm going to get you to try a scallop," he stated, folding his napkin next to his plate. Sean had relaxed about halfway to the restaurant when she'd caught him eyeing her suspiciously and told him to knock it off. She had rules. A strategy. Any time they were out of her apartment—which was her end goal, after all—Sean didn't need to worry about the flirt. He was safe.

From that moment on, they'd just been *them*. Easy and relaxed. Sean giving her crap about her psychological allergy to all things fishy and generally just catching up on each other's days. Which, she had to admit, she kind of needed.

Crossing her arms over her too-full belly, she eyed the last piece of crusty bread in the basket and wondered just how bad it would be if she finished it.

"Jesus, Moll. I'm going to be sick if you eat anything more." Then claiming it was for her own good, Sean flagged a passing waitress. "Any chance we could get the check and the rest of this bread and another loaf wrapped up to go?"

A flutter kicked up in Molly's heart, because that was the kind of sweet Sean was all about. "Thank you," she murmured, checking her phone to keep him from seeing anything in her eyes he shouldn't. She was having trouble regulating what she was putting out there, only hitting her mark about half the time, and she couldn't for the life of her figure out why.

Sean had looked ready to bolt when they'd been in the kitchen, and that had been an accident. He'd been so close, stretching up over her so his chest was right there and she could smell his cologne. It affected her, and he'd noticed. And freaked. But then when she'd tossed out that line about finding something to eat at home, offering up what she'd thought was a pretty good go at sexy? *Nada*.

Maybe she'd been too subtle, and he just hadn't noticed.

Outside the restaurant, Sean slung his arm around Molly's shoulders as they started down the sidewalk.

She smiled, that contented feeling filling her chest. Because this was the good stuff.

"You working Belfast this weekend?"

"Yeah, but I've got days, so I'll be out by seven." She pulled up her phone and scrolled through her texts until she found what she was looking for. "Suzanna's having that party Friday night, and Gib's band is playing Saturday. What are you thinking?"

Sean wagged his head back and forth in indecision. "I like hearing Gib, but the last two times we saw him, it got awkward after the show."

Letting out a short laugh, Molly shook her head. "You slept with his sister, Sean. What did you think… that *she'd* stop going to his shows?"

Sean was about to launch into some defense when she heard her name, and she drew up short, a sinking feeling settling in her belly. It might only have been a few days, but she'd gotten used to not having to brace for the interactions with Gary.

"Shit," Sean muttered from beside her.

Yeah, that was right.

"Be nice," she hissed as Gary jogged a few steps to greet her.

"Hey, Molly, long time," Gary joked. He had one of those creepy smiles that was probably totally genuine but still managed to make everyone a little uncomfortable.

"Yeah, sorry about the way everything worked out, Gary. I didn't…" She cut off uneasily. If she said kicking him out wasn't something she supported, there was a good chance he'd be back. And man, she didn't want him back. Still, she had to ask, "How's it going?"

"Good," he said, leaning into his answer with an eager nod. "I'm moving into my new place on Monday. The job is going great too."

Molly's heart lifted, and she relaxed a little. "Really? That's fantastic, Gary. See, it's all turning around."

Gary shook his head, a woe-is-me look threatening as he sighed. *Oh no*.

"Mostly. It's just now there's this—"

Sean's sharp whistle cut through the air just as her old roommate was about to launch into some story that would leave Molly feeling battered and bruised.

Sean was already firming his hold around her shoulders and propelling them toward the curb where a cab had pulled up. "Glad to hear it's all working out for you, Gary. A positive attitude can make all the difference."

The ride was quick, and Molly was still thinking about Gary when they climbed out of the cab at her building. She turned to Sean with a sigh. "Okay, I admit it. I'm grateful you handled the situation. Really grateful, especially with all the stuff you did to make sure he had a soft place to land and the means to go forward and…that was big, Sean. Thank you."

She was met with that half-cocked grin she'd fallen so hard for that first year.

"So you're okay with me staying now?" he asked, all confidence. All Sean.

Patting the center of his chest, she gave him a pitying look. "No. You still need to move out."

She only made it halfway up the stairs before he was cutting in front of her, that same smacked look on his face. "Whoa, Molly. What gives?"

She wouldn't expect him to totally get it. Using the back of her hand to nudge him aside, she started up again. "You didn't respect my boundaries, moving in the way you did. I'm firm on this, Sean."

At her door, she let herself into the apartment and then, before Sean could follow her in, turned in the doorway so he had to stop on the other side or mow her over. Arms outstretched so she was holding the frame with each hand, she gave him a level look.

"Your parents' place is open. You sure you want to cross this line again?" She hoped the answer was no, because she didn't know what her next move was going to be…but whatever it was, it was going to have to be good.

Those big shoulders sagged with his head. "Are we really going there again, Moll? Even after I bought you dinner and saved you with a quick escape from Gary?"

She checked her nails. Short and chipped to the point where there was more naked nail showing than deep-maroon polish. And she had a hangnail. "Up to you, Wyse. Are we?"

He sighed, and for a fraction of a breath, she thought he might relent and realized she was going to be a little disappointed to see him go. But then, his hands were on her hips, and she wasn't in the doorway anymore, having been bodily shifted out of the way. Sean scowled at her and walked into the apartment. Stalking into his room, he didn't bother to turn around as he muttered, "Fine, Moll. Whatever you've got. Bring it."

Chapter 6

Bring it. Sure, big talk from the tough guy.

Sean changed into jeans and a T-shirt and then stood in the center of his room, staring at the door and wondering what kind of beast he was going to encounter on the other side. Really, he just wanted to unwind and watch some TV with Molly. Listen to her laugh while they picked apart the ridiculous plotlines of some show she couldn't get enough of. He wanted Molly the way she was supposed to be with him. Kicking his hip with her foot when she wanted his popcorn or the remote. Just being—hell, just being his Molly. The one he didn't have to worry about what he said with and could relax with like no one else. *Fuck*.

Maybe he'd luck out, and she'd get distracted by the show and forget about coming on to him for a few hours. Maybe she wouldn't manage *that look* again—the one that was getting to him in all the wrong ways and had him a hairsbreadth from bringing it along with him to the shower and giving in to the kind of base need he'd successfully kept Molly separate from for the past twelve years.

Yeah, maybe.

Molly was watching some documentary on the fittest people in the world when he made it to the couch. Setting his laptop on the floor beside him, he leveled her with a glare before sitting.

It didn't work, because the minute she blinked up at

him, *that look* was back. If he hadn't already been standing, it would have had him leaping off the couch. Her big blues skimmed over his face, down his neck, and slowly over his stomach until—

"Christ, Molly!" he croaked, dropping his hands in front of his fly.

She sighed and sat back into her corner of the couch, letting her eyes linger just long enough to make her point—before she peered up at him with an appreciative smile.

"Have I ever mentioned how very nicely you fill out those jeans?" She swallowed, as if her mouth had gone dry or something, and then bit her lip. Only this time, it didn't look like she was trying to gnaw it off or bite through it or anything. It just looked—*fuck*, it looked like he really didn't want to know what she was thinking right then.

She was getting better at this. Which was a problem, because he did not want to be getting ideas about Molly's mouth.

"Knock it off, Moll. I just want to watch some TV in peace." There was another chair he could sit in, but this side of the couch was always his. He didn't want to give it up just because Molly was being a belligerent brat.

"Hmm. Pretty sure the TV at your parents' place is free."

No way. And to emphasize his point, he sat down, holding her stare as he did.

"Have it your way," she said with a sigh. "We'll just have to get comfortable here."

His head whipped around at that, because he could take the fake porn-star voice. The cheesy come-on lines were even kind of adorable. But every now and then, she gave him a taste of something that looked and sounded just a little too real and put a lot of bad ideas in his head.

He was handling it for now. But if she got any better, if she took things any further?

"That T-shirt is one of my favorites on you," she mentioned casually, her eyes back on the show. "The fabric's thin, and the way it hugs and hangs across your chest and stomach doesn't leave a whole lot to the imagination. Really nice."

Sean's brows pulled together, and he crossed his arms over his chest. Great. Not only was he thinking about his best friend in a way he didn't want to, but now he was thinking about his favorite shirt in a way he didn't want to either. It *was* super thin, but still hanging in there without any holes. And the fabric across his chest and stomach was damn soft.

A flash of Molly's hands sliding over it fired through his mind.

Enough, Wyse. She doesn't belong there.

He squinted his eyes shut, willing himself to sac up, because he was making this whole damn thing way too easy on Molly. And if he didn't get his shit together quickly, she was going to have him moved out before Max and Sarah even got home from the honeymoon on Monday.

No way.

Molly shifted beside him, and suddenly things got a whole lot worse, way too fast.

His eyes shot open as the cushion dipped beside him and Molly's hand settled on his shoulder.

"Excuse me, Sean. I just need to grab the remote," she said, throwing her knee over his hips so she was straddling him. He gulped. Trying hard not to stare at the hot-pink bra showing through her tank, getting closer and closer to his face as she reached for the remote on the end table beside him.

"Moll, don't," he warned through gritted teeth.

Instead of springing off him and retreating to her side of the couch the way he wanted, she cocked her head and looked down at him. "Something wrong, Sean?"

Her knees were on both sides of his hips, and his hands were balled against the cushion so they didn't fist in the shorts covering her ass. Yeah, something was wrong. And it got even more so when she rested both her hands on his shoulders and sat back on his thighs. Because another inch and she'd be right *there*.

His molars ground together. He couldn't think about it. About how close she was. About how it would feel to have her pressed against him like that.

Except *he was totally thinking about it*, and worse, he was thinking about it while he stared into those bright blue eyes.

And now there was *less* than an inch between him and Molly figuring out exactly what kind of victory she'd scored with this little stunt. If she knew, she'd do it again. She'd push further. And he'd let her, because as much as he didn't want to, *he liked this*.

"You're playing with fire, Molly. Enough."

"Am I?" she asked, watching him like she wanted the one thing he knew better than to give her.

It wasn't real. He knew it.

And even if it was, neither of them would ever act on it. Because Molly wasn't disposable. She wasn't someone he could take the edge off with and then walk away from like he did with all the other women. Not even if she kept looking at him the way she was right then.

Her lips parted, and the pink tip of her tongue peeked out to wet her bottom lip.

This was bad.

He could move her if he needed to. But then he'd have his hands on her hips, and what if he touched her thighs? What if he finally found out how it felt to have his fingers splayed wide across them, to feel how strong they were when they flexed? What would happen if his hands slid higher—

Her shriek cut through the fantasy that was rapidly spinning out of control.

"Sean!" she gasped, rising fast from where she'd been sitting back on his thighs, her hands clutching at his shoulders as she shifted in a panic from one knee to the other, which wasn't helping the situation in the slightest, because all that shifting around while she was practically mashing her chest into his face was sending the wrong signals to a part of him that wasn't very rational to begin with.

"Molly, stop!" he barked, capturing her hips with his hands and jerking his head back from a place that had been just the perfect amount of soft and sweet—and fuck, how was he going to keep that shit from following him into the shower?

Molly stopped her squirming and, safely out of his erection's way, glowered down at him, her face a very satisfying shade of beet. "You... That... I... It..." She sucked in a breath and scrunched her eyes closed, apparently giving up on the completely unnecessary recap.

About time the tables turned here. He knew he

shouldn't be thinking about the fact that his thumbs had brushed those sexy hip bones of hers or that the way he was holding her, half suspended above him, was feeding the part of him that liked a little control.

Because this was Molly.

And clearly she'd gotten more than she bargained for.

"Yeah, you straddled my lap, Moll. I'm a guy. What the fuck did you think was going to happen?"

When she opened her eyes again, all that saucy confidence was gone, and a part of him missed it. But the greater part of him recognized the woman looking down at him as the best friend he wasn't seeing enough of lately. The one who, despite all her hard edges and bluster, had a vulnerable side she didn't trust to many people.

"Yeah, but…you're you. And I didn't think…" Her eyes cut away, and she blushed even harder. Christ, she was so uncomfortable, it was killing him. Even if she'd brought it on herself, he couldn't watch her squirm. So he said the only thing he could think to make it better.

"Don't freak out. It's a physiological thing. Nothing else. You put any woman across my lap like that, and the man downstairs is going to get involved. It's not about *you*."

And shit, not only was that a lie, because it most definitely *had* been about her, but he also realized what a world-class dick thing it was to say. He opened his mouth to apologize and say he didn't even know what—but she was nodding like that flimsy-ass explanation had actually made her feel better.

"Okay, so we'll just forget about it then. Pretend it didn't happen."

He sure as hell was going to try, but he wasn't holding

his breath. Because for the first time in a dozen years, he knew exactly what Molly felt like above him. How soft and sweet those modest curves were against his cheek. How easily he could hold her. Guide her—yeah, forgetting about it wasn't happening any time soon. But pretending? Sean was a master at maintaining a facade.

Only… "This shit stops now, Molly. Keep it up, and you're going to start something we can't just forget about and pretend didn't happen. Is that what you want?"

Pinching her lips between her teeth, she shook her head.

"Me either," he said, finally releasing his hold on her hips and helping her up. Probably something he should have done immediately. Definitely. "You mean too much to me."

"Same here, Sean."

There was something about the way she said it that got him deep in the chest. Made him want to pull her back in to him and hold her for just a minute. But it wasn't the right time to get his hug on, so instead, he grabbed the remote she'd been going for in the first place and turned up the volume. "So CrossFit, huh? Those guys are huge."

Molly nodded. Then she shook her head and pushed off the couch, her shoulders low. "You know what? I think I'm going to hole up in my room for a while. See about getting some more work done since we're going out tomorrow night."

He sat up. "Molly, don't—"

But her hand was already up, waving him off. "I'm good. We're good. But…" Again, she pinched her lips together and looked away, which was bothering him more every time she did it. "Yeah, you just hang, and I'll catch you tomorrow night."

"You sure?"

She nodded.

Molly going to hide out in her room was the last thing he wanted, but maybe a little space wouldn't be the worst thing in the world.

—∿—

Working on the brewery website turned out to be a total fail when it came to distracting Molly from the train wreck her plan to flirt Sean out of her spare bedroom had ended up being. She'd wanted to make him uncomfortable. Well, she'd done it all right. But climbing over him like a sex kitten in training hadn't panned out the way she'd expected.

Sean wasn't moving out.

She hadn't won.

All she'd done was embarrass herself by acting like an idiot who didn't value their friendship enough to respect the lines that shouldn't be crossed and embarrassing Sean by…well, causing the physiological response that had nothing to actually do with her.

She was done.

Done pushing his buttons and done lying to herself about being able to handle it. Her feelings for Sean weren't just some passing crush, and they'd never totally gone away. She loved him like she always had. She'd just learned to manage it. And come morning, she was going to start managing it again.

—∿—

Sleep was hard to come by.

Molly heard the TV turn off around eleven. The sound

of Sean getting a glass of water. The door to his room
closing and then, a few minutes later, opening again,
followed shortly by a muffled curse and the shower starting to run. She shouldn't think of him in there, peeling
off his thin T-shirt and shucking his jeans. Like she
shouldn't think of the spray running hot over his back
muscles or what he'd look like soaping his chest.

She shouldn't have done a lot of things lately.

A torturous twenty minutes later, the water turned
off, and the apartment went quiet.

Eventually, she fell asleep, but it was fitful, her dreams
the kind she wanted to return to and avoid in equal measure.
She was awake before Sean but again waited in her room,
listening to the sounds she'd be hearing for the next month
or more. Yes, she could find a new roommate…or at least
she could try. But Sean didn't want to stay at the hotel or
in his parents' place, and after what she'd done this week?
She owed it to him to give him a room.

Once she heard the front door close and the apartment
was quiet again, she ventured out into the space where
Sean had been only minutes before. She was a chicken
for waiting until he was gone, but she was still feeling a
little tender, and it was only a few hours. She'd see him
at the party later. Following the scent of fresh-brewed
coffee, she found a sticky note on the mostly full pot.

Slept like shit. Today will be better. Brand-new day.

She pulled the note free and leaned back into the
counter, feeling some of the tension that had been
knotting up inside her ease.

Everything was going to be fine.

Chapter 7

SIX WASN'T COMING HOME EARLY.

Sean knew it. Kept trying to sell himself on the truth of it as he stepped out of the car in front of Molly's place and headed upstairs. Only thing was, he couldn't quite buy what he was selling. Probably because he'd had a shit ton of work left on his desk, and he usually just stayed a little longer and got it done—but today, he'd had other priorities.

Honestly, he wasn't looking forward to the party the way he'd thought he would. It wasn't that he didn't want to see everyone; he did. But with things so messed up with Molly this week, the greater part of him just wanted to hang out with her. Alone. Laugh about the both of them being idiots. Cuddle up on the couch and—

Shit—he stopped halfway up the stairs and gripped the keys in his fist. Maybe the cuddle should wait, because as soon as the couch crossed his mind, he was back there with Molly's legs spread across him and all the places *they hadn't gone* bombarding him like a dirty wish list of shame. The same dirty wish list that had followed him into the shower the night before. He wasn't proud, but there'd been no way back from what happened without some physical relief.

Maybe he should get her a new couch. Something untainted by his hard-on reaching out and grabbing a taste of the most forbidden part of Molly there was.

For as independent as she was, he suspected she wouldn't argue.

She'd gone too far last night, and she knew it.

On the upside, the games would stop. Small victory. Though even that wasn't quite right either. He hadn't won anything. In fact, he was pretty sure they both felt like losers after what happened. But at least it was safe to go back in the apartment.

Pushing open the door, Sean dumped his keys and slipped his messenger bag off his shoulder, stopping at his room to lose his coat and tie. "Hey, Moll," he called out, figuring she was in her room or around the corner in the kitchen area. "I talked to Jase and Em, and they're going to meet us at the party."

Folding his jacket before laying it across his bed, he toed off one shoe and then the other. "But Brody's up for some grub first."

Tugging his tie, he pulled it free and waited. "What do you think?"

Silence. He frowned. Her keys were here, but the apartment was silent. Unbuttoning his shirt, he went to check the kitchen and living area. "Moll?"

Empty. Weird. He'd been sure she was there.

Gut tightening, he started back to his room, hoping like hell she wasn't still avoiding him. But then he drew up short next to her room. The door was half open, and when he looked in, there she was. Facedown on her bed, in a black tank top with a fuchsia bra beneath and green-and-yellow polka-dotted cotton panties.

He should not be seeing this. Not after the assistant manager down south's latest takeover attempt.

Probably not at all.

He stepped back, tripped over his own foot, and stumbled into the wall with a thud.

Molly's breathing changed, and then she was making this little moany sound that was hitting all the wrong chords with him—because, fuck, that sleepy, soft *Mmm* was not what he wanted to hear.

"Sorry, Moll, I didn't realize you were sleeping," he said, taking another step back. He left her door open like he'd found it...except she was wearing those green-and-yellow narrow-hipped panties, and that wasn't really open door attire. So he stepped back to close it, not meaning to look, but fuck, that's exactly what he was doing.

"Sean?" she murmured softly, turning her head and looking at him with sleep-hazed eyes.

"Yeah, I, uh, just wasn't sure where you were, but, uh, now I see you were sleeping, and I'm sorry to have disturbed you. But I'll...uhh..." He shook his head, trying to catch the thread of what he'd been about to say. Where he'd been going. But all he could think was that Molly was pushing up on her forearms, and the low scoop of her black tank was giving him a criminally good view of that narrow well of cleavage.

Throat suddenly dry, he tried to swallow but only managed to choke.

Molly's eyes cleared, and slowly, her brows began to climb. He was so busted.

"I didn't mean to," he started, his tongue as clumsy in his mouth as a wad of Silly Putty. "I didn't realize you were, uhh, not all the way..." Closing his eyes, he stepped back and pulled the door shut. *One breath. Two.* "I'll catch you at the party. I've got to run back to the

office for some files I need for the weekend." His heart
was racing like it was about to bust out of his chest.
"Because I forgot them there." *Jesus*. "At the office. I
forgot them at the office." He pressed his palm to the
panel of her door, then pulled it back like he'd been
burned. "And I need them for this weekend."

The door swung open, and he jerked back, eyes
shooting to the ceiling.

"Relax, Sean," she said, cutting past him. "I'm
dressed."

Letting his breath out in a slow stream he hoped she
didn't notice, he nodded and dared a glance at where
she'd stopped by the butcher-block island. She was
still wearing the tank, but she'd pulled on a jean skirt.
Her feet were bare, and the way she was rolling out
her shoulders made him think she wasn't all the way
awake yet...and that she could probably use a back rub.
Which he definitely wasn't going to offer, even though
he'd rubbed the tension from her neck and shoulders
probably a hundred times before. And sure, he'd noticed
how soft and smooth her skin was. Maybe once or twice
he'd even needed to remind himself not to get carried
away with it. But in the past, it hadn't taken more than
the single mental shake to remember that the silky neck
and shoulders he'd had his hands on were off-limits to
his mouth and to get his head back in the right space.

Today? He'd been mentally chanting Molly's name
since he walked into her room so he wouldn't forget who
she was, and his fingers *still* burned with a less-than-
platonic need to get hold of her. So yeah, no touching.

Walking over to the sink, she ducked down to grab
the long-spouted watering can. After filling it from the

tap, she started to feed her collection of sickly plants on the shelf in front of the window.

"I didn't do that on purpose," she said, sounding almost angry. "I didn't think you'd be home for a few hours and was getting dressed when I heard my email ping. I crawled into bed to check it out, and the next thing I knew, you were there."

He nodded, desperately trying not to think about her panties.

She glanced over her shoulder, the worried furrow between her eyes telling him he should have answered her.

Clearing his throat, he crossed around to the counter. "Yeah, totally. I mean, you were in your room. It was my fault."

The look in her eyes said she wasn't sure she believed him. But then she shrugged, and he was pretty sure it meant they were good. Christ, he wanted them to be good.

"So see you at the party, Moll."

Turning back to pick a few dead leaves from one of the plants, she nodded. "See you there."

Molly loved her apartment, but when it came to throwing summer parties, she'd been coveting Suzanna's place for years. The Southport apartment was a wide-open space on the second floor with tons of windows, all of which were open wide as Molly walked through the front door, waving to a few familiar faces in the crowded living room and hall. The kitchen was in the rear of the apartment, overlooking a good-sized balcony and the backyard below. It was modern, stainless, and stocked with all the foodie essentials Molly found at

Brody's place but on a smaller scale. Suzanna's brother
was mixing drinks in the corner breakfast nook and
called out to her as she walked in.

"How's it going, Ben?" she asked, weaving around
another cluster of friends. Giving him a hip bump in
greeting, she checked out his drink fixin's. He had two
dozen tall glasses lined up on the counter, along with
several bowls filled with limes and mint and sugar.
"Mojitos?"

"You know it, gorgeous." He rinsed his hands and
wiped them on the white towel thrown over his shoulder
before handing her a drink. "What do you think?"

It was fresh and delicious. She made an appreciative
sound and shook her head, looking up into his face.
"You sure you don't want to quit trading and come work
at Belfast? You've got a gift."

He wagged his dark brows at her. "Not my only gift,
Moll."

She laughed and stepped back. "Yeah, I actually
heard that from Tonya last week."

The guy was a relentless flirt, and he got around.
But not with Molly—though it had been a close thing.
Ben was only a year older than she was and had been a
sophomore when the guys were seniors. There'd been a
party, and they'd been talking. And then he'd brought
her a drink—one with booze in it—and Sean had stepped
in to *talk* with him. That had been the end of that.

Ever since, he'd been flirting with her like it was his
job, but it had never been the same. There was no spark
behind the charm. It was strictly friendly. Fine by her.

They joked back and forth about him wearing her
down one of these days and then caught up some, since

it had been a few months. He was telling her about the trip he was planning to Alaska when Suzanna came in from the back.

"Molly, you made it!" she greeted her, wrapping her in a tight squeeze. "Hey, mind if I borrow Ben here for a few minutes? Brody brought three trays of those marinated steak appetizers, and my fire's about to die." Turning to her brother, she pulled an anxious face. "We bought more charcoal, but where did it end up?"

"No problem, Suzanna," Molly cut in. "Give me your keys, and I'll go grab another bag."

Ben snorted out a laugh as Suzanna coughed in shock at the suggestion that Molly would drive her precious baby BMW. Molly had only thrown it out there to mess with her, knowing Ben wasn't even allowed to drive it.

"Kidding," she assured Suzanna.

"You're trouble, Molly."

She curtsied and headed out the back door, leaving the siblings to sort out their charcoal situation. Passing another group occupying a few chairs on the patio, she followed the wide stairs leading down to the backyard where she found the guys crowded around a picnic table with a few friends. Sean saw her first, not quite meeting her eyes before burying his face in his phone. She didn't have time to wonder what to read into a greeting so different from their usual before Brody was up and shuffling people around in a flash to make room for her to sit. Maybe it was nothing.

She hadn't even been naked. He'd seen her in her underwear before and never batted an eye. So what was the big deal this time?

But she knew. The big deal was that all week, she'd

been coming at him in the one way he'd warned her not to.

"Thanks, Brody," she said, tousling his mane of red-brown waves with her fingers as she settled onto the bench between the two men and across from Jase and Emily. "Hey, Sean," she started, hoping it sounded normal and not like she was panicked the guy was going to get up and leave. "Get your files?"

He stiffened and then rubbed the back of his neck. "Oh yeah. All set. Thanks."

Her heart stopped, the air going still in her lungs as the silence stretched between them. She waited, because this wasn't how it was with them. Ever.

Sean didn't avoid her or ignore her. If he was mad, he'd lay into her just the way she did with him. He'd tell her to knock it off. But this—God, she could feel the tension coming off him. She tried to come up with something to say, something to lighten things up, but all she could think was that *Sean wouldn't look at her*.

Brody turned to her, one brow raised in question as he mouthed "You okay?"

She gave a tight, too-fast nod, and then one to Emily, whose concerned expression said she hadn't missed the tension clogging the air around them either.

Heat burned its way up Molly's neck into her cheeks as she tried to hold on to her smile. But pretending was beyond her.

Finally, she turned back to her friends at the table— who were all staring. All except for Sean, who seemed well and truly mesmerized by the neat shrubs bordering the fence of the yard.

That heat in her cheeks pushed higher, getting hotter

as it did. Finally, she stood with a jerk and sucked in a deep lungful of air. "Fine. It's totally my fault. I was pissed at Sean for moving into my apartment and kicking my old roommate out without talking to me about it first. And I did something stupid, okay?"

There was a round of slow nods from the table, except for Sean, whose head had come up in a snap, a smacked look on his face like he couldn't believe she was putting it out there.

"I tried to get him to move out by flirting with him, because I knew how uncomfortable it would make him." She sucked a shaky breath and fought the tears threatening to break with the best defense she had. *Anger*. "But the total *ween* wouldn't go, so I kept trying and trying, except then he got a boner, and it touched me, and now it's all weird and uncomfortable, which is why Sean's sitting there looking like he'd rather be anywhere else."

Four people started talking at once, but she didn't hear a word of it.

Throwing her hands out to the sides, she cut them off. "I'm going back upstairs, because I'm embarrassed and upset. And you guys…" She met each of their eyes in turn, landing on Sean's last. He looked agonized, and she hated it, but they needed some more space. "…are just going to let me."

Hands shaking, she launched away from the table, wondering what the hell she'd just done. She needed to get away. There were two dozen people she could talk to at this party, easy. People who wouldn't make her feel like she'd threatened the very fabric of their tightly woven world.

The truth of it slammed into her.

That was exactly what she'd done. This wasn't just about what she might lose with Sean. It wasn't just *their* friendship on the line.

It was everyone.

And it wasn't like she'd never thought about it before. Like she wasn't aware of how interlocked all their relationships were. She'd known from the very first year. It was why she'd always worked so hard to keep her feelings under wraps.

Because there was too much at stake.

But she hadn't been thinking about that last night.

Molly hit the stairs without looking back. She was halfway up when Ben came out the kitchen door laughing, a bag of charcoal under his arm.

Catching her eye, he grinned. "It was in the trunk."

Hugging the rail, she forced herself to laugh back, latching on to the exchange like a lifeline. "Exactly where I would have expected it to be."

Nodding at her, he asked, "Which way you heading?"

"I was going up. Need any help with the drink prep?" she offered.

"Hell yes. Let me drop the briquettes, and I'll meet you back up there in a minute. There's another bag of limes ready to go if you want to start on that."

"Deal." Honestly, something to keep her hands busy would be fantastic. Ben was always good for chitchat, and watching him work the girls was entertainment of the highest order. Or, more specifically, ribbing him over how he worked the girls. Besides, being at the bar station would give her a slew of people to talk to. Anything to keep her mind off this thing with Sean.

Chapter 8

TWICE, SEAN HAD STARTED TO GET UP TO GO AFTER MOLLY, and twice, Brody's meaty hand had shoved him back down on the bench. This was the worst-case scenario. Molly thinking he was avoiding her because he was upset about what had happened the night before, when really the reason he couldn't look at her for more than five seconds was because apparently in the last few hours, the doors had blown off the vault where he stored all his most forbidden Molly fantasies, and every time his eyes landed on her—his best fucking friend—he started mentally peeling off her clothes to get down to those polka-dot panties stretched across her perfect ass. And then he was putting her back across his lap, and this time, his hands were coasting over the backs of her bare thighs, stealing inside those panties so he could cup—

"See, I *told* you," Emily gloated, the smile she was giving her husband smug and superior and enough to yank Sean's attention back to the table and his friends who were still trying to make heads or tails of the bomb Molly had just dropped on them.

"Told him what?" he asked, feeling shitty on every count.

Emily shrugged, waving toward him. "This business with you and Molly. I told him there was something going on there. But typical guy"—she looked from Sean to Jase to Brody—"sorry, but you guys can be seriously dense when it comes to this business. Anyway, he said I was off the mark. Didn't know what I was talking about." She tossed her strawberry-blond waves off her shoulder and leaned forward on folded arms. "I'll accept your apology now."

Jase gave Sean a narrow-eyed look. "Wood?"

This was bullshit. He needed to talk to Molly. Explain what a low-down shit he was and make sure she understood that no matter what, she was still his girl. She'd always be his girl. He just had to put the perv who saw her as more back in the attic. Pushing to his feet again, he made it about halfway before Brody had him back down.

Firing the guy a hot look, Sean stopped and pulled his chin back. "You're texting?"

Brody shot him a grin and set his phone down on the table. "Yeah. Just letting Max know your dirty dog bone touched his sister."

Fucker. This wasn't the time to joke around.

Brody's phone sounded with a text. And then a second one, and Sean's stare widened, shifting to Brody, who looked way too pleased with himself.

A second later, Sean's phone pinged and then almost immediately started to ring.

Jase was stifling a laugh, and Emily tapped a finger on the table. "You should probably answer that."

Scowling at Brody, Sean dug out his phone from his pocket and stepped away from the bench. This time, he didn't get any resistance from Brody.

"Hey, Max, how's the honeymoon?" he asked as Emily chimed in from behind to say hi to Sarah.

"What in the fuck is your dick doing anywhere near my little sister?" came the slow, threatening growl of one of Sean's oldest friends. A guy Sean thought of as a brother but who, from the sound of it, was contemplating putting his fist through Sean's face. Because…he hadn't said *Molly*. Not *his sister* either.

No, Max had gone straight to his *little sister*.

Who was a twenty-seven-year-old woman, last Sean had checked.

He sighed, not in the mood for one Max's overprotective tantrums. Not when Molly was legitimately upset and he was flipping out with the need to make things right.

"It was an accident. Don't worry about it."

"Accident?" The guy's voice went up an entire octave. "You call—"

"Look, have a good last couple days. Molly and I are fine, but I gotta go."

He disconnected the call, and this time when Brody moved to block him, Sean put his own hand on the bigger guy's shoulder, pushing *him* firmly back into his seat. "I got this."

Taking the stairs two at a time, Sean wanted to kick his own ass for letting Molly walk away. He should have followed her immediately.

He hit the patio and scanned the crowd, nodding at the friends he recognized while he kept moving. And then he heard it, that laugh that had a way of filling his chest even when he felt completely empty. Following the sound, he stopped at the open door and found her behind the bar, head down, slicing limes beside Ben. Ben who kept cutting looks Molly's way, teasing her about her slicing technique and making her laugh again.

She was having fun and, hell, he didn't want to ruin it. So he hung back a minute, trying to figure out what he was going to say.

And then Ben stopped what he was doing and leaned a hip into the counter where they were working so he could look at her. No big deal. Sean liked looking at her too. She was beautiful, and when she smiled, it felt like the first sunny day after a month of rain.

That's how it had been for him since the first time he'd seen it. Of course, that first smile hadn't come until she'd been living with them for months. Months of trying to get a laugh out of the kid with the saddest, most guarded eyes he'd ever seen. And then one day, he'd made some stupid joke, and it had happened. The sun came out, warm and sweet and so damn bright, it cracked something open inside him.

One smile, and he'd been hooked. One smile, and that had been it for him. He'd been a goner.

Not like this. Not back then. But the way she'd looked at him from then on made him feel like he was *something*. It didn't have anything to do with his last name, who his father was, or what everyone knew was ahead for him. The way Molly had looked at him was about the guy he was at the core…and that was some addictive shit.

He loved her. And as she grew up, that protective, quasi-brotherly love had grown into a friendship like no other he had. Not even with her brother.

Ben grabbed a sprig of mint and tucked it behind Molly's ear.

She stopped slicing the second Ben reached for her, and then she was looking at the guy, gingerly touching the little green leaves peeking out from behind that silky bit of hot-pink hair. Sean closed his eyes, trying to quell the possessive beast clawing at his chest. He had no right. No business. No fucking reason for his fists to be balling up at his sides and his gut to be telling him it was time to take Ben apart once and for all. The guy had been sniffing around Molly for the better part of a decade and—and what? Sean's breath left his lungs in a rush as it hit him.

So what if Ben had been after Molly? The guy was kind of a dog, but no worse than Sean.

Ben might get around, but that didn't mean he wouldn't be serious about Molly.

Sean swallowed hard and pushed his feet to move. When he reached the front, he texted Brody that he was taking off. He wasn't in any mood for a party.

A stiff drink though? He could definitely go for one of those. Walking another block, he saw a bar on the corner. One he'd never been to or heard of. Perfect.

It looked like a neighborhood place, filled with a midtwenties crowd in casual summer clothes. Comfortable. He ordered a whiskey and looked down the bar to flash a grin at the girls who'd been watching him since he walked in.

He needed to stop thinking about the way Ben had touched Molly's hair or how she'd been giving him her smile. He needed to stop thinking about her at all.

The blond with the wild curls, bold red mouth, and tight Captain America T-shirt cocked her head to the side and asked if he wanted to join them for a drink. She had a hint of edge to her. Maybe this was just what he needed.

Coming home had been stupid. Molly sat forward on the couch, letting her eyes roam the empty apartment.

It had taken her a while to lick her wounds and scrape her pride back together before returning to her friends, fully expecting the hard-core razzing she totally deserved. But when she got back, Brody let her know that Sean had taken off. So she'd come home to find him. Only he wasn't there.

Turning her phone over in her hands, she swiped it to life and, for the tenth time, let it go dark without sending the text asking where he was.

She'd never been hesitant to contact him before. She'd text him if it was slow at Belfast just to ask what he was doing. Once she'd gotten a response back that he was in a meeting with the guys from the Rome, Paris, and Vienna Wyse locations. With a follow-up question asking what she was doing. She'd laughed, figuring he didn't need to know that she was marrying the ketchups. But then she'd gotten his next text with a series of question marks, and when she'd replied, he'd texted back within five minutes, calling her a hopeless romantic.

He'd been in an international sales and marketing meeting, and somehow, he'd still made sure she knew he always had time for her. And yet tonight, she couldn't bring herself to send the simple text asking where he was. Because she was afraid of the answer.

Tossing the phone on the couch, she pushed to her feet with a huff and walked back to the kitchen. All the freezer had to offer was an old takeout box encased in freezer burn. The fridge wasn't much better. Maybe she'd go shop. Stock up. Sitting around waiting for a guy who might or might not be coming home was making her feel pathetic. Especially since she wasn't sure he was going to want to talk to her when he did get home.

Checking her phone again, she thought about texting to see if there was anything he wanted her to pick up. It wasn't even nine. Totally reasonable.

Gah, she was being ridiculous. She circled the apartment looking for the canvas tote she used for shopping. Shoes, wallet, keys—

The apartment door swung open, and suddenly, there was Sean—her heart sank—with a smudge of fire-engine-red lipstick below his ear.

So now she knew where he'd been.

"You're here," he said, looking confused and something else she couldn't quite put her finger on. Guilty maybe.

Which he shouldn't.

Just like she shouldn't be feeling hurt to know he'd found a woman for a little off-hours recreation. This was Sean. That was his thing, and she'd grown out of it bothering her years ago. Mostly.

She set her bag down by the door. "You didn't tell me you were leaving. I came home to find you, but"—she stepped into his space to brush her thumb across his jaw, showing him the smudge of lipstick—"I guess you made other plans."

His eyes narrowed on her thumb and then went wide. "Shit, that's not what—" His hand closed around her wrist, warm and strong, and then he was tugging her down the hall to the bathroom with him. "That's not what I was doing."

Molly watched, stunned, as he turned on the water and pumped a squirt of soap into his hand.

"I went for a drink, just trying to get my head together and chill out. I feel like I keep fucking everything up and… Shit, Moll, I just wanted to stop. I wanted to get out of the way and let you have some fun, even if it meant you were with…" He shook his head and drew her hand down to the tap and began washing the red off her skin. "Okay, so I thought for a minute about taking her up on her offer when she made it. But then, hell." Sean released her hand and turned his attention to the now-faint streak of red by his ear. Soaping the spot and rinsing it, he met her eyes in the mirror. "I guess I just didn't want to. I didn't want her."

She shouldn't ask. She didn't need to know. But with Sean's deep-brown eyes locked with hers, she couldn't stop the question from whispering past her lips. "Why not?"

He held her reflected stare before turning to face her and taking a slow breath. "Because I couldn't stop thinking of you."

She shook her head. He didn't mean the words the way they sounded.

"I know it's not what you want to hear, Moll. And I'm sorry. But that's what was going on at the party and before. I couldn't look at you without seeing…" He blew out a harsh breath. "Without seeing something that's not mine to imagine. I didn't want you to know what was going through my head, so I was trying to dodge you until I could get it out."

That wasn't possible. She couldn't be hearing him right. Her head bowed as she fought for the breath coming too thin through her lungs. Because it sounded like Sean was telling her something she'd given up on hearing years ago. Like maybe, finally, he wanted—

"Molly, it's killing me that you think this is your fault or that you'd done something wrong." Ducking down, Sean caught her chin with the crook of his finger to bring her face up to his. Searching her eyes, he looked like he was about to say something more when his expression shifted. He straightened, pulling back as a furrow marred his brow.

"That look," he muttered, his voice low. "Jesus, Molly, you aren't supposed to be looking at me like that."

Her racing heart stalled as the floor dropped out from beneath her. She hadn't meant to let him see, hadn't been thinking anything other than that Sean wasn't mad at her. That maybe there was actually a chance for them. But the way Sean was looking at her didn't make her feel like that at all.

Running his big hand down his face, he swore into his palm, understanding filling his eyes. "I thought you were doing it on purpose. I thought it was part of some game, but that's not what this is, is it?"

Oh God. Anxiety knotted her stomach. She needed to answer him.

"I didn't mean to," she whispered, her throat going tight as tears inexplicably pushed at her eyes.

"No, I know," he assured her, as if he completely understood the grievous nature of what had happened. "Me either. You know what you mean to me. What our friendship means to me. I would never willingly risk it."

It was supposed to make her feel better, but all she

felt was an impending sense of dread. Because where did they go from here?

"Obviously, we can't change our living arrangements until this is resolved."

Huh? "We can't?" she asked, not sure if her ears were playing tricks on her and she was just hearing what she wanted to hear.

His eyes met hers, steady and clear. "No. I mean, not unless you feel like you still want me to go. I mean, if you do, Molly, I'll go. Tonight. It's just that I don't want to put any more distance between us until things are back to normal. Christ, Moll, I *need* us to get back to normal."

She was nodding fast, reaching for him as he pulled her into a hug. "I love you, Sean."

Burying his nose in her hair, he answered, "You too. We'll get through this, Moll."

Snug in the hold of Sean's strong arms, no secrets or lies between them for the first time in a week, she believed him.

His hold tightened. "I think we'll be okay so long as I don't get another look at those sex kitten yellow-and-green polka-dot panties."

Molly froze, then pulled back with a snort to look into his face. "You're serious."

Her panties were cotton briefs. Probably the least sexy thing she could imagine.

"As a heart attack, Moll. Those panties"—he bit his lip, closing his eyes as he shook his head—"with that little loopy edging. *Fuck*."

Was he talking about that little elastic scalloping around the top and legs? Crossing her arms, she asked, "Just how close a look at my panties did you get?"

"Believe me, not nearly as close as I wanted," he said, giving her one of those *sorry, not sorry* looks as he wrapped an arm around her back and led her out of the bathroom and into the kitchen.

"So the panties were the proverbial straw that broke the camel's back." It was weird, but the part of her that had always wished there was something about her that could attract Sean preened just a little.

"Pretty much." He walked to the fridge and pulled out a couple of beers. "What about you?"

Curling into her corner of the couch, she bit her lip as the realization hit her. This had been the one thing in her life, the only thing she hadn't been able to talk to Sean about…and now she could. He walked back and dropped down beside her, legs splayed in that comfortable, at-home way, and she grinned, cocking her head at him. "Shirtless, post-workout Sean is burn-the-house-down hot."

His brows shot high, and he took a long swallow of his beer. "I always figured post-workout Sean was pretty gross. In fact, I'm pretty sure I've had you running from him several times over the years."

She grinned into her beer, remembering the way Sean used to chase her around for a hug after getting back from a game of hoops when he'd been in school. "No, don't get me wrong, the cold, damp T-shirt is nothing I want to be pressed up against. But lose the shirt, and it's just all that warm skin and hard muscle, flushed red and beaded up with sweat." She smacked her lips for emphasis. "They could make a Tumblr GIF out of you, for real."

"Shut up," he said, laughing.

"No. It's that hot. Especially when your hair is going every which way. That's like the cherry on top of the Sean-candy sundae. The messy hair might even be more potent than the shirtless part."

"Messy, huh?" He looked like he couldn't quite believe her, but then this wasn't something she'd ever shared with him before.

"Messy Sean is my favorite Sean." She turned to him. "Not just because he looks so good on you, but because I like you best when you're all relaxed instead of watching your words to maintain an appropriate public image for Wyse. I like the Sean I get behind closed doors. The one who sits like a guy and says everything he thinks and makes me laugh at all his inappropriate jokes."

Throwing his arm over the back of the couch, he turned to face her, his eyes serious. "I'm not that Sean very often anymore."

She shrugged. "You are to me. Even when you're all suited up and on your best, most bland behavior, when you're looking at me, that's the guy I see."

"That's why you're my favorite." Stretching out the arm behind the couch, he caught a bit of her hair between his fingers and met her eyes again. "All the time, Moll."

"Sean, you're kind of giving me that swollen-heart feeling," she warned quietly.

Their eyes held a moment longer, and then he blew out a short breath. "Yeah, and I'm getting a semi." He shifted back into the cushions, not so much putting more distance between them as adjusting it with his posture. Removing the deep-eye staring and potential for an escalating situation. "Time for some negative reinforcement." Rolling his head against the cushion to look at her, he asked, "You ready for this?"

She laughed, enjoying the return to a state of full disclosure with her best friend. "I don't know, what are we talking about?"

Grabbing the remote, Sean scrolled through the offerings. "Brace yourself, Moll. This is going to be rough."

A close-up of what looked like a half-finished sweater lit up the screen as a woman's gentle lilting voice ran like nails down a blackboard, immediately drawing every muscle in Molly's back tight. "No," she snapped, reaching for the remote and failing when one of Sean's hands planted against her forehead and the other held the remote out of reach.

"Sorry, Moll." He laughed, fighting her off. "It's for the greater good. Drastic times, drastic measures and all that."

Squirming, she stuffed her bare foot into his armpit and wiggled her toes. "You sound like a girl," she taunted at his shocked squeak. "I will not watch this knitting show. I work three jobs, Sean. My downtime is precious."

"All the better," he countered, dropping the remote behind the couch to catch her foot. "Every time we get a case of the wayward thoughts, we turn this shit on as punishment. Pretty soon, we'll be safely back in the land of Platonica."

Molly shuddered and withdrew her foot as Sean eased off her forehead. "God, I hate you."

Clinking his beer to hers, he eased back into the cushions, a smug smile stretching his lips. "See? It's working already."

"Your boner's gone?" she asked, forcing herself to watch the camera pan across the yarn. They were going to need more beer, she thought, taking a long swallow.

"Not even close," Sean replied casually, causing beer to snort out her nose. He shook his head. "Damn, not even now."

Chapter 9

SATURDAY MORNING WAS ROUGH, THANKS IN NO SMALL PART to the drinking game Molly had come up with the night before. Every time the camera zoomed in when a new length of yarn slipped free of the ball for what Molly called "the money shot," they had to drink. Sean had only planned to force ten minutes of the yarn porn on them, but then there'd be another infraction, and they'd had to add more to the tally. It had been a long night, and at its end, Sean knew more about the value of maintaining a steady tension than he'd ever wanted to.

And waking up to a cacophony of ringing phones, pinging texts, repetitive buzzing from the intercom, and then incessant hammering at the front door hadn't been his favorite way to meet the day. Molly's either, considering the bleary-eyed scowl on her face when he'd run into her stumbling for the door.

"It's after ten." Emily laughed, shaking her head as if Sean was crazy for demanding to know what she and Jase were thinking, barging in on them at the crack of dawn. "And we made plans last night, right?"

The hell they had.

Jase at least had the good grace to keep his eyes trained on the far corner of the ceiling as his leggy wife strutted into the apartment like she owned the place.

"Oh, you know what?" She stopped and looked from Molly to Sean, one finger tapping her chin.

"You guys might have already left when we decided to do breakfast. Well, you're always up for anything, so you don't mind, right? I mean, we shopped, and Brody said he'd cook, even though he thinks you need a new cooktop."

Jesus, apparently Emily wasn't going to stop talking until they just gave up.

"Jase, baby, you want to unload this stuff over on the counters? Just move the beer bottles. Wow, looks like you guys had a good time," she stated, her eyes glinting expectantly as she again looked from Molly back to him.

Ahh. Now he got it.

And Molly must have too. "Okay," she mumbled through a yawn. "You're trying to figure out if Sean nailed me."

Sean cut her a look. "Way to cheapen it."

The corner of her mouth kicked up as she padded into the kitchen and pulled a can of coffee from the cabinet. "Sorry. I meant that Em was trying to figure out if you made sweet, sweet love to me."

Emily's hands clasped beneath her chin, and she bounced in place. "Yes! That's what I want to know. Tell me you did." Turning that laser stare on Sean, she did that whisper-at-full-volume thing, pleading, "Please tell me you were waiting for her when she went after you, and then you kind of caught her up against you and kissed her with everything you've been holding back for...for, what, like twelve years?"

Sean was about to cut in when Brody's voice boomed from the front of the apartment. "Better not have been that long. Max'd tear your head off if he found out you've been after his little sister since she was fifteen."

Head dropping, Sean prayed for patience. But on the next breath, he smelled something even better. "Coffee?"

"Got you covered, my man," Brody said, stopping beside him with two carriers filled with hot, steamy goodness. "Front right is yours."

Molly had shoved the canister away and was biting her lip as she moved in for her cup. "Brody, I take back all the terrible things I tell people at work about you."

He answered with a gruff laugh and passed Em and Jase theirs before taking the last cup for himself. There was a moment of silence, followed by a round of low appreciative moans. But it was the one closest to him that Sean couldn't ignore. Molly's eyes were closed, those dark-blond lashes dusting her cheekbones as her tongue peeked out to catch a stray bit of foam from her top lip.

He swallowed hard and stepped back a pace to get the remote from where it was resting on the back of the couch.

The TV came to life, and Molly arched a brow. "Really?"

Working hard to keep his thoughts on the blissed-out narrator channeling 1977, Sean nodded.

Molly's eyes hazed as they ran over him. Slowly.

Fuck.

She reached behind her and grabbed the kitchen timer. When she set it on the butcher block facing him, it was set to twenty minutes.

Ten for him.

He gulped.

Ten for her.

Emily was talking again, rewinding her fantasy about

events that hadn't happened. "Okay, just tell me what happened when you guys took off. Sean looked like he was about to do physical violence to Ben when he stuck that mint in your ear."

Okay, now she had his full attention. "What?"

"I followed you up to make sure you didn't do anything crazy. Which you looked like you were about to do. But then you just…left. And I went back down to the party."

Sean turned to Molly, who was looking at him. He rolled his eyes as if Emily was making more of it than there had been. She wasn't.

Molly walked over to Emily and, gently rubbing her arms, broke the news. "Sorry, Emily. There was no sweet, sweet lovemaking. We just needed to talk and let things get back to normal."

Emily looked to Sean, obviously hoping he'd call Molly a bald-faced liar. "Sorry, Em."

Brody was separating egg whites over at the counter. "So gotta ask. What's with the yarn work? I didn't think you were the crafty type, Moll."

She grinned. "I'm not. Sean's trying out a few new stress-management techniques."

Brat. But damn, that smile on her when she knew she'd gotten him good. "Add another ten to the clock, Moll."

The smile she flashed him made him feel like he'd just been thanked for paying her a compliment. So he gave her a wink before turning to Brody. "It's negative conditioning. When we get a case of inappropriate thoughts, we add ten minutes to the clock. This show is brutal. We'll be past this stuff in no time."

Jase rubbed at the back of his neck and looked to his wife. "I told you they were idiots."

Brow furrowed, Emily waved him aside. "So after the boner incident, you guys are suffering from a case of mutual attraction? And instead of say…giving in to it… you're watching knitting?" When they both shrugged, she straightened, huffing out a breath. "That's the most asinine thing I've ever heard. What's the matter with you two?"

Sean turned to Molly and saw the clock was up to forty minutes now. She was sweet. "You got this?"

She nodded, pulling her hair back with one of those little elastics that were always materializing out of nowhere. "It's not like with you and Jase, where you suddenly realized you were in love and wanted forever."

"Well, that's not exactly how it went down," Emily corrected slowly.

Molly rolled her eyes. "Okay, Em, you haven't known Sean as long as the rest of us, but I'm sure you're familiar with his plans to land a specific *quality* of wife, thus ensuring a certain *standard* of marriage. Those plans haven't changed, and in case it isn't obvious, I don't really stack up to be a future Mrs. Wyse."

Sean was nodding—mostly because Molly was the one talking and he figured whatever it was she said, he'd be agreeing with—but as the words passed from her lips to his ears, that mindless bobble action slowed to a stop. If Molly thought the reason he didn't consider her marriage material was because she was in some way lacking, she was dead wrong.

They'd all given him shit about his plans before, Molly more than anyone. But it had always been in the abstract or at the very least about someone other than Molly. He never thought of the girls he casually hooked up with as not being good enough. And as far as Molly went? It was because of everything she *was* that he wouldn't put her through the kind of life being with him would mean. Not because of what she wasn't.

Molly lived her life out loud. She was a free spirit, bursting with energy and excitement and laughter and love. And his life—hell, it was restrictive and locked down. His life was about being proper and polite. About remembering there was a time and a place. About presenting a public image in line with the legacy he'd been born into. His life was about business. And the idea of Molly trying to conform—trying to turn down the vibrancy that was his very fucking favorite thing about her—he'd never want that.

But hearing Molly suggest that she was somehow less than what he'd been looking for in a wife—or more specifically, than what had been drilled into his head about the kind of woman who would be an appropriate partner in the life he'd been born into—was nuts.

"I'm…I'm like an itch that's going to go away on its own," she was saying now. "Without getting scratched."

"You fit into my plans, Moll," Sean said, cutting her off. "I can't imagine my future without you being a part of it. But I'm pretty sure the kind of marriage you're looking for isn't the kind just as easily referred to as an arrangement." Hell, he wasn't even sure it was enough for him anymore. "You're more than that, Moll. Not less."

He shrugged, looking at each of the guys in turn. "That's why we're watching yarn porn. Because what

Moll and I have together, *our friendship*, is too important to risk screwing up with…screwing."

Molly turned to him and cocked her head. "You say
the sweetest things."

He winked at her and got on with the impromptu
brunch they'd both have preferred to sleep through.
After adding another ten to the clock.

———

"Max, I told you already, nothing happened." Molly
sighed, pinching the bridge of her nose. Cutting a look
across the apartment to where Sean was heaping the
leftovers from brunch onto a giant tortilla, she covered
the receiver. "This is the sixth call in less than twenty-
four hours."

Sean pointed an oversize spoon filled with cold goat-
cheese-and-chive scrambled eggs at her. "And who do
we have to thank for that, little Miss Runs-at-the-Mouth-
about-Private Roommate-Happenings?" A glob of eggs
hit the counter, and Sean scooped it up and popped it in
his mouth. "Besides, I don't want to hear it. I stopped
answering after the fourth call last night."

Grabbing a dishrag, he wiped the counter.

Man, he was the best roommate.

Max was droning on in the background about making
smart choices and how she knew better than to let herself
get into a situation that would leave her vulnerable. She
wanted to ask if he'd forgotten that he was talking about
one of his best friends but instead took a steadying
breath and did what had to be done. "Max, you're on
your honeymoon for another two days. Pay attention to
your bride before she decides to stamp Return to Sender

on your ass and lets one of those saucy scuba guides give her a few buddy breathing lessons."

Sean raised a brow in her direction, and she had to pinch her lips together not to laugh. Because all she was getting from the other end of the line was silence. It was low, but as Sean had said the other night, desperate times and all that.

"Okay, Moll," Max stated, sounding uneasy enough to cause a stab of guilt. "Be good, and I'll see you Monday night."

"Make it Tuesday. Love you, Big Brother." She disconnected the call and pushed up from the couch to meet Sean in the kitchen.

He'd microwaved his burrito and had the thing cradled between his hands, half of it miraculously gone already. The guy could seriously eat.

"So I think I scored us a reprieve. At least until they get back."

"Yeah," Sean said around another obscene bite. "And when he does, I have a feeling I'll be looking at a sit-down with him to explain in exacting detail what my dick was doing anywhere near your no-fly zone."

Molly waved the burrito over, because it smelled crazy good. She took a bite and then grabbed his arm so she could take another. "Oh my God, that's even better left over than it was fresh," she said, chewing around her words.

Sean grinned and leaned back into the counter. "We going to hear Gib play tonight?"

"You were the one worried about his sister always being there."

He nodded and chewed some more. Then shrugged.

"True, but it'd be good to get out of the apartment. Get a break from this." He grunted, pointing to the sweater in progress on the screen. They were zooming in on some really fine cable work in a soft peach.

"Nice tension there," Molly commented, and when Sean agreed with a considering nod, she knew he was right. "We definitely need to get out of here."

It was starting to get kind of hot, the way he actually paid attention to the show.

Three hours later, Molly and Sean walked into the dark club, nodded once, and split up. It was almost a relief to get some space, not because she was trying to hide anything from him, but because at least if he wasn't in her direct line of sight, there was a chance she might not have to add any more minutes to the yarn porn.

The bar where Gib was playing was one they'd been to many times and always enjoyed. It was an older place, not quite half the size of Belfast, with a worn but welcoming feel to it. Heading for the bar, she saw Jill and waved.

"I forgot you were off tonight too," Jill chirped, greeting Molly with a hip bump before craning her head around. "Damn, no Sean? I was hoping for a few fireworks, Moll."

This was what she got for being all open and honest with everyone. Still, it was better than that sick feeling she got when she was trying to hide things from her friends.

"Relax, he's here." She turned around on her stool to check out the back where the band would be playing and found Sean across the crowd. His head came up, and when their eyes met, the corner of his mouth pulled into her favorite crooked grin. "But don't get excited about any fireworks. Our little public tiff has been resolved, and we're back to our chummy selves."

Jill flagged the bartender for another beer, handing hers to Molly. "Not that kind of fireworks. Please, I can watch you guys bicker any time. I'm thinking more about the sizzle-and-pop kind that ends with the authorities having to break out the fire hoses to get you apart. I mean, since they don't have the knitting channel here at the bar."

Molly choked on her swallow of beer, smacking the bottle down on the bar as she gaped at Jill, who was shamelessly grinning at her.

"You heard?" she coughed out.

Jill nodded back at her. "So how's the knitting aversion-therapy thing working out so far?"

Slumping against the bar, Molly sighed. "Not as well as we'd hoped. At least from my end." They'd been tuned into the channel for almost the entire day, and Sean had even found some app for their phones to track all the hours they'd been racking up. The only problem was that just hearing Jill mention yarn had Molly's body reacting in ways it shouldn't. "Honestly, I'm starting to worry the knitting thing might be reinforcing the bad behavior."

Jill squinted at her over the top of her beer. "So you remember when I first started at Belfast and I was still trying to take off those extra pounds?"

Molly thought back and then shook her head. For as long as she'd known Jill, the girl had been giving Molly a serious case of curve envy. She couldn't ever remember Jill looking like anything but a bombshell.

"Whatever. I was dieting, and it took months to get back to where I wanted to be. Months of fighting cravings for all the things I wanted but couldn't have."

Jill had her attention. "Go on."

"So here's the deal. When you want something— say, like a doughnut—and you keep telling yourself you can't have it, not to even think about it, that doughnut starts taking over your world. You can't function right because it's there, dripping warm chocolate over your every thought."

"Yeah." Molly was nodding, because Sean was dripping his hotness all over her world, and if he didn't stop, it was going to get messy.

And now she was thinking about him giving her that all-trouble smile of his as chocolate ran in a hot mess down her fingers. Fingers he was bringing to his mouth to… *Dang it!* "What do you do to get the doughnut out of your head?"

"Simple," Jill said with a shrug. "Eat it."

And this time when Molly choked, she couldn't even blame it on the beer.

Jill was rolling her eyes now, laughing. Which was so going to cost her when Molly was putting the schedule together for the next week. "Settle, Moll. I'm not talking about the *whole doughnut*…but you have maybe a bite. A nibble." Her eyes lit up. "A doughnut hole. Just enough to satisfy the craving before you go off the deep end at Dunkin' Donuts, snarfing down a baker's dozen in one sitting. 'Cause you know you won't feel good about it if you do."

Molly was pretty sure her mouth was hanging open, and if Sean happened to glance over from his end of the place, the way she looked in that moment would probably be enough to curb whatever cravings he'd been suffering on the spot. Giving her head a shake, she pushed off the stool and took another long swallow. "So, have you ever actually applied this technique to a guy? Or is this all theory?"

"Theory," Jill admitted, then waved past her to the girls who'd just cleared the front door. "Hey, my friends are here. Good luck, and let me know how it goes."

Pass on that. Sean might be a lot of things, but a doughnut hole wasn't one of them.

Though as Molly started toward the end of the bar where the band was setting up in front of the small dance area, she caught sight of Gib's sister, Amber, swaying back and forth to the overhead music while she stood much too close to Sean. The way she was nibbling at her bottom lip while she stared at him looked like *she* was after a bite of his doughnut.

Molly hung back a minute, waiting to see how it would unfold this time. Sean had taken her home once a few years ago and then made the mistake of doing it a second time about a year later. Now, every time their paths crossed, there was a gleam of expectation in Amber's eyes, and she wasn't very subtle about letting Sean know what she wanted.

Amber reached out and plucked what Molly was willing to bet her boots was a bit of nothing from Sean's shirt. He flashed one of those charming smiles, the kind he had for the camera and visiting dignitaries, and smoothly took a step back. With the way he rolled through the women in this city, Sean could handle situations like this one in his sleep. But tonight, when his eyes came up and met hers, Molly could see pleading there. Or maybe she just wanted to, but either way, in the next blink, she was closing the distance between them, stepping into the space he had waiting for her. She hooked an arm around Sean's waist as he slung his around her shoulders. And like that, the situation was defused, which was nice, because Amber was pretty cool, and the three of them talked a while before she left to greet a few other friends.

When she was gone, Sean leaned in close to her ear. "Thanks, Moll."

And that warm rush of air… Add ten minutes to the log.

Slipping out of his hold, she nodded toward the worn stage, where the band was ready to play. The front man, dressed in a loose T-shirt and a pair of beat-up jeans that looked like he might have painted a house in them, started off with an introduction to the rest of the aggressively casual band members and then within minutes had the entire place rocking their bodies in time to an upbeat indie sound. They were covering the Revivalists and Big Head Todd and the Monsters, mixing new hits with old favorites. The air heated with the press of bodies in motion, and soon Molly was slick, covered in a thin layer of perspiration, her heart pounding in time with the heavy beat as she let herself go.

Eyes closed, she gave in to the pull of the music, letting her arms drift overhead. Her T-shirt crept higher on her midriff, allowing a bit of air from the overhead fan and air-conditioning to reach her warm skin.

And then he was there. Without looking, she knew it was Sean moving in time with her hips, his muscular

arms wrapped loosely around her waist, the hard planes
of his chest brushing against her back.

When she turned to face him, there was a sheen of
sweat on his forehead, and she could see the roots of
his sun-god hair were damp. His eyes were locked with
hers, and he was wearing that half smile she'd never
been able to resist. Giving herself over to the music and
the moment, she reached for all that too-neat hair.

"Molly," he warned with a single shake of his head,
but she couldn't resist.

Pushing her fingers through the damp strands, she
ran them around until Sean looked every bit as unruly
as she felt. He shook her off, catching her wrists in his
hands. This was where he would throw his head back
and laugh, maybe sending her out in a quick spin as
they returned their attention to the band—but that's
not what happened. Where there should have been
laughter, Sean's brows drew forward and his jaw went
hard. Instead of reeling her out, he used the hold on her
wrists to pull her closer. His hands moved to her hips,
his fingers spreading wide. Flexing. The band and the
bar and the crowd pressing in on them seemed to fall
away as they tumbled deep and deeper still into each
other's eyes.

It was just dancing. That was what she was telling
herself, even as the hot churn low in her belly called her
a liar. Promising it was more.

The last notes sounded, and suddenly, the crowd
that had been pushing at them from every direction was
thinning out, the house lights coming on as the sound
system started playing overhead. Sean looked around,
withdrawing one hand from her hip and then the other.

Retrieving his phone, he pulled up his new app and shook his head. "Why don't we just call it an even hour?"

He was being conservative. An hour probably wouldn't have covered her infractions alone, but at this point, she wasn't sure it mattered. The knitting wasn't doing anything but possibly spurring a kink she wasn't sure she'd ever be able to share with anyone else.

"Forget the app, Sean. Just"—she drew a long breath and took his hand—"come with me a minute. We've got to talk."

They cut around to the back hallway. Half a dozen girls were waiting for the ladies' room, and while the men's was open…gross. This wasn't going to take long, but even a second in a public men's room was more than Molly could handle. Pulling Sean farther, she pushed out the back door and waited for him to prop it open with a broken slat of wood. They could still hear the music—one of those Ed Sheeran songs was playing—but it was quieter outside, and they were alone in the alley.

Sean took a step back and ran his hand through his hair, pausing when he realized the state of disarray she'd left it in. "You messed up my hair," he accused, his grin telling her that he knew how much she'd liked doing it.

She shook her head, unable to play along. "You're messing up my mind."

The half smile fell away, and then Sean was stepping closer, his eyes going serious. "If this is about the dancing, Moll—"

"It's not. It's about you and me figuring out something besides aversion therapy, because the knitting isn't working."

Sean sighed, looking relieved. "I wasn't going to say

anything, because it was still early and I was hoping…
but you're right. I want to say whatever's going on
between us will go away on its own. That if we just
ignore it, eventually it will stop being an issue."

Molly nodded, then shook her head and stepped into
Sean's space. "Or maybe… Okay, I know this is going
to sound nuts, and it probably is, but I was talking to Jill
inside and…" And this sounded so stupid, she couldn't
believe she was even thinking about suggesting it, but
then Sean ducked low, putting his face back into her
line of sight and giving her that smile that promised she
could tell him anything.

"What is it?"

"Do you ever really wish you could have a doughnut,
but you know you shouldn't? Like you're trying to cut
back on bad carbs or processed sugar, or maybe they
were just out of doughnuts when you went to the stand
and you figured you'd just wait until you could get one
another day, but then all day you think about the doughnut, because you didn't just have it when you wanted
it, so when you finally, *finally* see a chance to get the
doughnut again, you make a really bad decision and buy,
like, all the doughnuts they have and eat and eat and eat
until you're sick to your stomach and filled with regret?"

That endearing smile had left Sean's face, but being
Sean, he was taking her question to heart. He rubbed a
hand along his jaw and cocked his head to the side. "No.
I bust my ass at the gym so I don't worry about carbs
and sugar, and when I want a doughnut, I get one. And I
mean, this sounds pretty obnoxious, but if I really want
a doughnut and the stand doesn't have one, I call down
to Jerry, and I've got one in the next twenty minutes."

Molly blew out a breath in a silent plea for patience. This guy ran the most successful hotel in the city, could do her taxes in his head, and knew the answer to every *Jeopardy* question every time they watched the show… and yet he couldn't see where she was going with this?

"Say it's a special doughnut and—"

"I'm more of a bagel guy."

Maybe she should have used an éclair.

"*You're the doughnut, Sean!*" she snapped, exasperation wearing her thin. "*You* are the doughnut I'm craving. The one I keep thinking about when I'm supposed to be thinking of other things. You. And all I was saying is that maybe what we need to do is give in just a little. Have a taste to curb the craving… Before we crack and wake up surrounded by shredded Dunkin' Donut bags and a bed filled with crumbs."

Sean had stopped moving. Heck, he looked like he might not even be breathing, he was so still. Except for his eyes, which had gone dark and serious as they searched hers.

"Molly, what kind of a taste are you talking about?" he asked, his voice gone gravelly rough.

She swallowed past the anxious knot in her throat. "A kiss. Not more than a doughnut hole."

His stare dropped to her mouth. "You're talking about now? Here?"

She angled her head, taking in the setting. The concrete was cracked, and Dumpsters lined one side of the alley, while fire escapes hung overhead. She looked at someone's discarded McDonald's bag and nodded. "Yeah, this is probably perfect for our needs." At Sean's raised brow, she explained. "It's not romantic, so I don't have to worry about you getting caught up in some princess fantasy. We're only semiprivate out here. While if we were at home, we'd have zero chance of getting interrupted."

"Plus, the assortment of sexable surfaces on hand back at your place."

"I know. Don't get me started. But here, the atmosphere isn't really conducive to going too far. You know what I mean?"

The muscle in his jaw bounced, and he met her eyes. "You worried about things going too far?"

He wasn't? "No. But better safe than sorry, right?"

He moved a step closer, his single slow breath seeming to fill out his chest and broaden his shoulders. "Sure."

She swallowed hard. "Honestly, it's probably going to be gross when we finally do it."

Sean nodded, close enough now for his hands to settle on her hips. "If you say so."

Her hands met his stomach, her fingers briefly catching the fabric of his shirt before coasting up to rest lightly on his shoulders. "Just a taste," she whispered, her lungs tight as their eyes met.

"Just enough to satisfy the craving," he corrected, lowering his mouth to hers so slowly, she knew he was giving her this last chance to back out. Maybe she should have, but after all the years of wondering, being this close to knowing what Sean's kiss tasted like was something she couldn't back away from.

And then…*contact*.

Chapter 10

His kiss was firm and bold. No hesitation, no tentative whisper of his lips meeting hers. But then Sean wasn't the kind of man who ever did anything he wasn't committed to. And based on the skilled glide and draw of his mouth against hers, he had most definitely committed to this. The flick of his tongue at the seam of her lips had her gasping as a tingling heat shot straight through her to her center. She clutched at his shoulders, opening beneath the press of his mouth. Moaning at his tightening hold as his hands shifted, smoothing across her lower back and pulling her in close.

Wow. Closer to Sean was incredibly good. All those muscles she'd been valiantly trying to ignore were right there. Flush against her thighs, belly, and breasts and, yeah, they were every bit as amazing as they'd looked.

His tongue dipped past her lips, sweeping over hers in a wet velvet caress that had her humming against him, pushing to her toes for more. He bowed over her, kissing her harder, giving her what her body had been begging for. Her arms linked around his neck, holding tight. Their tongues were moving in time, one sliding over the other, stroking soft and firm, slipping from her mouth to his and back. It was so good, so right. So hot and sweet and—*yes*.

His hand moved over her bottom in a greedy press,

continuing to the top of her thigh where his fingers splayed wide.

He groaned into her mouth. *Groaned* like somehow the feel of her leg in his grip was more than he could contain. And that *so* worked for her. She opened beneath the thrust of his tongue, burying her fingers in the thick strands of his hair and cocking her knee to give him more access to the back of her thigh.

Access he made ready use of, pulling her leg up along the outside of his. Running his hand to her ass and back, squeezing and gripping and groaning along the way. The kiss turned ravenous. Like blow-the-top-off-the-meter hot.

Another demanding thrust, and a spasm ripped through her center, wringing a needy cry from her.

"Fuck, Molly," he growled, and the tortured sound of his voice was almost as good as when, in the next breath, he bowed over her again, catching her other leg and pulling her up.

"*Yes!*" she hissed, hooking her legs around his hips and then moaning at the feel of him, so hard, at the place where their bodies met. She couldn't get enough of his mouth, of the way his hands felt like they were every-where, of this man she'd ached for, panting for breath as he muttered her name again and again.

Her back met the rough bricks behind her, and she kissed Sean harder, gasping his name like a plea as he rocked into her, hitting that perfect spot again and again. Nothing had ever felt this good before, this right. So completely perfect while being not nearly enough.

Sean was growling something against that tender spot where her neck met her shoulder.

"Uh-huh," she replied blindly, because she was good with whatever he was saying as long as it meant *more*. More of his wicked mouth and hot grasping hands. More of her name rumbling low against her ear. More of Sean's arms around her, his breath in her hair, and—

"Oh shit!" A female voice giggled a second before the back door slammed closed with a clang.

Molly's eyes snapped open, and those roving, needy hands that had been all over her froze where they were, the body they were attached to going as stiff as her own. A horn blared, and a few shouts sounded from a distance, the typical city night noise landing like reality slapping her in the face.

Her heart hadn't stopped pounding, her body burned, and her breath came in ragged draws, but with every thunk of a car door, roar of an engine, and wail of a siren that passed, more of her ability to reason returned. Until she was aware with crystal clarity of just how far things had gone in the Dumpster-lined alley behind the bar where they'd been hanging out with friends.

Oh shit. What had they done?

Her legs unraveled from Sean's waist. He helped her to her feet and then turned away before she'd even gotten a look at his eyes. A hint at how he was taking what had just happened.

The metal door to the bar opened again, and Jill popped her head out, offering a weak "Sorry" as she returned the broken slat of wood to where it had been propping the door open before.

Jill. The floor dropped out of her belly, and Molly spun back to Sean, who was still facing the other way and appeared to be adjusting his pants.

"Everything okay over there?" she asked with a nervous laugh.

Sean's head dropped forward, and then he laughed too. Not the big, full laugh she loved to hear out of him, but a quiet, thoughtful laugh that hit all the right chords within her. This was going to be okay.

Walking back to her, he smoothed her flyaway hair and then helped her adjust her shirt and skirt. "Yeah, but just barely." His eyes fixed on her mouth, and he brushed it with his thumb, softly and only once. "That was—"

"Not gross," she supplied, still a little lost in the look he was giving her.

"No. Not at all." Gently unhooking her fingers from where they'd found their way between the buttons of his shirt, he cleared his throat. "But what I was going to say was that it was definitely enough to satisfy the craving. Right?"

Umm. No. Not even a little bit. That craving she'd been bitching and moaning about prior to the kiss hadn't been anything. Not compared to the inferno of need raging through her veins right then. But if it worked for Sean… "Sure. Right. You bet. Totally."

Sean nodded, his smile looking strained. But then he wasn't nodding, and he wasn't smiling either. He'd somehow switched to shaking his head, and that frown on his face matched the darkness in his eyes. "Fuck. Your mouth, Molly," he groaned, taking another step back. "I never should have gotten a taste of it."

Relieved not to be the only one feeling a little mixed up over what had just happened, she sagged back into the wall where she'd just been pinned, then remembering it was a dank alley—and even though it didn't stink or look gross, it probably was—she pushed back up and stepped away from it.

Sean waved a hand toward the wall. "Sorry about that."

"I don't think either of us was thinking totally clearly. I mean, I was touching it, and I didn't even notice. If it hadn't been for Jill, I would have let you—"

Sean's hands came up in front of him like he was warding her off. "Jesus, don't say it. Having that kiss in my head is bad enough. I don't think I could handle you putting any more ideas in there."

That was not what she'd been expecting.

He cleared his throat. "Seriously, Moll, you can't look at me like that."

She blinked, her brows furrowing. "What?"

"You're doing that thing again with the eyes. You know, where I thought it was just a play, but it turned out to be real."

That thing? She looked down at the broken concrete between their feet, because if she'd had any control over *that thing* she'd been doing with her eyes, none of this would be an issue at all. That thing had been the harbinger of this escalating nonplatonic situation.

"That kiss was probably a mistake." She didn't want it to be true, but the writing was on the wall.

"Sorry, Moll. But the whole taste-to-curb-the-craving thing? Not even close to working. We need to shut this down now."

"Totally," she agreed, wanting to mean it. Certain she would too, as soon as every nerve and sense stopped sizzling with a need for more of what Sean had just given her.

Sean was still half hard as they returned to the bar
through the door they'd left. Jill was standing at the end
of the hallway, hopping around, her grin stretching from
ear to ear.

Molly headed over to her, hands patting the air in
front of her in an effort to calm the other woman down,
while Sean headed straight for the bar. To cool himself
off, fast.

The bartender pushed a pint in front of him, and he
downed half of it. What had he been thinking? Not that
kissing Molly would be a good idea. Or that there was
even a chance one kiss would be enough to take the edge
off. Ha. He wasn't an idiot. He'd been to high school and
remembered well enough how every inch the girls had
given him had only served to make him work harder for
the mile. No way he'd thought it would be any different
with Molly. But when she'd suggested it… *Fuck*. The
opportunity was there, and he'd wanted to know what it
would be like. So even knowing better, he'd gone along.

Turning so he was leaning back against the bar, he
scanned the crowd for the white blond of her hair, thinking about its silky texture slipping through his fingers
and falling around his face when he'd hoisted her up.
And when her legs wrapped around him, those fucking
amazing legs, clutching at his hips. Her skirt shoved up
so he could feel her heat and—

Yeah, he'd messed up but good.

Molly was standing with the band, nodding her
head to whatever the guy with the overeager smile was
saying. She looked…well, shit, she looked normal. Not

like she was going crazy thinking about the taste of him on her tongue. Not like he felt.

Maybe she was doing what he'd suggested and just shutting it down.

But then she turned her head, her eyes finding his across the room. And he knew—he could see it in that look she couldn't stop giving him—that she wasn't any better off than he was.

Tossing back the rest of his beer, he pulled out his phone and texted her.

Sean: You're making it worse.

A second later, Molly had her phone out, a smile playing at the corners of her lips. At least that was better. No matter how badly they screwed up, as long as he could see that smile, he knew somehow everything was going to be okay. The conversation with the guys from the band was still going on around her, but she seemed to have shifted to the fringe edge of the group.

Molly: Pot meet kettle. Fix your hair. You look... played with

He turned, checking to see if there was a mirror behind the bar, but already another message was coming through. A picture of him, with his hair tangled in too many directions to count. Jesus.

Finger combing the mess, he raised a brow at her.

Molly: Marginally better.

But there was a glint of amusement in her eyes that said she was lying. More than that, the glint was tempting him to get closer. To forget about the "space" they were violating in spirit, if not action, and just—

A slim set of shoulders bumped into him, jerking his attention from Molly to the woman taking a quick step back from him, an apologetic look on her face.

"I'm so sorry. I knew I shouldn't have worn these stupid heels." She shook her head, sending a half-wild mop of corkscrew curls tumbling around her shoulders. "I didn't spill your drink, did I? I'd be happy to buy you another."

Sean was shaking his head, trying to be polite to the obviously embarrassed woman in front of him, while simultaneously trying and failing to keep his attention from skating past her to the far side of the bar.

"I'm fine"—he held up his empty glass—"and my beer was gone already."

"So the only thing hurt is my pride?" she asked with a nice laugh and edged past him to the open stool at the bar. She sat and, pulling her feet up, sighed. "Oh my God, that's almost better than sex."

Wow.

But then her eyes bugged, as if she'd just realized what she'd said, before she squinted them shut again in what he would guess was deep embarrassment. Molly would love this. And she'd make this poor girl feel better too.

Sean glanced back across the bar, ready to wave her over, but this time, Molly wasn't looking at him. Returning his attention to the woman, he caught sight of her shoes and coughed out a laugh. Because damn, they had to be five-inch heels. Intense.

"Now I get it. How do you balance with those skinny… Never mind. If I were you, I'd hold on to that seat all night and then pay the bartender to piggyback you out to a cab."

Rotating her ankle this way and that, she nodded. "I wonder if I could upgrade to a princess hold instead of piggy for an extra twenty. You know, because with the dress and all."

He laughed. "Worth a shot."

Molly would definitely like this girl.

Smiling up at him, she held out her hand and introduced herself, then nodded to the bartender. "I'm going to order something incredibly strong from this guy." Her head cocked to the side, and she peered up at him from beneath her lashes. "Can I get a drink for you too?"

He hadn't really noticed it before, but she was a very good-looking woman. And that was most definitely interest in her eyes.

Which sort of put a damper on the easy exchange between them. Because—well, because of Molly.

But as soon as the thought rolled through his head, he stopped short. There wasn't anything between him and Molly. Or at least there wasn't supposed to be. They'd said they were going to shut this thing between them down, so they would.

A lot of women had passed through Sean's life over the years. Women he'd had fun with but knew weren't what he'd been looking for long term. With most, it had been easy to move on and let a few nights of fun be the end of it. But from time to time, there had been that one who'd been the kind of fun he hadn't quite been ready to give up. Those had been the ones he'd needed to move past the quickest, cut off without a second glance, because he'd known there wouldn't be a future with them, and it wouldn't have been fair to either of them to let that natural connection grow when it would need to be severed later. And from as far back as he'd been thinking that way, the best way he'd known to get one woman out of his head had been to move on to another.

Jesus. He couldn't imagine trying something like that with Molly. He wouldn't want to. But even if he did…he had to wonder if it would even work with her.

Rapping his knuckles on the bar, he pushed off his seat and wished the woman in the next seat luck with the heels. And then he crossed the bar to join Molly and the guys from the band.

Chapter 11

THE REST OF THE NIGHT HAD BEEN PRETTY MELLOW. SEAN
and Molly both did their best to act like what happened in the alley wasn't completely messing with
their minds. Both pretended everything was cool.
Both feigned fatigue when normally neither of them
would even be thinking about calling it a night. Both
kept a minimum two feet of distance between them.
Neither joked about the kiss that had nearly set them
on fire.

Sean had called an Uber, and they'd ridden home
at opposite sides of the little economy's bench seat,
Molly offering strained small talk before retreating to
the sanctuary of her phone and then Sean following suit.

But Molly could practically feel that kiss dismantling
the foundation between them, changing the terrain of
their relationship. Or maybe she was just imagining
the lingering tension in the air between them. The eye
contact they didn't break quite fast enough. The heat
in that single extra glance back after they finally had.
Maybe she was the only one who felt like something
inside her had been twisting slowly into an agonized
knot since they'd done the "right thing" and put a stop
to the kiss that had felt more *right* than anything she
could remember in her entire life.

She looked across the car at Sean, aching for some
sign she wasn't alone in this. Not that it would make

things any easier or better…but a part of her had become dependent on Sean being with her in everything.

Sensing her eyes on him, he glanced up and gave her a tight smile before returning to his phone. Maybe it was better if they weren't in this together. Because if Sean could be strong—well, she would have to be too.

The car stopped outside their building, and Molly headed up to the apartment, trying to ignore her awareness of Sean's proximity. Trying to be cool. Failing.

Inside, Sean went to his room and closed the door. Molly only made it another three steps before stopping, completely at loose ends and irrationally wanting to turn around and rush back to him, because he was the one who made everything better.

But he'd just closed the door. So that was that.

She didn't know how long she'd been standing there when she finally forced her feet to move. She went into her room and pulled out a pair of cutoff sweats and a clean tank to sleep in. But first a shower. Maybe she'd be able to wash away the feel of Sean's hands on her.

Sean's door was still closed, no sounds emanating from beyond it, when she headed to the bathroom. Probably for the best, considering she still wasn't quite right in the head about the two of them. Rationally, she knew there was no way that kiss could ever be repeated. She knew what a bad idea it was to give in to this attraction even a little. But the part of her that wasn't entirely rational still *wanted* more.

Turning on the tap, she stripped out of her T-shirt and skirt, leaving them in a little heap next to the radiator. Her fingers were on the front clasp of her bra when she heard Sean. His muttered curse was followed by a loud thud. There wasn't time to question what it was before the bathroom door swung open and her breath rushed out in a whoosh.

Sean stood in the frame, his hands gripping either side as he raked a dark look over her. He was fully dressed, his breathing strained and ragged.

"Tell me to get the fuck out of here, Molly," he bit out, his voice different than she'd ever heard it before, rough enough to scrape against her every straining sense and nerve.

She should. Of course, she should. And yet if someone had tried to pry the words past her lips, she wouldn't have been able to give them up. *Because that wasn't what she wanted.* Not when Sean was practically vibrating with a tension that matched her own, his body looking like it was a blink away from propelling itself into her space.

And then it happened.

Pushing off the frame, he reached over his head and grabbed a fistful of the back of his shirt, yanking it off. Moving into the small room, he caught her by the back of the neck and pulled her in to all that muscle and hot, bare skin. He kissed her hard, crushing her against him as her arms flew around his neck. They were beyond desperate, picking up where they'd left off in the alley and then catapulting past it in the next heartbeat.

A flick of his tongue, and that burning need low in her belly was reignited in a flash flame. The ache to have him inside her was almost unbearable.

Sean clutched her closer and kissed her harder, growling against her mouth. "I'm sorry, Moll."

"Don't be," she panted in response, jerking at his belt

and fly until his cargo shorts dropped and hit the floor with a clack that sounded like his phone might still have been in his pocket. "I'm not sorry."

A tiny voice in the back of her head whispered, *"Yet."*

His tongue swept through her mouth, setting off a needy pulse deep in her belly. *So good. Too good.* Sean's hands tightened at the nape of her neck and over her ass, that borderline rough touch ratcheting the tension within her all the higher.

The hand at her rear shifted inward over her panties so it was splayed wide and covering both her cheeks, the curve of his fingers following the seam between her legs. Another deep kiss and sweep of his tongue, and he pulled her against the thick length of him.

Her mind briefly blanked as his steely pressure met the sweet spot of her sex. She still wore her panties, and he was covered by his boxer briefs, but the way he'd lifted her against him, letting her slide the few friction-filled inches down his hot length, had her closer to satisfaction than most of her past boyfriends had gotten her in a whole night. Sean lifted her again, and it was just right, making her breath catch and her inner walls spasm. And then again, and oh God, if he kept doing that, she was going to—

"Sean!" she gasped when sensation burst through her center on a crashing wave.

His head jerked back, eyes burning like coals as he studied her face. "Fuck, Molly."

The hand he'd been using to guide her shifted, sliding back up over her ass in what she recognized as a retreat.

Her heart sank. *No.*

But it made sense that Sean would come to his senses

and rein them back in before it was too late. Prevent things from going any further than they already had to minimize the damage.

He'd probably make a joke, something to lighten the mood and remind her of their friendship before he told her they had to stop. And she'd nod and laugh and agree, because she never forgot about their friendship. Which was why, even though what was about to happen would hurt, she wasn't going to let it show.

Bracing for the rejection she didn't want to hear, Molly bowed her head and waited.

It wasn't going to be that simple though. Not with Sean. He caught her chin in the cradle of his warm palm, tipping her face to his. She could do this. Another breath, and she slowly lifted her eyes.

Those dark eyes staring back at her were hard, intense. Totally devoid of the gentle apology she'd expected to find in their depths. Even if she'd wanted to, she didn't think she would have been able to break from the contact.

"There won't be any coming back from this," he warned, the quiet of his voice adding to the weight of the words.

She nodded, a shiver of anticipation spearing through her. "I know." Then resting her hand against his heart, she asked for the clarification she knew they needed. "Just this once?"

The corner of his mouth hitched, blurring the lines between all the versions of Sean she knew. "Just this once."

And then he was sliding into her panties from behind, those long fingers stroking through her wetness as he told her how fucking hot she was, how he was about to lose it, how he needed to feel her come again. His words spilled over her neck and down between her breasts, where he licked and kissed her before returning to her mouth with a growl that curled her toes. So sexy. So a side of Sean he'd never shared with her before.

Wrapping his arms around her, he pulled her off her feet. Her legs locked around his hips, and it was like coming home. Like this was where she was meant to be.

It wasn't. She was too smart and had known Sean too long to believe anything else. But tonight, everything she knew was shoved aside. Tonight, she just wanted to give in to the moment completely.

Her back met a bed, and she distantly registered that he'd brought her to his room. Then his mouth was covering the fuchsia cups of her bra, catching the bead of her nipple with his teeth and groaning with her when he gave it a little pull.

"Take it off," she begged into the thick silk of his hair. The plastic clasp was in the front, and she gasped when he managed it *with his mouth*. "Whoa."

One golden brow arched up at her. "Mad skills, Moll," he offered, his voice thick.

She nodded, not certain she was still capable of speech. Sean was braced on one strong arm above her, his deep-brown eyes fixed on that inch of exposed skin between her breasts.

The cocky smile slipped from his lips as he gently, almost reverently peeled away the thin cup from her left breast and then her right. Sean's breath washed over her skin in a rush as he cupped the small mound.

"Beautiful," he managed hoarsely, his thumb brushing back and forth across the sensitive peak.

The frantic, grappling desperation that had been the driving force between them in those first minutes had quieted, giving way to something almost calm. Like maybe they'd each realized the other wasn't going to back out, and they could just…take their time.

Threading her fingers through Sean's hair, she whispered his name as he ran his tongue around her nipple and then kissed the very tip.

"I shouldn't know how sweet you are." He looked into her eyes. "I was never supposed to know."

What could she say to that? They both seemed to understand what they were doing was a mistake, but for whatever reason, neither could stop. "Now you do."

"Not quite. Not the way I need to." His nostrils flared. "But I will."

He backed off the bed and went to the drawer where he left his watch and wallet each night and, apparently, kept his condoms.

Just the sight of Sean holding that foil packet was making her squirm.

This was happening.

Pushing up on her elbows, Molly shrugged free of her bra and scooted to the edge of the bed, where she hooked a finger into the side of Sean's boxer briefs and tugged him to stand between her knees.

"You look really good in these," she said quietly, letting her palms smooth over the sides, down the leg to where they ended, but not quite mustering the courage to venture to the front where the fabric strained against the swell of him. He looked big.

Tossing the condom to the bed, Sean took her hands in his, moving them to the place she'd been too intimidated to touch. Her hand curved around him, molding to his shape as she eased up and down the length that seemed to grow more with her every stroke.

"I never let myself think about what it would be like to have your hands on me," he confided, his fingers sifting through her hair before moving lower. "But now that I know, I'm afraid I'll never be able to stop."

Molly peered up at him as he leaned closer. But instead of kissing her the way she expected, he caught her by the backs of her knees and tugged.

"Sean!" she squeaked, her back hitting the bed.

"Panties," he growled, hooking his fingers into the waistband and pulling them off.

She was naked. With the light on. In front of Sean. And not just artfully bare, like some tasteful nude in a gallery. She was brazenly exposed, her thighs spread to Sean's urging touch.

Dropping to his knees, he stared at her sex like a starving man. Then, eyes flicking up to hers, he gave her a peek at that half smile again. "You remember all the times you told me to bite you?"

Her eyes went wide as he leaned into the space he'd made for himself. "You wouldn't."

"Oh, I would," he assured. "I will."

And then he was kissing her there, making love to her with his mouth, slow and sweet. Running his tongue through all that wetness before dipping inside and tipping her world off its axis.

Dropping a kiss against the spread of her sex, he looked up at her. "Do you have any idea what it did to me, hearing you come?" Easing a finger inside her, he thrust slowly. "I'd barely touched you, and you were falling apart in my arms. Is it always like that with you?"

"No," she answered, the single word unsteady but true. Because while she was not a virgin, getting off had never been an easy feat. She'd been with guys she was really into, guys she'd been less into but who had been built or beautiful or talked a big game about everything they were going to do to her and how much she was going to like it. She'd tried to be polite, putting on a good show so their egos didn't have to take the hit when she couldn't get past lukewarm—and most of the time, she couldn't. But tonight, with Sean, she'd come less than ten minutes before, and already her body was winding tight again, the heat in her center ready to boil over and spill through every part of her.

Her inner walls clenched around him, and he raised a brow as he lowered his mouth to her again. "No?"

"Aghh," she cried out as the sensation intensified. "Only with you."

Sean's eyes met hers again, the amusement and teasing gone. "You can't say that to me, Molly." Adding a second finger to the first, he stroked in and out. "It makes me want things I shouldn't have." Then curling them, he hit the spot that until that very moment she hadn't totally believed existed. "It makes me want to take all your 'only with yous.'"

Just imagining what that would be like had her fingers digging into the comforter and her back arching hard.

"You like that, Molly?" he asked with another beckoning stroke.

"Yes," she panted, her hips lifting to meet him. "Oh God, yes."

"So fucking hot, Moll." Another stroke, and she was *there*, her body seizing around his thrusting touch, her head thrown back as she shattered.

Sean leaned over her, kissing her hot and deep, giving her a taste of her own pleasure as he moved them back up the bed and reached for the condom.

"Last chance, Molly," he said, restraint tightening his features as he searched her eyes.

Sliding her heel up the back of his thigh, she asked, "Trying to back out?"

But she knew that wasn't it. He was trying to make sure they didn't regret this night any more than they had to.

Sean's mouth met hers in another soul-shattering kiss, and then he was pushing inside her, stretching her as, inch by inch, he took her deeper, filled her more, until finally, she had him all.

Her breath left on a shuddering gasp as emotion and sensation tangled together, overwhelming her. Everything she'd wanted was, in that minute, hers.

"Molly, look at me," he urged, bracing on his elbows so his hands could cup her face. "It's just us. You and me."

She nodded, tears pricking her eyes. "It's just…so much."

She knew he understood what she was saying, could see it in his eyes. They were connected in a way they never had been before. It was powerfully overwhelming, in the very best way.

"I know, Moll." And then because he was Sean and he always knew exactly what she needed, he added, "I'm a big guy."

She laughed, which made him laugh too, which was

really weird considering the way they were connected but was also the most perfect thing that could have happened. She touched his cheek and sighed. "Only you."

The corner of his mouth pulled up, his eyes going tender as he started to move. "Don't forget it."

"Never."

―――∾∾∾―――

Just once.

That's what they'd said. What *Molly* had said. So it wasn't even like Sean could pretend she'd been agreeing with him just to be cool. She'd brought it up. She'd said it first. And like the total fuckwit he was, he'd thought she couldn't be any more perfect, because *once* was supposed to be enough to scratch the itch.

But now Sean was breathing in the sweet, sexy coconut smell of her neck, the five seconds he'd allotted himself to collapse on top of her well past expired already. He needed to get up. He needed to deal with the rubber. He needed to figure out how to stop thinking of Molly in terms of how insanely hot it was being inside her…how wet her kisses were…what she tasted like.

He needed to stop thinking about what it had been like making her come for him *four times*.

"Mmm," she moaned from beneath him, still doing that thing with his hair that he was also going to have to stop thinking about, because friends didn't run their fingers through each other's hair, and friends definitely didn't get hard thinking about how fucking good it felt either.

How was he going to come back from this?

Start by getting off the girl, numbnuts.

It was time, much as he wished it wasn't. Because this thing with Molly…was just *a thing with Molly*. It wasn't their first step toward forever.

And it wasn't like he and Molly could just *date* and see where it went. For one, it was Molly, his go-to girl for everything short of, well, *this*. He couldn't risk what would happen if things didn't work out. He couldn't risk hurting her.

Which meant it was time.

Reluctantly, he started to push up on his arms, making it less than an inch before Molly moaned in protest, wrapping her arms and legs around him tighter.

"Just one more minute?" she murmured with a contented purr when he gave her back his weight. "You just feel so good like this."

"I'm not squishing the life out of you or cutting off your air supply?" He checked, burrowing his face into her neck, because apparently it was okay.

"No." Her breath washed over his ear, soft and warm. "Feels good."

Yeah, it did. Especially when she started sliding one knee up and down at his side. It felt good everywhere, silky soft, but especially where he was still buried inside her. He was already getting hard again. He definitely needed to get out of her. Get rid of this cond—

"Mmm, *Sean*," she half moaned, her blue eyes startled as they met his. "Are you…*already*?"

The tip of her tongue touched her bottom lip, and his cock swelled even more, triggering her lips parting on one of those tiny gasps that hit him like a wrecking ball.

"We said just once." Okay, and maybe things would

have gone differently from there if he hadn't rocked his hips into her...while licking the lobe of her ear before sucking it between his teeth.

"I won't tell...if you... *Sean*!" she cried out, her inner walls grasping at him like hungry hands.

Two thrusts, and she was sucking on his tongue while he took his fill of those insane legs of hers.

So fucking good.

So fucking hot.

So fucking perfect—

"Jesus!" he choked, pulling out before another second passed and, from the looks of it, not a second too soon. "New condom, baby—*Molly*," he promised, backing off the bed in record time to change out the equipment. Heart slamming, he shook his head.

What the fuck, man?

That was the closest he'd ever come to flaking on the safe part of sex. And it had happened with Molly. Who he cared about more than any other woman he'd ever been with. It was inexcusable and—

"Sean?"

He looked back, ready to beg forgiveness, when instead, that racing heart skidded to a stop.

Because the way Molly was looking at him—*holy fuck*. He'd never seen anything so sexy in his life. Those smooth, long legs shifted restlessly together as one hand stroked lightly across her breast and the other played with the pink ends of her hair. She bit softly into her bottom lip, pulling it through the clasp of her teeth before whispering, "Hurry."

His breath hissed out, that last word tightening every damn inch of his body, flipping switches he didn't even realize he had. She was killing him, and he never wanted her to stop.

Turning back to her, he rolled the condom on, and catching the flare of interest in her eyes as she watched, he gripped himself, running up and down his length a couple of times just to see how she would react.

"So hot," she whispered, that hand playing at her chest teasing lower, coasting past her belly until—

"Show me, Molly," he gritted out through clenched teeth, and when she did, parting her knees for him as she slipped her fingers down to where she was glossy and slick *because of him*, he groaned, "Fuck."

And then he was back on top of her, pushing her already-spread legs wider with his knees and pinning her wrists above her head. She took him full length in one long stroke that ended with their mingled moans, their eyes locked, and smiles on their lips.

Just once…*more*.

Chapter 12

THEY'D SHOWERED SEPARATELY. SHE'D BEEN FIRST, BRUSH-ing her teeth when she finished and laughing when Sean shouldered into the small bathroom naked, shrugged, and stepped into the shower while she was still standing there, minty-white foam overflowing from her lips.

As much as she would have liked to, it would have been weird to just stand there and watch him shower, so she'd gone to her room and pulled on a pair of panties and a tank top to sleep in. She'd been on her bed when Sean walked in ten minutes later. He was wearing his boxer briefs, light blue this time, and his hair was a sexy, wet mess that looked almost as good as it had after she'd had her fingers in it through two rolls in the hay. She'd been about to comment when, without a word, he scooped her off the bed and tossed her over his shoulder and marched out of her room.

"Sean!" she squealed, futilely grappling for a hold. "What are you doing?"

"I put out, *twice*," he announced above her laugh-ter, dumping her onto his bed with a bounce and then following her down. "I *earned* the cuddle."

"You think?" she teased, not even trying to keep a straight face because oh man, oh man, had he ever earned a cuddle or anything else he wanted.

"Sit up."

She did as he asked, checking around the bed beneath her to see if she was on top of something. But that wasn't what he wanted.

"Arms up, Moll," he ordered, pulling at the hem of her tank top until she complied.

"So this is going to be a naked cuddle?"

"Don't be crazy. Friends don't cuddle naked." The tank landed on the floor in a little heap, and for one second, Sean just stared at her chest like a kid on Christmas morning.

"Sean?"

"Right," he said with a contented sigh. "We're getting a friendly topless cuddle. Just tonight." He punched his pillow and then lay back, that amazingly muscled arm outstretched like a pillow too perfect to resist.

Sean was a pretty cuddly guy, so it wasn't like they'd never curled up before. But this was something else. This was skin-to-skin contact, warm and comforting and so very right. Her head settled against his shoulder, and he pulled her closer. Their legs were tangled together, and she was in Sean's arms. And even though she'd thought she'd never be able to unwind after what they'd done, already she could feel her muscles loosening and that contented fog settling in her mind.

Sean pressed his lips to her brow. "You know I'm going to have to move out after this."

"I know." He'd have to. They'd crossed a line that couldn't be uncrossed. There wouldn't be any more pretending salvation could be found in the yarn channel. They'd have to rely on good old-fashioned will and, short of that, space.

Still… "I'll miss having you here."

His gruff laugh ruffled her hair, and even with her eyes closed, she could sense the smile on his lips as he held her closer.

"I know."

The last thing she remembered before drifting off was the too-good feeling of Sean's arms tightening around her as if he wasn't ready to let her go.

———

Molly had been so sure the morning after was going to be hell. Filled with regret and all the awkward tension she'd been accumulating since Sean moved in, times a million. But it wasn't. Sean was at the office when she dragged herself out of his bed around eleven, and in her room was the most beautiful bouquet of flowers she'd ever laid eyes on. There were roses, peonies, and stargazer lilies in every shade of pink, and on the card, there were two words written in Sean's script.

Only you…

Molly hadn't stopped smiling since. Which was something of a feat considering no small portion of her day had been spent scrubbing grout and toilets for the Goudins, whose newly remodeled kitchen was going to be featured in some design magazine, and before the shoot, they wanted the entire condo scoured to a high-polish gleam. She'd been happy for the job, they were paying her double to come in on a Sunday, and Carla was a breeze to work for.

Finished by three, Molly had time for a shower and

change before heading over to Belfast for the evening shift. She'd been telling Brody about their latest vendor issues when he sat back in his chair and pushed both hands through that wild mane of hair.

"That's great, Moll. If you want to try out the other guys, set it up."

"Got it." Pushing up from her seat, she asked, "Anything else?"

The eyes that met hers were patiently amused. "You tell me."

Jill must have told Brody what she'd seen the night before behind the bar.

Mouth pursed, Molly crossed her arms and looked down at her boots. "It wasn't that big of a deal."

The gruff burst of laughter from her boss said about the same thing as her heart. She was a liar.

"Try again. Or better, have someone cover so we can grab a beer. I think you're going to want one."

He rounded the desk and threw a heavy arm around her shoulders, pulling her in close to his side. They walked past the bar where a couple of regulars sat, more there for the game and the meal in front of them than the beer. She thought Brody would head for their usual table, but instead, he guided them right rather than left. They didn't open the restaurant side on Sunday nights, so the room was only lit by a handful of spots around the perimeter.

"Grab the table in the corner, Moll, and I'll get the beer."

Molly crossed to the far side of the room where the wall was lined with booths and slid in. A minute later, Brody was back with a couple of pints. Sitting across from her, he rapped his knuckles on the glossy surface of the table.

"Here's what I know," he said, pushing his phone across the table, screen side up.

Molly choked, heat surging to her cheeks.

The small screen had captured a kiss that looked like it had been seconds from becoming flat-out porn. Sean had Molly wrapped around him, her jean skirt pushed up enough that she could see where every one of his fingers dug into her ass. Their mouths were fused together, his shoulders hunched forward as he held her close, her chest pressed into his, and her hands knotted in his hair. This stolen snapshot had captured their kiss completely, the need and heat etched on their features frozen in digital clarity.

"Oh, Jill is so dead." *How could she?*

"Not Jill. Or at least not what you think," Brody corrected. "One of the girls she was out with had been looking for a place to grab a smoke and headed out the back door. I guess she saw you guys, snapped a picture, and then went back in, laughing about the couple out back. Which was when Jill looked out. She didn't even realize her friend had taken the picture until she posted it on Instagram. Jill saw it pretty fast and had her take it down. She even went over to her house and made sure her friend deleted it from her phone and backup storage… but she sent a copy to me first. I don't know, maybe she figured you'd want to know what had been out there, just in case."

Molly's breath left her in a slow leak. Sean tried really hard to keep a handle on his public image. He practically lived two lives to make sure pictures like this one didn't happen.

Brody reached for his phone, but Molly got it first, pulling it all the way in front of her.

This was so bad. But it could have been much worse if Jill hadn't acted so quickly. "Okay, so I guess I won't be scheduling Jill for back-to-back closing and opening shifts until time eternal. Has Sean seen this?"

"Not yet."

Molly tapped the screen, bringing up the messaging program, and then sent the picture to herself. When the image arrived, she deleted the shot from Brody's phone before returning the device to him.

"I'll tell him," she said, hating the sinking feeling in her gut. He'd be fine, but last night had been perfect. She hadn't wanted anything to taint it.

Brody took a long swallow from his beer. When he set it down, he shrugged. "Why Sean?"

The question caught Molly off guard, and she opened her mouth in a sputtering protest.

Brody cut her off with the wave of his hand. His soulful green eyes locked on hers as he folded his arms on the table in front of him. "Because it's always been him, right?"

She wanted to deny it—to Brody, to herself. But there it was. It had always been Sean, and at least in some way, it always would be. Because he'd made her laugh when she'd forgotten how. Because he needed her as much as she'd needed him. And because one day, he'd looked at her, and suddenly, she hadn't been able to catch her breath…and just like that, it was him.

She slumped back in her seat, giving in to the helpless smile. "Yeah, it has."

It was hard to admit, even to Brody, who was

arguably one of her best friends. She could confide in him about almost anything. But Sean—Sean had always been a secret too close to her heart. Even once she'd grown out of the most crushing emotions, she'd kept them close. "But the kiss…" She couldn't admit to more than the kiss. Not even to Brody. "That never happened before last night. And the rest, me all caught up in him… It hadn't been like that for a long time."

"I know. I wouldn't have asked you out myself if I'd thought you were still into him."

Molly smiled, looking into her beer. Brody had been a lot of things to her over the years, and she loved him… but only like a brother.

"So what changed?" he asked, nothing in that rumbly deep voice of his but curiosity based on caring.

"Sean walking around my apartment, stripped down to nothing but those silky basketball shorts and a sheen of sweat. Some friend, right?" She laughed and looked away, not wanting Brody to see her eyes. Because while what she'd given him was the simplest truth, it wasn't the whole truth. Which seemed to be a pattern with her lately, and one she wasn't too proud of.

Why couldn't that shallow objectification be the whole story?

Why couldn't she really have outgrown the feelings for Sean that had plagued her since that first year they met?

They'd been tamed to a degree. Managed enough so she could function…date…smile.

Get out of bed.

And most importantly, be around the friends who were the foundation of her life without giving anything away that would threaten that bond. But as adept as she'd gotten at pretending those forbidden feelings for Sean didn't exist, they were never far away. She was always working to keep them in check, because they were deep, and they were strong, and they were a very real part of who she was.

"You sure a friend is all you are? Because that picture, Moll?" He let out a low whistle.

She knew. That picture said more than she wanted about her feelings for Sean. The look on their faces had been almost pained, as if it hurt not to be closer than they were. And what had been captured in that image was nothing compared to what had been going on a couple of hours later.

After another long swallow of her beer, she scrunched back in the booth. "I'm sure. Whatever was in that picture, we got out of our systems last night." And even if they hadn't, Sean had the movers coming first thing the next morning.

———————

"Just what the fuck was your dirty fucking dick doing anywhere near Molly?" Max demanded, stalking out of the Wyse private elevator two days later.

Sean uncrossed his legs and stood from where he'd been leaning against an incredibly uncomfortable wingback chair in the foyer of his parents' incredibly uncomfortable apartment. He'd been expecting something like this, but even for Max, ninety-seven minutes after touchdown seemed extreme.

"I'm guessing this is a straight-from-the-airport visit?" Sean asked, fairly sure his favorite employee,

Sarah Brandt, was going to skin him alive the next morning for screwing up her honeymoon. "Where's the lovely bride, anyway?"

Max rubbed the back of his short brush cut. "Dropped me here and then took the cab back to our place."

Sean was dead meat, for sure. And it was definitely going to be the newest Brandt taking him down. Not his buddy, who just looked like he wanted to.

"I'm serious, Sean." Max crossed his arms over his chest and glared at him. "What the fuck were you doing? Because I know it wasn't putting some bullshit move on her like you do with all your other disposable dates. I know you wouldn't be that stupid." Then, as if the guy couldn't live with leaving it at that insulting threat, his head dropped forward, and he added, "I know you wouldn't be so selfish with Molly. Not unless you were wrecked or something, and even if you were, that's no fucking excuse."

Jesus, Sean wouldn't have thought there was anything worse than Max looking at him like he wanted to take his head off, but knowing that one of his best friends in the world couldn't look at him at all was definitely worse. Especially when Sean was about to do what he was going to do.

Lie.

Code or no code, Molly was a grown fucking woman, and what happened between them was no one's business but their own. If she wanted her brother to know they'd slept together, she was welcome to tell him, and Sean would gladly own it. But that information wasn't coming from him, and not just because said brother was standing there looking like he was about to have an aneurysm waiting for Sean to put his fears to rest.

Still, if he wanted to defuse the situation, he was going to have to give the guy something. Hell, Molly was Max's little sister…and that bro code of ethics they'd all adhered to back in college mattered. He knew it did.

"Look, Max, we were screwing around, and it got out of hand. She wanted me out of the apartment, and I wanted to make sure that dipshit didn't have an opportunity to weasel his way back in."

The frown etched into Max's face went deeper. "I'm not seeing how your dick gets involved from there."

"Right," Sean admitted, not even sure himself how to connect all those dots without giving Max even more to worry about. Because Sean was pretty sure the only way big brother was able to sleep at night was believing his friends had blinders on when it came to Molly and that none of them had the slightest clue how fucking gorgeous or desirable she was. Or hell, maybe that she was a woman at all.

Clearing his throat, Sean nodded back toward the kitchen and started walking. He needed a beer.

Max hung back, then heaved a sigh and followed along. "You managing okay, staying in your parents' place?"

Barely. Every damn night, he had to talk himself out of driving back to Molly's and begging her to let him in. Not for a repeat of the night they'd had together. Hell, he knew better than that. What he wanted was just more Molly. He wanted to hang out. To kick back in that way he was only really comfortable enough to do with her. He wanted to see her smile and know the most important thing in his life was still as solid as ever.

But that wasn't what Max had been asking. Sean shrugged and waved a hand at the showplace his parents called one of their homes. "What do you think?"

Max stopped beside a Victorian settee in shades of white matching the rest of the decor and shuddered.

"Exactly."

In the kitchen, Sean pulled a couple of bottles of beer from the fridge and handed Max one before propping a hip against the white marble-topped island. Explanation time.

"She thought the best way to get me out of the apartment was to freak me out by pretending to flirt with me." It wasn't the whole truth—it wasn't even most of it—but it was the part Sean could give Max.

Max's expression grew steely, and Sean rolled his eyes.

"Don't get on her case about it, Max. It worked. I freaked." Not exactly for the reasons Max would believe, but whatever. "Only you know how it is with me and Moll. I wasn't about to let her win."

He couldn't bring himself to say that he probably should have, because he didn't even want to think about the idea of not having shared what he had with Molly. Of not knowing about that last layer of the friendship between them.

"So, what are you saying?" Max prompted, sounding almost hopeful as he asked, "You got a bone to one-up her?"

What?

"No, I got a bone because she crawled into my lap, and she's fucking beautiful," he snapped back before he'd thought about the filter he might have used.

But Max seemed to have missed the urgent truth in his delivery and nodded. "She got to you."

More than he'd ever let on. "Yeah, but we both realized the line we'd crossed and took steps to ensure it didn't happen again." And this is where it got dicey. Because while that much was true, the omissions that followed—about the failure of those steps and just how far past the line they'd ended up going—made this conversation a lie. But it had to be done. "Dude, this isn't something you need to worry about. Molly and I have got it figured out. We're past it, so go home to your wife before she tosses your clothes from the honeymoon onto the front grass."

Max stared a minute longer until he finally nodded, the furrow between his eyes smoothing. "Okay, man. If you guys are good, then I'm good. I know you'd never do that shit with Molly—treat her the way you treat those other women. Just had to ask anyway."

Sean clapped him on the shoulder, covering the sick feeling in his gut with a practiced smile. He wasn't sure what bothered him more…that he'd essentially lied to a guy he thought of like a brother or the idea of Molly being lumped in with any of the women Sean had spent the night with, despite the fact that he'd never been anything but respectful, up-front, and—he'd like to believe—good to them.

Molly didn't belong anywhere near that group of casual encounters, because that's not what she was to him. She was critical, not casual.

—∿∿∿—

It shouldn't be this easy between them, but a week after he'd moved out, Sean still couldn't scrape together a single regret about the night he'd spent with Molly. Even moving out wasn't the end of the world. He'd gotten rid of the freeloader. Paid Molly for a full month of living there. And as it stood, they were closer than ever.

Temptation eliminated. *Mostly*.

"Hey, man." Jase greeted him with a fist bump at the front door to his place. "Glad you made it."

"Sorry for the holdup. Dad decided to cut his trip short, and every time they change their plans, it throws a world of shit out of whack."

Jase grunted in that way that suggested he knew exactly what Sean meant. He got it.

Cutting straight back to the kitchen, Sean bit back what he wanted to know most. Whether Molly was there already. He'd have his answer in less than ten seconds, so whatever pressure was building in his chest, he ought to be able to handle it.

Fine, so maybe there had been a few residual effects of sleeping with Molly.

She was on his mind more and, admittedly, in a way she hadn't been before. He'd been inside her, heard her moan his name, and felt her come apart for him. But aside from needing to talk his dick down from time to time when he thought about what they'd done or when he accidentally on purpose stumbled across that photo Molly had brought to him from the back alley—the one he was supposed to have deleted but hadn't quite managed to—there was this other thing happening too. A need to talk to her…more. To hear her laugh. To touch her and see for himself that there wasn't anything broken or hurt in her eyes. That what they'd done hadn't cost him something immeasurably precious.

Laughter bubbled over the sounds and scents emanating from the kitchen, and that pressure in his chest instantly eased, replaced by something warm and easy.

Molly.

She was there.

As he stepped through the wide cutout doorway, their eyes met across the room, sending a satisfied pulse through his system. Her smile stretched wide as she nodded toward Emily and Brody, who were shoulder to shoulder, each whisking some kind of sauce while exchanging backhanded compliments about the other's product.

"Tell me this means what I think it means," Sean pleaded, rubbing his hands together.

Molly nodded, an eager smile lighting her face. "Oh yeah. The taste-off is *on*. Emily is challenging Brody's mustard cream sauce." Edging out from behind the cooks, Molly shimmied around Jase and stopped beside Sean, leaving an inch of space between them. An inch he couldn't leave alone.

Leaning in to her so their arms brushed, he waited for it. The slow shift of her eyes meeting his, the flicker of a smile that was only about them. The relief he shouldn't need to feel. And yeah, the pull of an attraction he could only manage as easily as he was because of how completely *she'd* fallen back into their routine.

Whatever had gone haywire between them was shut down, at least from her side. Which made it a hell of a lot easier to keep his side in check. Thoughts were one thing, but those impulses weren't getting off the leash.

A commitment totally reinforced when Max and Sarah showed up a few minutes later.

"Let's see those tan lines," Emily urged, abandoning

her sauce to greet the newlyweds, who'd been back for almost a week but hadn't been able to meet up with everyone until that night. Though Sean had seen them both, Sarah because she'd become something of his right hand at Wyse, and Max because of his little visit on the way back in from the airport.

Donning a pair of ovenproof mitts, Brody hunkered down in front of the oven, coming back up with a broiler pan loaded with juicy medallions of perfectly charred steak.

"Rare all around, yes?" he asked, not actually listening for an answer, because Brody had a knack for remembering everyone's tastes the way Sean had a knack with numbers.

Sarah was leaning forward over the counter, looking like her nose had led her. "That's it, Max. I'm throwing you back and running off with Brody."

Emily was moving a stack of small white plates from the counter to the island. "Yeah, Brody knows his way around a choice piece of meat, but after you taste my sauce over it, you'll be begging me for a three-way."

Molly leaned back into Sean's space, her shoulder meeting his chest as she grinned back at him, eyes gleaming.

He knew exactly what she was thinking. Emily hated to lose more than any person he'd ever met. She was physically incapable of not competing, and it was hilarious.

A flick of Molly's eyes toward Jase, and Sean gave her a nod. He'd seen it. While Max was aspirating his beer over Emily's quasi proposition, Jase was sitting there nodding, with that same smacked look of love on his face he'd had since Em had agreed to marry him.

Agreeing to a three-way his wife hadn't even offered to include him in. Over a *sauce*.

Damn, he loved these guys. Slinging his arm around Molly's shoulder, Sean pulled her closer. She smelled like coconut, and when his thoughts veered to how she'd smelled like coconut *everywhere*, he pulled her closer still, reminding himself about what was really important.

———

Two weeks later, Molly was huffing and puffing after the four-block sprint from the Armitage L stop. Her last Brandt Housekeeping job for the morning had asked her to stay after she'd finished cleaning to talk about a friend who was interested in getting on Molly's wait list. It had cost her most of the time she'd budgeted for lunch with Emily and Sarah, but they still needed to get some planning in for the camping trip, so she'd been hustling.

Pushing through the front door, she waved to Jill by the till. Then catching sight of the girls at a four-seater in the main bar, she headed over.

"Sorry I'm late," Molly apologized, quickly weaving through the tail end of Belfast's lunch crowd to where Emily and Sarah were already done with their meals.

Looking around, she caught one of the servers' eyes, giving a nod toward the empty plates before sliding into her open seat. She wasn't on for another hour, but she'd been around as long as Brody, and whether she was working or not, when she was in the bar, the staff tended to look to her first.

"What, did you run here?" Sarah teased, pushing her water in front of Molly.

"Feels like I'm running everywhere these days."

Molly laughed, shaking her head at the offered glass, figuring she'd have her own in a matter of minutes. "Sorry I missed lunch."

"That stinks, but we totally get it," Emily assured her, and Molly knew she meant it.

If anyone understood about work demands, it was these two. Even if they were working in high-rise corner offices and Molly was down on her knees scrubbing the corners of Gold Coast homes, they were all ambitious women who understood goals.

"How many employees are you up to?" Sarah asked, straightening her silk blouse as she sat back.

"Twelve, but I've got a couple of prospects, and if they work out, it'll bring me up to fifteen. Which would be great, because it's killing me to turn down customers."

If she wanted to, she could hire the staff she needed by the afternoon, but she wouldn't risk the reputation she'd worked so hard to build on people she couldn't vouch for personally. Her plans were long term and depended on consistent revenue streams. Satisfied clients were the key.

Emily nodded and picked up her phone. "So what do you think? Should we start figuring out the logistics for the trip?"

Molly grabbed her own phone, bringing up the calendar. The trip was still two weeks away, which would have been two weeks more time than she needed to plan if they were camping like they had when it was just her, Max, and Sean.

They'd have decided to go at five and left at six, and it would have been perfect.

And while planning wasn't Molly's favorite part, she

loved how their group had grown and how every new addition brought something wonderful to their experience. So change was good.

Phones out, Sarah and Emily were a blur of thumbs, looking things up and taking notes on games, food, and drinks. Then breaking down each of those categories — not just into meals, but snacks, appetizers, and late-night snacks with alternatives based on whether it was warm or rainy. Because you didn't want to be making s'mores if it was pouring.

"I know we just had our honeymoon, and that vacation was spectacular," Sarah said, a dreamy expression on her face. "But the buildup to the wedding was so intense, and there've been a million things to do since we got back. Max and I are really looking forward to a weekend off the grid."

"Jase too," Emily added, her brows furrowing in concentration as her thumbs sped across the screen of her phone. "Do we know if Brody confirmed the campsites again?"

Molly laughed, because Emily took everything so seriously. To her, this camping trip was being handled the way she handled a promo spot for one of her campaigns.

"I'll double-check with him," Molly promised. Then thought better of it. "Forget that. Let's just find out."

Five minutes later, she'd grabbed Brody from the back. When they were all settled at the table, he slapped down a pad of paper in front of them and started scribbling notes. While the rest of the world would be using their phones, Molly imagined those thick fingers of Brody's couldn't make more than the simplest texting very easy.

"I'd been planning to get organized next weekend, but since you girls are all here and your lesser halves tend toward last-minute preparations, let's work it all out ourselves."

"Speaking of lesser halves," Emily sang, leaning in toward Molly. "Think you and Sean will be able to share a tent without another boner incident to report?"

Sarah chuckled lightly. "God, I hope so. I don't think I can handle a replay of the groin-to-groin contact that nearly blew my husband's head off during our honeymoon."

Molly froze where she was, her iced tea halfway to her mouth, a sense of dread spooling through her stomach. "You okay, Moll?" Brody asked, looking over his phone, then turning it to show Emily the picture of the new tent he'd ordered. Thankfully, neither of them was paying too much attention, because Molly felt like she'd just swallowed a frog. She'd been working overtime to remind herself that Sean was not her other half. The two of them together did not make a whole. And yet on some level, even their friends saw her and Sean as another couple within this group.

Things had been going smoothly with Sean. He seemed to have gotten past their night together without a glitch. And she was getting there. Absolutely. But suddenly, those two weeks she had until she was sharing a tent with him didn't seem like much time at all.

———～～～———

Mature adult men didn't throw tantrums about their parents bugging them. But Sean was about to blow a gasket if his didn't exit his office, *his sanctuary*, in the next thirty seconds. They were driving him nuts, going on about who would *represent* Wyse for this commitment or that. How *dreadful* some coming event would be, but how it was their *responsibility* to attend regardless. Obligations that couldn't be avoided, and opportunities to advance relationships.

None of it was new.

Sean had been participating in conversations like this one, and doing so without complaint, from the time he was twelve. But in almost twenty years, this was the first time the conversation felt truly *old*.

It was the first time he felt as if every second that ticked past was another second lost.

Finally, he snapped. "Every year, we attend that dinner, and every year, it's a complete waste of time. I say we decline." When he was met with silence, he pressed, "Why not?"

His mother sat neatly folded at the edge of her seat across the low coffee table, looking at him like she didn't know who he was. When she deigned to answer, it was only to say, "Appearances, Sean. That is why."

Of course. He shouldn't have asked when he already knew.

It was just that everything felt off with him lately. His fuse was just a little shorter, his patience taxed just that much. It was as if he had the constant sense he ought to be somewhere else.

Even the office wasn't the balm it once was…and he *loved* work. He loved the Wyse.

Hell, he loved his family, but in that moment, his mother's voice was hitting him like nails down a blackboard.

Enough of this. "Fine, whatever you decide. Copy Carson on the schedule, and I'll make it work."

The sun was setting, and he could see the elongated shadows falling across the Drive from his window. By his standards, it was still pretty early, but he wanted out.

"Are we about done for the night?" Sean rose from his seat on the couch with purpose and headed back to his desk.

"Are we keeping you from a meeting?" his father asked, sinking farther back into his chair. "I thought Carson said your schedule was clear."

Sean closed his eyes and drew an even breath. "No meeting."

"Dinner plans, then?" his mother probed.

"No dinner plans either. I was going to head over to the gym. I've missed a few days this week and could use a good workout." He could use about two hours to burn off some of this pent-up whatever-the-hell-it-was that had gotten into him. He'd swim and then hit the weights, and if he wasn't on a more even keel when he was done with that, there was always the treadmill. Or maybe he could head over to Belfast and say hi to Molly. And Brody. Molly and Brody.

"So the work on your apartment is finished?" his mother asked, and Sean suddenly wondered if he was being an ass.

Maybe his parents were just looking for an opportunity to talk with him. To spend some time as a family, and this was the only way they knew how. Things hadn't really been right since everything had come out about his father and—

"We were relieved when you came to your senses about

that Molly situation," his mother added, her eyes locked on him as if she was studying his face for a reaction.

The muscles down his spine started to knot. He would definitely be hitting the treadmill.

And if his mother was waiting for a reaction, she wasn't going to get it. After all, Sean had been schooling his emotions for appearances' sake since he was old enough to walk.

He began flipping through a report Sarah had left for him, and after a moment, his father stood. "We had lunch with Valerie this afternoon. Did you know she was back from Rome?"

"No." He hadn't known she'd left.

"Well, she is," his mother stated, standing. She straightened her skirt and adjusted the heavy gold bracelet at her wrist. "She made some exceptional connections while she was there. You ought to set something up this week." Then, meeting his eyes, she added, "She's still receptive, Sean."

That tension that had been ratcheting tighter and tighter down his spine suddenly released, and he took a deep, easy breath. He smiled a genuine smile at his mother and rolled up his sleeves. "You know, I think I'll call her tonight."

The sharpness of his mother's features softened, making her look more like the woman she'd been to him growing up. The woman who was so proud of his efforts to follow in his father's footsteps.

That softer side of his mom was nice.

He just wasn't sure it was entirely real anymore.

—∿∿—

Ninety minutes later, Sean was seated in the back corner of a mostly empty coffee shop with Valerie across from him. Her hair fell in immaculate glossy waves to a few inches past her shoulders, and her clothes looked like her personal shoppers probably earned enough in commissions to buy their own summer place in the Hamptons. It was no mystery why his parents had pinned their hopes on this woman.

Valerie laughed, recounting the hard press his parents had given her at lunch, and sat back in her chair, smiling over her espresso at him. "I must admit, Sean, I was surprised you called."

He nodded, setting his own coffee aside. "Thanks for meeting me on such short notice. I imagine your calendar is booked for months."

She laughed politely, but he knew from when they'd dated it was true. "It was easy enough to push my dinner plans back."

"David?" he asked, remembering he'd seen her and Stanthorpe in the paper not too far back.

She shook her head. "Alan Ryder."

Right. He knew the name. "Serious?"

"I suppose it could be."

The answer was just ambiguous enough to leave the door open, validating his decision to contact her. "Valerie, I've been reconsidering my stance on marriage, and with the somewhat open-ended way we've left things"—and considering his parents' conversation with her at lunch—"I thought you deserved to know."

It was time to close the door.

Chapter 13

MOLLY SHOULD'VE KNOWN THAT WITH BRODY, EMILY, AND Sarah coordinating the camping trip, there was no way it wasn't going to be perfect. Or over-the-top. Or as unlike traditional camping as you could get while still sleeping in tents in the woods. They'd gone to Google Earth and scouted out the available sites, securing the last four backing up to the woods with a decent distance between them and the next campers in front of them.

She'd ridden up with Emily and Sarah Friday morning, leaving around ten. Both the girls had a few things to handle at their respective offices, which left Molly an extra couple of hours of sleep. But mostly it had given her a handy excuse not to ride up with Sean.

No matter how she sliced it, the two of them were a pair. Not that it was something new or something terrible. It was just that with the way her brain had been misfiring recently, anything she could do to avoid that coupled-up feeling seemed wise. So she'd ridden with the girls in Max's Charger, Sean had gone with Jase in the SUV, and Max had ridden along in the truck Brody rented to transport all the necessities.

Sarah pulled to a stop, both hands secure around the wheel as she leaned forward, her mouth hanging open.

Emily's hands clutched between her breasts as she practically bounced in her seat. "This is going to be awesome!"

Awesome? Definitely. Over-the-top to the point of ridiculous? Already there.

The girls piled out of the car and walked down to the campsite where Brody was manning a gleaming six-burner grill parked beside the half-rusted-out traditional pit provided at the site. Jase and Max were assembling a screened-in gazebo, and where any other campsite might've had an assortment of folding chairs, theirs was littered with a deep-cushioned set of wicker patio chairs, end tables, a love seat, and this crazy sort of blow-up tube that looked like it might be a cross between an inflatable couch and hammock.

The girls ran down to greet their husbands. Emily got dipped back into one of those showy kisses Molly never would've guessed Jase had in him but had become all but standard since the two had gotten together. And Sarah stepped into Max's arms, pushing up to her toes to meet him for a kiss Molly ended up having to turn away from. He was her brother, for crying out loud.

They had a routine. Each couple, their own thing. And seeing it usually made Molly smile, but then usually, she wasn't fighting *her own thing*. Because she had one too. She and Sean. And right then, he was stepping out from behind the truck, dressed in a Wyse Hotel T-shirt that had found the perfect balance between fitted and tight, a pair of ripped-up cargo shorts, and hiking boots with socks. There were two coolers stacked in his hold, and it took everything she had not to give in to the pull of habit, skip down the gravelly slope, and cuddle into Sean's side for a minute before helping out with whatever she could.

Not today.

Sean scanned the site, checking out the couples who were greeting each other as though it had been weeks rather than hours since they'd last had the chance. And then his eyes landed on her, his smile going wide and crooked as he jutted his chin in a nod of greeting.

Offering up a wave, she forced herself to go to Brody first.

"Hey, Moll, how was the drive up?" he asked, that too observant stare shifting between her and Sean.

"Great. Little later start than we intended, but Sarah made good time."

A chuckle rumbled deep from Brody's chest "For being married to a cop, the girl's got a lead foot on her, doesn't she?" His eyes flicked past Molly's shoulder. "Hey, man, let me take one of those."

Molly turned to find Sean standing beside her, an expectant look on his face. Because whether he'd dissected it or analyzed it or not, Sean knew the routine too. He handed the top cooler off to Brody with thanks, and when the other man walked it back to the prep area, Sean searched her face.

"You okay?" His biceps were flexing as he stood there holding the oversize cooler. "We okay?"

She sighed, feeling like a jerk. Of course, Sean would notice something off.

With a shake of her head, she sighed. "Yeah, we are. It's just me being weird."

"Weird how?" He raised a brow, pulling the corner of his mouth a bit higher in the process.

She stepped closer, her eyes trailing around the campsite where everyone was laughing and starting to come together. Everyone except for them. "Residually weird?"

"Ahh, because of…" He let his voice trail off, but they both knew what he meant. Because of that night.

"Yes. It's stupid, and I'm sorry. But every now and then, I feel like maybe things are different, and I really want them to be the same."

He turned, angling his back to the rest of the group so it was just them. "What's different?"

She might as well tell him. "Me seeing everyone couple off and maybe thinking of us that way a little too. I mean, not like I want to run and jump into your arms, showering kisses all over your face because I haven't seen you for three and a half hours. But"—she looked behind her again—"I don't know, it's always Emily and Jase, Max and Sarah, and in my head, I guess I realized I always add us like that too. Sean and Molly. I know we're not a couple, but in certain ways, we are."

Like it was just understood that they would share a tent. That they sat together. That all their private jokes were for each other.

"Don't overthink it, Moll." Hefting the cooler to readjust his grip, Sean started toward the area where they'd been piling everything up. "We are together. Not like they are, but I can't remember a time when we haven't been paired up. Can you?"

"No, I guess not."

"I think we're both sensitive about making sure everything is okay between us. After what happened, there's bound to be a *little* residual weirdness, but we're good, Moll. We're just us. Even if occasionally one of us thinks something about the other they shouldn't."

Molly stopped walking and turned to face him.
Their eyes met, and again, she found herself caught
in a hold that made her heart beat faster, her skin heat,
and her belly start that slow needy churn she only
associated with Sean. His eyes slowly dropped to her
mouth, and she felt something deep inside threatening
to break free.

But then Sean looked away and cleared his throat.
"I'm sure it will pass."

⟶∿⟵

Once the campsite was set up to Brody's liking and
he had his feast under way, everyone else donned their
hiking shoes and sneakers and took off down the trail
toward the swimming hole. About a mile in, the trail
split. One way was an easy path directly down to the
beach, and the other wound farther around the lake,
following a steeper trail dead-ending at a rocky over-
hang protruding far enough over the water so swimmers
could jump in.

"It's not that high," Molly urged, practically
bouncing on her toes, she was so excited to get there.
"There's a windy walkway on the side where you can
leave your stuff and climb back up." Her breath came
out in an adorable rush. "Even Sean jumps off it, and
you know what a chicken he is."

Or not so adorable. He barked out a laugh, shaking
his head.

"Once," he countered, throwing his hands up with
a laugh. "One time. I suggest that maybe we take the
trail down to the beach and go in there." And it hadn't
been because he was afraid to jump—he'd been afraid

to watch Molly jump. Even years and dozens of jumps later, he still had to keep himself from trying to talk her out of it.

"Come on, you guys! Don't be a bunch of babies," she goaded. "It's, like, fifteen feet up."

Max stood behind Sarah, his hands resting on her shoulders. "Twenty-two feet, seven inches," he clarified.

Sarah gave a firm shake of her head. "I'll pass. But don't let me stop you."

Emily and Jase shared one of those looks where a whole conversation took place without words. And then Jase grinned, taking his wife's hand as they started back toward the site. "You know, we're kind of beat actually. You guys go. Have a good long swim, and we'll see you back at the campground."

Christ.

"Mmm-hmm, I think maybe a nap," Emily added unnecessarily, because seriously, like everyone didn't know what was going on.

Molly snorted quietly. "Subtle, guys."

"Okay, so, Moll, you and I will take the high road, and Sarah and Max will take the low road," Sean said.

They split up, hiking the last mile and a half separate from the group. Sean didn't mind. It wasn't like he'd been plotting to get Molly alone, but sometimes when it was just the two of them, he relaxed in ways he couldn't when everyone else was there.

"This is it." Molly stopped next to the sign for the overlook, kicking off her shoes while Sean did the same.

He'd just pulled his T-shirt over his head when he looked up to find Molly doing the same.

He swallowed. Hard. She was wearing a bikini he'd

seen before. Hell, she'd probably been wearing it last
year this time, but for some reason, today, it was different. Today, that bikini seemed criminally small and
painfully sexy. Today, he found himself looking around,
with the insane need to prevent anyone else from seeing
what he was. Like somehow he had the right to keep her
all for himself.

"Hurry up, hotshot," she said, waving her hand all
let's go, let's go.

"Relax, babe. The water's not going anywhere."
Dropping his shirt over his sandals, he stood back up
and found Molly missing the eager smile that had been
on her face seconds ago. "What?"

Her eyes cut away uneasily. And she shook her head.
"You just called me 'babe,' and it sounded funny."

He hadn't, had he? *Babe* wasn't what you called your
best friend. It was one of those intimately affectionate
names he rarely used with anyone. The women he dated,
the ones he was photographed with and who usually
knew his parents before they knew him, never went by
babe. And the girls he hooked up with? There generally wasn't time to establish that level of intimacy. He
wasn't the kind of guy to call just anyone *babe* either,
and he never used it as a crutch when he'd forgotten
someone's name.

So calling Molly *babe*?

"Don't worry about it," she insisted. "I'm just being
weird again." She started to leave, but Sean reached out
and caught her wrist, pulling her back a step.

"No, you're not. It's me." Those big blue eyes peered
up at him, bright as the sky above, and suddenly, Sean
was aware of the way his hand had drifted from her

wrist, and now his fingers were caught in a loose tangle with hers. Jesus, what was wrong with him?

He needed to look away, but instead, he found himself searching deeper, getting caught in all that blue, looking for...hell, looking for something he wasn't going to find.

Releasing her, he took a step back and smiled. She'd just told him it was weird that he'd called her *babe*. Standing there getting lost in her eyes probably wasn't the best way to come back from that.

"All right, Moll. Let's see what you've got."

A smile flitted across her lips, and then she was turning toward the lake, starting to run, and then launching herself out into the open air. And just like every time he'd seen her take that leap before, his gut clenched as he watched her plunge deep, holding his breath until she broke the surface again.

A second later, she bobbed up and, treading water, pushed her hair back from her face. The smile stretching her lips was one of pure delight.

"Come on in. The water's great!"

He was betting the water was cold as shit, just like every year. Taking their things, he dropped down to a lower rock formation and then the one a few feet below that, where he set their stuff. Pushing himself back up, he returned to the top and waved for Molly to swim a few more feet to the side before taking off and jumping himself. It was pure exhilaration, those seconds of free fall, and then he was taking the plunge as well. Cutting through the icy water, he kicked toward the surface and came up a few feet from where Molly was swimming over. The sun glistened across her wet skin, while the water turned the white blond of her hair golden beneath its rays.

She was beautiful.

"See? Wasn't that worth it?" she asked, grinning ear to ear.

Jesus, that smile. "It always is."

———

Turned out Sarah wasn't really interested in more than getting her feet wet and Max wasn't interested in anything more than following his new wife around, so they'd headed back after a few minutes, leaving Sean and Molly to splash around in the lake for a good half hour on their own before returning to the campsite themselves. It was quiet when they got back. Brody's car was gone, and there was a note on the picnic table letting them know they'd all gone into town to grab a few extra ingredients for dessert.

"Think I'm gonna head over to the showers," Molly said, ducking into their tent to grab her things. She was still wearing her bikini, and Sean was still feeling like a shit for the way he kept looking at her and it. For the things he kept thinking.

Like how he never had fun with the women he dated the way he did with her. How no one's smile had ever done to him what hers did. How when she was looking up at him with those eyes, for the first time in his life, his heart and head had started to say the same thing.

She popped back out, holding her little satchel of toiletries, and he tried to imagine what it would be like if that wasn't his tent she'd been crawling out of. What it would be like when she found her someone…and it wasn't him.

"Want me to zip it up?" she asked, holding the tent flap closed.

Clearing his throat, he shook his head. "Nah. I'll get cleaned up too. You saw where the bathrooms were when we drove in?" They'd been to this park half a dozen times probably but had never stayed on this side of the campground before.

"Yep, I'm good. Meet you back here when we're done," she said, already walking toward the road.

Sean nodded, waiting until she turned around and then waiting some more before grabbing his own stuff. He was just tucking his phone into his boot when it lit up with a call from his assistant.

As a rule, when they went camping, they tried to leave work behind. But with everybody doing their own thing, he gave in to the pull and answered. He was glad he did, since the question took less than two minutes to answer and probably saved the guy an afternoon of hassle. When he was done, he headed up toward the showers, still thinking about Molly and that suit…about Molly in the water…about Molly in his arms and in his bed and all the places and all the ways he wasn't supposed to think about her at all.

The showers at this campground looked like they did at every other one he'd ever been to. A brown wooden structure with empty windows and the doorway partly obscured by more brown fencing at either side. Out front, there was a waterspout on a concrete slab surrounded by a bunch of soupy mud.

Through the open windows, he could hear Molly singing "Radioactive." Damn, he loved it when she sang. She didn't hit even half the notes, but when she sang, he knew she wasn't just happy. She was bubbling over with happiness. And it just didn't get any better than that.

He walked up to the hut, following the sidewalk to the men's side, but his steps slowed as he neared the door. The singing was louder, not quieter. He looked up and checked the sign again. Men's.

Uh-oh.

Sean tentatively stepped through the doorway, knowing what he was about to encounter but hoping against hope he was wrong.

"Hey, Moll?" he called above the spray of the shower, stepping down the row of open stalls.

Holy hell, there was no way he was going to survive this. Molly stood beneath the spray, rinsing a thick lather from her hair so the suds spilled over her shoulders and chest, slipping past her belly button and down her back…making a playground of that body he hadn't been able to get out of his head. But this wasn't fun and games. This wasn't about getting an eyeful of the girl he needed to remember was his best friend. This was about getting Molly out of the men's room before she completely lost her shit when she realized where she was. Thank God she was still wearing her bikini and a pair of sandals. Hopefully, that would be enough.

"Um, Molly?" he said again, calmly, quietly, not wanting to startle her.

Her eyes blinked open, going wide at the sight of him standing there, and then she laughed, her arms crossing over her chest even though she was wearing the bikini she'd been swimming with him in for the last hour. But standing there, with the water and suds and his dirty thoughts, it felt different to him too.

JUST THIS ONCE 173

"Sean! What are you doing? This is the *ladies'* shower. You can't be in here."

He nodded, holding up one hand and knowing she wasn't going to like what he had to say.

"Okay, thing is, Moll, it's not the ladies' shower."

That knockout smile went brittle and stiff before cracking just enough for one lip to curl. Molly had a thing about men's showers. Back in college, Max found out she'd been slipping into the showers on their floor, despite it being guys only. She'd thought it was no big deal since she only snuck in at odd hours when it was deserted. No surprise, big brother didn't feel the same.

So he'd told her all the depraved and dirty things guys did in their bathrooms—the most obvious true, while other accounts had been embellished or flat-out fabricated to the furthest degree his imagination would allow. And based on Molly's posttraumatic response to whatever details he'd given her, Max Brandt must have been way more creative than Sean had given him credit for. Because even a decade later, Moll was about to lose it, finding out where she was.

"Oh no," she croaked, her eyes shooting to the concrete floor where the water was sloshing through the open toes of her sandals. And then more urgently, "*No.*"

She raised one foot and then the other, as if she was trying to keep from getting contaminated but didn't know which foot to sacrifice first, while her increasing stomping only served to splash more water around her ankles. "Sean...Sean, Sean, Seanseansean..."

Shit. "Yeah, I know. It's touching you." He stepped closer. "Not a big deal, Moll. Just come with me."

"*It's touching me.*"

One look at those wild eyes, and he recognized the crazy train had left the station. Molly was beyond reason, and the only thing he could do was get her out of there before it got any worse.

"Not anymore." He ducked down, catching her around the waist and backs of her thighs, and picked her up against his chest. "Come on, Moll, wrap your arms around my neck."

She did, holding tight to him as though her life depended on it. "Get it off!"

"We will. Just bend your knees and kick your feet back. We'll get them rinsed off, and I'll carry you out."

She looked at him with pleading eyes. "Hurry."

Seconds later, he was carrying her outside, promising her she was clean and that she could put her feet down. Finally, he felt the rigid muscles of her body relax against him.

"I'm completely nuts," she whimpered into his neck where her face was burrowed.

"No," Sean soothed, rubbing her back with one hand while he held her against him with his other arm beneath her ass. "Not completely. I mean, sure, a little, but I've always kind of liked that best about you, so it's okay."

She laughed and lifted her head to look him in the eyes. "Thank you, Sean."

And shit, she wasn't giving him that look—the one that had brought him to his knees and pushed him past sense the weeks before—but something in those too-blue eyes was pulling at a spot in his chest he couldn't quite ignore.

It was time to set her down. Time to take that

necessary step back and let her go, but her arms were still wound around his neck, and fuck if holding her like this didn't make him feel like he could take a full breath for the first time since they'd promised nothing would change between them.

"Sean?" she asked quietly, searching his face for answers he knew weren't there, answers he didn't have. "Are you going to let me go?"

Was he?

"I've been trying," he said solemnly. "But the truth is, I'm not sure I want to anymore. Molly, I'm not sure I even can."

He'd said it. The truth he hadn't been able to admit to himself until that very moment, but now that it was out... Yeah.

Her eyes filled with shock, and her breath stalled in that small space between her parted lips. *Way to blind-side the girl.*

He ought to tell her it was up to her. That he'd respect her feelings, but that thing that had been beating against his ribs for the last weeks had finally found its voice. "I want you, Molly."

"Sean, we agreed—"

"We shouldn't have," he interrupted, his heart starting to pound. "We shouldn't have agreed to anything, because we both still feel it. This thing between us isn't going away."

She was nodding, her eyes a little too wide, her voice a little too calm. "Sean, I get that you feel this way right now. But you know this isn't what you want."

He shook his head, more certain with every second that passed. "No. Molly—"

"Hey, there you two are," Max called from down the road. "What's going on?"

Molly shook her head, pushing back from Sean's hold.

He let her slide down his body, half tempted to turn to her brother and lay it out there. Tell Max that he'd just realized he was in love with his little sister.

"I wasn't paying attention and ended up in the guys' shower." Molly sent him a pleading look before turning back to her brother. "Sean rescued me."

Max let out a hearty laugh, his eyes squinting shut as he shook his head. "Shit, Molly, you know I was making half that stuff up, right?"

She nodded tightly, peering back at the showers, and Sean couldn't help but wonder if it was because she didn't want her brother to see her face. "Regardless, the damage is done. I hope you feel guilty forever."

Max stepped closer to Sean, clapping him on the shoulder. "Probably not as guilty as I should." Then, hitching a thumb over his shoulder, he added, "Everyone's back, and Brody's got some assortment of snacks set out, so don't take too long."

"No problem." Molly started walking toward the road. "Sean's still got to shower, but I'll head back now."

Sean watched her go, rubbing his chest when she cast him a single uncertain glance over her shoulder.

So, this wasn't going to be easy.

Chapter 14

MOLLY WALKED BACK TO THE SITE IN A DAZE.

She couldn't believe what he'd said. *He wanted her*.

Maybe it was true. Fine, she knew it was...*for now*. Temporarily. But the future Sean's parents had outlined for him, the one he'd been working for all these years, didn't include her.

What was she supposed to do with that? She wanted Sean. She'd always wanted him...but to set herself up for heartbreak like this? She couldn't do it.

She'd be insane to even think about it.

"Molly, you've got to try this," Sarah called from beside the table where cocktails were set out in tall, narrow glasses with a pitcher beside them for refills. After the bomb Sean had just dropped, one of Brody's concoctions was just what the doctor ordered.

She wondered if anyone would notice if she just took the pitcher and skipped the glass.

Sarah stirred through her ice with her straw and took a long pull.

"Whoa, you may want to go easy on those, Sarah," Molly offered with a laugh. "Brody's drinks are known for their punch."

Sarah's eyes gleamed as she nodded, taking the straw out of her drink and pointing it at Molly. "I am aware. In fact, I'm banking on it to help me get through."

At Molly's curious look, Sarah went on, waving her

hand around as though whatever she was about to reveal was no big deal, but something in her eyes said it was. "I have a little *thing* about bugs where I'm sleeping. They don't bother me when I'm up. Sitting out here around the campfire? No big deal. It's when I have my guard down. When I'm sleeping. I don't like being vulnerable to them."

Molly set her drink back on the table and pulled Sarah in for a tight hug. She couldn't tell her about what had happened with Sean. Heck, she didn't even know what had just happened with Sean. But she could share what happened before. "You do not know how much better I feel hearing that. I just made a complete scene because of my hang-up about guys' showers."

Sarah's face scrunched up. "Like Max's shower?"

Molly shook her head and looped her arm through Sarah's, recapping what had happened up at the shed and why she couldn't get past the whole public shower thing. Sean was back by the time she finished her story, and Sarah couldn't stop laughing as she stumbled over to her husband and laid into him for being the worst big brother of all time.

That wasn't true. Max was probably the best big brother on the books. But he was still a big brother, and Molly didn't know one who could resist the lure of tormenting a little sister from time to time. Besides, what goes around comes around, and while she'd never given him any real trouble, she'd made sure he paid in the little ways little sisters knew best.

Sean climbed out of the tent. He'd changed into a long-sleeved fitted shirt and a pair of jeans. He straightened and started walking toward them, his eyes landing on hers as he scrubbed the top of his head a few times, leaving his hair in a wild state of damp disarray.

Geez, he knew exactly what he was doing. Pushing buttons she probably should've known better than to reveal to him.

They needed to talk, but she'd been too chicken to stay and finish what he'd started up at the showers. She hadn't seen it coming, wasn't prepared, and had run off before clearing the air between them. And now she was looking at serving out the rest of her night surrounded by an audience she wasn't ready to share her drama with.

Sean dropped into the chair Sarah had just vacated. Leaning over, he pulled Molly's chair closer. Her eyes cut to his, a warning he wouldn't miss in them.

The corner of his mouth hitched up, and he stretched an arm over the back of her shoulders, casual as can be.

"We need to talk, Sean."

"We were talking. You ran off."

She nodded, letting out a slow breath. "You're lucky I did, with Max right there."

His eyes twinkled with mischief. "True. I definitely wasn't thinking about your brother."

Molly turned in her seat, taking a closer look at the man beside her. He looked utterly delighted. And something about that hitched-up smile pulled at hers too. "Just what are you grinning at?"

He leaned closer, dropping his voice to barely above a whisper. "Thinking about all the things I'm going to do to you tonight. About your hands in my hair and how I'm going to keep you quiet when you're panting my name."

Molly gulped, her body getting on board all too easily

with Sean's plans. His completely presumptuous, totally flawed plans that absolutely were not going to pan out.

"What's gotten into you?"

Sean laughed, giving her a look like the answer was the most obvious thing in the world. "You have."

When she couldn't do more than stare, he stretched back in his chair, looking up at the evening sky before he stood. Taking Molly's glass from her hand, he rattled the ice. "Get you another one?"

Her eyes bugged. She'd sucked down the whole thing without even realizing it. Molly shook her head. "Just bring me the pitcher."

Sean spent the rest of the night sitting too close, touching her at every opportunity, and repeatedly violating her personal space to whisper one outrageous thing after another in her ear. By the time Brody's Friday night feast had been devoured and the dishes all cleaned, not only were Molly's cheeks blazing, but all those dirty suggestions had more than warmed up the rest of her as well.

She'd asked him what had gotten into him, and he'd told her she had.

It was exactly the kind of thing she had dreamed of hearing those first years when he'd been her hardest crush. But now, suddenly all she could think about was how much there was at risk. Because this didn't feel the same as it had a couple of weeks ago. This didn't seem like just one night...because it wouldn't be. They'd already had their one night. So this was *more*.

Maybe it was Brody's drinks or the nearly newly-wed status of their company, but as obvious as it seemed to her, the rest of the group seemed oblivious to what was happening. Completely missing the way Sean's fingers were playing at the back of her hair or how his eyes burned when he looked at her. Whatever the reason, she was grateful for it.

Finally, Sarah stretched her arms overhead in an exaggerated yawn that set off an avalanche more from everyone else.

Standing up, she conceded, "That's it. I can't fight it any longer. I'm going to have to risk the bugs." Max grinned, wrapping his hands around her hips as he stood as well.

"Don't worry, baby. I'll protect you."

Sean tilted his head toward Molly's. "He added an extra lining to their tent and used some kind of perimeter spray along the door. So unless she's got a spider hitching a ride on that sweatshirt of hers, I'm guessing she'll be good."

Molly gaped. "He installed a second liner? You remember when we came out here those first years, and he wouldn't even let me bring a pillow. We had to roll our jeans up to make one, because he wanted it to be authentic."

"I remember. He was a hard-ass. But those trips were fun."

Brody and Jase loaded the coolers into the truck and locked it up, while Emily stared down at her phone from across the fire, periodically rubbing her eyes or covering her mouth for a yawn.

"Crowd's getting thin," Sean commented, his eyes cutting to Molly's.

He was right, but it wouldn't take more than a single look at Brody, and the guy would stay up as late as she wanted. Only what good would that do, really? Eventually, they'd have to go to bed, and when they did, Brody had his own tent, and she and Sean were sharing. Like they did every year.

Sooner or later, she was going to have to finish this conversation, and it was going to kill her when she did. She was going to have to tell him *no*. And of all the scenarios she'd imagined over the years, that had never been one of them.

———∞———

Sean unzipped the mesh flap of their tent and crawled inside, moving quickly in the darkness to close up behind him. A couple of fires were still going strong farther up the loop, but with the exception of Brody's air mattress inflating, from this end of the campground, things were quiet. Too quiet.

Molly wasn't ribbing him the way she always did. She wasn't gasping about something she'd forgotten to tell him or sticking her foot out of her sleeping bag to shove at his ass while he dug through his stuff. She was just lying there silent at the farthest edge of her side of the tent.

"I know you're not asleep," he said, keeping his voice low enough so the words wouldn't carry.

Her sigh was his only answer.

"Molly." He reached for the end of the mat and found her ankle beneath a layer of sleeping bag. Not exactly the kind of scorching move he'd been promising all night, but now that they were alone and he could literally feel the tension coming off her, a *move* didn't feel right. "Talk to me."

He'd been so sure earlier with Molly in his arms. It had been as if the clouds had parted and suddenly the answer was right there in a clear blue sky as bright as Molly's eyes. He'd been fucking giddy with the revelation—laughing at her shock, because he'd been so damn sure it wouldn't take more than a few minutes before she was right there with him. But the minutes passed and then the hours, and despite him playing with her in ways he knew she liked, she still hadn't turned to him with that too-bright, too-beautiful smile and tried to drag him off to find some place private to celebrate the two of them finally seeing the most obvious thing in the world.

They weren't just friends.

When Molly still didn't answer, Sean found the zipper of her sleeping bag and opened it up, easing down onto the mat beside her. Arms wrapped around her waist, his feet tucked in with hers and most everything else hanging out, he closed his eyes and breathed her in. A second later, she turned into him, pressing her forehead into the center of his chest above where her hands had balled in the fabric of his T-shirt.

Jesus, when she clung to him like that. Like somehow she thought he was the answer, when they both knew he was the problem. He was the one pushing them past the lines that had framed their relationship to this point.

He stroked a hand through her hair and pressed a kiss to the top of her head.

"It would be a mistake," she whispered against his heart, breaking it just a little. "We were lucky that first time. Lucky to be able to slip back into things being normal between us. But I can't risk it again."

He sighed into the space above them. He got it. "Moll, I was freaking out about things changing too. After what we did, I was panicked we wouldn't be able to go back to how we were. But then we did, and I was grateful, except…somehow, the way we were didn't feel like it fit anymore. It didn't feel like enough."

He could hear her swallow, feel the unsteady breath filling her lungs. Did she even realize how tightly she was clinging to him?

"How can you say that?" she asked, her voice so low, he could barely hear her. "How can you think what we have isn't enough? To me, it's everything."

"Molly, don't misunderstand. You do mean everything to me. I've never questioned that. It's just that suddenly…it feels like there could be even more. Like maybe there already is."

Like maybe there always was, and he'd just refused to see it.

She was shaking her head slowly against his chest. "Sean, I-I know it feels good being together. Believe me, I know. But it's not as simple as that. I don't think I can be with you without getting invested."

He let out a quiet laugh, holding her closer. "'Invested' doesn't sound like a bad thing to me. Not at all. In fact, it's pretty much where I'm going with this whole thing. Invested. Committed. The whole shebang."

"For now," she whispered.

His hand stilled at the back of her head, the air seeming to go solid in his lungs. *For now?*

"Molly, no—"

She pushed back from him, going to her knees. "Sean, I know this stuff with your parents hit you hard. I know you're angry, and right now, it feels like maybe the last thing you want is the life they have. But one of these days, you may realize your feelings about the mistakes they've made don't matter when it comes to the kind of future you want. And when that happens, I don't want to be what's holding you back."

Sean pushed to his knees as well, his heart hammering. "What happened with my parents changed a lot of things. It made me take a look at what I was doing with my life. And yeah, it made me question the priorities I'd taken for granted all these years. But, Molly, this isn't just some whim or passing phase. For Christ's sake, I'm not some fifteen-year-old kid rebelling against my folks…and you sure as hell aren't some bad decision I'm using to do it."

"I know. And I'm not trying to make light of what you're feeling. It's just"—she bit her lip, searching his eyes—"I'm not sure you completely understand where *I'm* coming from. Why I'm afraid to let things go any further than they already have."

"Then tell me." So he could tell her why she didn't need to worry.

"I was in love with you, Sean," she admitted in a whispered rush, her brows furrowed, her big blue eyes pleading for understanding.

They were the kinds of words he'd spent his adult life consistently working to avoid. But hearing them come from Molly's lips—Jesus, he didn't know if his heart could take what was happening to it. He wanted to grab her shoulders and pull her in to his chest so she could feel what she was doing to him. Only one thing stopped him.

"*Was?*" he clarified, the single word sounding like it had rolled around in gravel and glass. He didn't like *was*. As in past tense and no longer. It wasn't what he wanted to hear. Which was crazy—but man, it also felt like the most sane reaction he'd ever had.

Molly pinched her lips together and nodded. "For years. From the time I was sixteen until I was twenty-three, you were the beginning, the end, and everything in the middle. I was just a kid, and eventually, I got over it. I have my heart under control now, but, Sean, there's no way I'd be able to maintain that control if we were adding some kind of regular benefits package to the mix."

She was killing him.

"Molly, you've got this all wrong. I'm not asking you for some 'benefits package.'" Unable to hold himself back any longer, he pushed his hands over her hips and pulled her in tight to him. "What I'm talking about— asking you for—is you and me, together. Giving *more than friends* a chance, because this is the first time in my life that I'm not *waiting* for what feels right. I've found it. It's you… Damn it, Molly, it's this."

He took her by the back of the head, pulling her into his kiss, telling her everything he'd meant but couldn't get right with words, reminding her of all the reasons why.

Her hands were in his hair, her fingers pulling as she opened beneath him. All that stiff resistance gone within a single breath.

Couldn't she feel this?

Tearing her mouth from his, she sucked in a breath and then another. But she was still holding him, her hands at his shoulders now, her fingers bunched in his shirt. "So this isn't just another night or another string of nights? You aren't trying to get me out of your system?"

Molly, Molly, Molly.

"No. I don't think there's any getting you out of my system. And more than that, it feels so fucking good having you there, I don't even want to try." His hands coasted up her sides, following the dip of her waist and the rise of her ribs before reversing their paths and starting back down again.

"So you want—?" She sounded so vulnerable, but beneath that soft tremble, there was something else making his heart start to pound. Because she sounded hopeful too.

"I want you, Molly. I want us."

"But what about your plans?"

He could hear her swallow, hear the doubt and the hope just beneath it in the words she could barely whisper.

His fucking plans.

"There's got to be a reason I haven't been able to follow through on the plans I had, and I think you're it. I think you're my plan, Molly." Just saying it out loud felt so good. So right. So fucking different from those conversations with Valerie, where they talked about compatibility, discussed their acceptable levels of attraction with the distance he would never have been able to manage with Molly.

Now, here in the dark, with Molly trembling beneath his hands, he couldn't believe he'd been so blind to this woman who had been in front of him the whole time.

She'd been in love with him.

He wanted that back.

"What if it doesn't work?" she hedged. "What if we try this being together in front of all the friends we share and love…and we realize we made a mistake?"

It wouldn't be a mistake. "Then we go back to being friends, Molly. Because that will *never* change."

"Do you think that's even possible?"

"I swear to you, I do." He believed the two of them could do anything.

The silence stretched, and then she whispered, "I'm afraid to tell them. I'm not sure—"

"Maybe we leave them out of it for now, if it makes you more comfortable." It wasn't what he wanted, but if there was anything he could do or say that would put Molly's mind at ease, he was in. "See how we feel about just being us?"

He waited for her answer, the seconds stretching.

His heart sank, a cold chill slicing through him as she pulled away.

Too late. He'd figured out what he wanted too late, and now she wasn't willing to risk a relationship. After she'd admitted to having loved him for years, he'd finally seen what was there in front of him the whole time, and it was too damn late. Which meant now it was going to be his turn to make sure his feelings didn't get in the way of the friendship that meant more than anything.

He had to say something. Make sure she knew it was going to be okay.

"Molly—"

The velvet touch of her fingertips at his lips interrupted his words, and then he felt the soft press of her breasts against his chest as she leaned in to him. "I'm scared, Sean. Terrified. But I don't want to say no."

His arms locked around her waist, hauling her in closer still as he caught her in a crushing kiss. Because *she didn't want to say no*. "Molly, you won't regret this. It's going to be so good with us. I know it."

"It's already pretty good with us," she said, her words coming breathless and soft. "You sure you're going to be able to improve on perfection?"

He could hear the smile behind her words, the teasing challenge as she tested the new ground beneath them.

"Oh, baby, let me show you the ways."

And with that, he laid her back on her mat and followed her down.

Chapter 15

THIS WAS CRAZY. BUT AFTER ALL THE YEARS, ALL THE wishing, there was no way Molly couldn't say yes. And now Sean was on top of her, taking her mouth like he couldn't get enough of her taste. Like each kiss was a claim, both victory and celebration. Like he truly believed this was what they were meant to be.

He kissed her like he believed it could last forever. And more than anything, she wanted to believe too. More than anything, she wanted to forget about all the years before. She wanted to erase all the nights they'd haggled over the kind of future Sean saw ahead for himself. The kind of woman he planned to have by his side. Sophisticated...educated...poised...elegant.

Women so different from her.

Sean couldn't want her. Not really.

The low growl rumbling from deep in his chest as he palmed her ass and rocked between her legs called her a liar.

Okay, so he did want her. But for how long? How long before he began to notice the ways she didn't quite fit into his world? Before frustration replaced passion?

He said they would always be friends. No matter what else they became.

She needed to believe it.

Threading her fingers through the hair that had always been her weakness, she opened beneath the thrust of his tongue and arched into the sweet pressure of his weight on top of her.

Sean's mouth moved down her neck, hungrily devouring that sensitive stretch of skin.

His gruff laugh sounded against her breast, cocky and assured. "You gotta know how hard I get hearing all those sexy little sounds you make when I put my mouth on you," he told her, still rocking his hips into hers. "But, baby, if you don't want your brother finding out about us like this, you've got to be quiet."

She sucked in a breath, mortification burning through her veins. "We should stop. I didn't even think… Oh my God, Sean, do you think he—?"

"No way. They haven't heard anything."

"How do you know?"

After a beat of silence, he shifted back on his knees. "Because your brother isn't tearing this tent apart trying to get at me. Now put your arms up." Finding the hem of her sweatshirt, he whisked it overhead and into the darkness. The cool air touched her skin, but then Sean was back warming it again. With his hands and his mouth. Covering her with his body. And when that wasn't enough for him, pulling back to tear off his own shirt before returning for the skin-to-skin contact so good, it was driving her past sense.

"Shh, baby," he warned again when his mouth reached her belly button.

"Right…yes…quiet. Quiet," she agreed, probably louder than she should have, but when he wet her flesh with his tongue and then sucked… Oh God, when he bit—"*Quiet*!"

She was pretty sure he was laughing against her

stomach again, but she didn't care. Not when he'd hooked his fingers into her pj's and dragged them down her hips. Not when out of the darkness, she could feel the teasing scrape of his day's worth of stubble moving up her thighs. And not when he kissed her *there*. Softly, gently…*deeply*.

"Quiet… *Oh, Sean…quiet!*" The tension was building within her, pulsing heavily at her center.

Strong fingers dug into her hips. "Christ, Molly, you taste so fucking good, baby," he groaned, and that deep rumble against her sex was her breaking point.

Her entire body was working for what had in that moment become critical. She was pulling at him with her hands and feet, her arms and legs, arching her back to propel him up.

And then he was there on top of her, crushing her with his kiss, one hand fisted in her hair, the other gripping her ass with a rough hold that had her ready to combust on the spot.

He was thick between her legs, steely hard as he ran his length back and forth through her slickness, each pass pushing her closer to that place only he could take her.

"Please…please," she begged, her knees hitching higher up his sides as he drew back. Her hips canted as he rocked forward—and he was inside her, the penetration sending her over the edge.

"Fuck, Molly. Wait—" Sean choked, starting to pull back. "Baby, no condom."

But she was already there, her body seizing hard around him.

"What?" she cried, panic edging past the pleasure

slipping through her fingers. "No, can't we just…just one…oh…Sean…just one more second."

Sean's arms wrapped around her, holding her tight, as he bore down, taking her so deep, she saw stars. "Come on, baby," he growled. "Let me feel you."

Her release slammed through her in one brutal wave after another.

She clutched at him harder, muffling the cries she couldn't contain against his chest.

When it was over, her every muscle was lax and lazy. Her head dropped back against the mat, and her legs slid into a tangle with Sean's. Threading her fingers though his sweat-damp hair, she sighed. "That was… I don't even have words." She was never going to be the same.

"This is going to kill me," Sean groaned, the sound as sexy as any she'd ever heard. He kissed her briefly, his tongue dipping past her lips for a single sexy taste before he slowly withdrew.

"Do you have something?" she asked, sitting up, her legs still draped over the spread of his knees. The crinkle of plastic was her answer. Following the dim outline of his arm, she took the condom from him. "Let me."

"Yeah?"

Tucking the wrapper under the edge of the mat so she'd be able to find and discard it later, she laughed. "You ask like I've just offered you some dirty, taboo treat."

The fingers tracing a light path over her thighs stilled when she found him and carefully began rolling the thin latex down his shaft.

"I've always done it." His breath caught and then hissed through his teeth as she stroked him. "Just to be sure, you know."

She blinked, his meaning becoming clear. "So…no one gets to do this but me?" Something so simple shouldn't turn her on so much, but knowing how he trusted her… how he wanted her…she ached for him again.

Sean urged her to her knees, guiding her over him and then slowly down to take him again. And when she was seated completely, filled to the point where she could barely find the room to take a breath, he pressed his forehead to hers and groaned. "Only you."

Morning came too soon.

Okay, so nothing new there. It's how Molly felt most days. But then most days, she hadn't been kept up until dawn with Sean finding new and creative ways to test her ability to stay quiet.

Somehow, she mustered the strength to turn her head.

A shirtless Sean grinned down at her as he cinched up a hiking boot. He was wearing those same sexy beat-to-hell cargo shorts and a smile that, if he didn't figure out how to tone that sucker down, would have her brother's fist in his teeth before he could blink. Not such a terrible way to wake up after all.

"Morning, gorgeous," he greeted her, keeping his voice low. "Only found three wrappers so far, but the guys have been up for a while, and I heard them starting to joke about who was going to have to risk waking us."

The sleepy haze cleared in a blink, and she was scrambling up, patting herself down for an inventory— tank, panties…*socks*?

She stuck her foot into the space between them, raising a questioning brow.

Casting her a wink, he switched to the other boot. "I thought you might get cold."

When she didn't say anything else, he bit his bottom lip and ran a hand through his spectacularly messy hair. "Okay, I admit it. I think it's fucking hot seeing you in my socks." And in case she didn't believe him—because why the heck would she—he turned, prowling over her until she was on her back with the hard press of him between her legs. "When we get back…I want to see you in my socks and not one fucking thing more."

Okay, and certain things couldn't be faked. So… "You're serious?" She giggled, her knees sliding up his sides. He looked down at where her sock-clad foot perched against his hip and groaned.

"Fuck it, I don't care if they hear."

And wow, that man-possessed look in his eyes was all the confirmation she needed to know he was serious. Bringing her hands up between them, she laughed, trying to hold him back. "Sean!"

The corner of his mouth kicked up. "That's nice, Molly, but my favorite is 'Sean, please,' followed closely by 'Sean, yes.' Or maybe it's the other way around." Giving her his weight, he easily pushed past her arms and buried his face in her hair. "How about we give them both another try and figure it out for sure."

The clang of metal against metal rang through the site, followed by her brother's sharp call. "I know you're working in there, Wyse. Put the laptop down, and wake Molly up. Brody's got…*brunch* ready, and he says you'll never forgive yourself if you don't get it hot."

Molly froze, panic choking off her air as her eyes locked with Sean's above her.

What if Max decided to wake her up himself? What if he came to their tent and found Sean on top of her?

Max would kill him. Or at the very least hurt him. And what about Sean and Max's friendship? What if she ruined everything because she couldn't just say no?

Sean's eyes narrowed as he searched her face. "You're white as a sheet." And then, "Shit, Molly, *breathe*."

The breath she'd been holding burst out on a rush, and she started to squirm. "We can't let him find you. *Hurry*."

One dark-blond brow arched above her. "Because you're worried about what he'll think if we're together?"

Please. "Because I'm worried he's going to kill you," she hissed, wriggling again. But while that reminder would have been enough to launch any sane man back into the farthest corner of the tent, Sean merely smiled.

"Well, if that's all…" Holding her stare, he lowered his head to hers and eased his tongue between her lips, sliding it in and out, licking and rubbing, until he'd slowly, methodically kissed the life out of her.

Message received.

Her brother wasn't going to get in the way.

<hr />

"Molly's up. She'll be out in a minute," Sean stated, zipping the tent closed. He squinted up at a crystal-blue sky dotted with a few cotton-ball clouds and stretched out his arms. "Damn fine morning, huh?"

Max stared at him a minute, a tub of plates and silverware in his hands. Then, looking around as if just noticing, he shrugged. "Yeah, I guess. You guys get any sleep, or those fucking raccoons keep you up too?"

Raccoons? He hadn't heard a single thing other than Molly's panting breaths and desperate moans. His name on her lips again and again, each variation better than the one before.

"Wyse?"

Sean's head snapped up, his eyes landing on Molly's brother. *Shit*. Running a palm over his mouth, he tried to wipe away the grin he was damn sure her brother wouldn't appreciate if he had any idea what had put it there. Clearing his throat, he made a show of looking around the campground. "Yeah, some. But you know. Raccoons. Noisy fuckers."

Max nodded toward the table still set up next to where Brody was working the grill, and they started walking. "It was nuts. You guys must have gotten the worst of it though. One of the sites farther down left a Styrofoam cooler out, and the raccoons must have dragged it down here. The thing was demolished, bits and pieces covering the entire site. Emily took a bunch of pictures before they picked it up."

Sean had heard raccoons get into stuff during the night before, and it sounded like a war zone. But a cooler? How the hell had they missed it? Sure, he'd been distracted in the best way—but to not even know a gang of vermin was looting the place? To not have a clue?

Christ, the last woman he'd been with had been pissed because he'd heard his phone ping from two rooms away while they'd been in the act.

But she hadn't been Molly.

Max jutted his chin over Sean's shoulder. "Sleeping Beauty awakes."

Damn straight she had. Molly was bundled in his

sweatshirt again, along with the cutoff jean shorts that showed off her legs and the pair of his thick socks he'd put on her the night before wedged into her flip-flops. She looked good. Her cheeks were pink, her lips rosy, and that shock of pink was pulled back into a lopsided ponytail with the rest of her white-blond hair.

So hot.

He swallowed hard, momentarily overwhelmed by the realization that she was *his*.

Brody called out a greeting, and Sean focused on staying rooted where he was instead of walking over and kissing her right there in front of everyone.

But one step at a time. For now, Molly was more comfortable keeping their relationship just between them while they tried it on for size. He got it, but... *Damn*.

Beside him, Brody started bitching at Max about a serving tray he knew was in the tote. Sean stood there as if he was doing something to help, but in truth, he was just watching his girl, grinning at the flick of her eyes to his. The soft curve at the corner of her mouth and the near-electric charge that seemed to run between them through a single, brief look.

Laughter sounded from beyond the trees, and then Emily and Sarah rounded the drive, Jase close on their heels.

"Morning, guys," Molly called, turning around to greet them with a wide wave. Which was when Sean saw it.

Oh shit.

The missing condom wrapper dangled precariously from a fold in the hood of her sweatshirt.

He needed to catch her eye. Get her to turn around

and wait for him to clear the evidence. But the psychic hotline that usually ran between them must have been overloaded this morning, because no amount of willing her to turn back around was working.

Molly threw her hands out to the sides and stared up at the sky, announcing, "Wow, what a gorgeous morning, huh? It's still morning, isn't it? Man, I slept like the dead. How about you guys?"

Sean's head snapped around, expecting to greet a punch midthrow, but Max was still on his knees, grumbling as he dug through the tote while Brody snapped his tongs at him.

Moving fast, Sean jogged around the fire pit.

"All that fresh air and quiet, right?" she asked again, jumping lightly from foot to foot. Okay, so she hadn't noticed the raccoons either. Nice to know he wasn't the only one that distracted, but seriously, was it possible to attract any more attention? "Who's hungry? I'm starving."

Dodging three chairs, he came up behind her and threw his arms around her, laughing loudly. "Funny, Moll. But hey, you know what all that racket was?" he asked pointedly, giving her midriff a squeeze. "The raccoons stole a cooler. Ripped the thing to shreds outside our tent."

Her eyes went wide. No doubt she was wondering what he was doing all over her after they'd agreed not to share their new status with the gang just yet. He'd explain later. But for now, he pulled her close enough to pluck the damning evidence from her hood before discreetly stuffing it into his pocket.

Stepping clear of his hold, she turned to him and

crossed her arms, mischief in her eyes. "See, I told you it wasn't a bear."

That got everyone's attention.

"A bear?" Jase coughed out with a laugh.

"Were you huddled up behind Molly all night, begging her to protect you?" Max joked, walking over with the serving platter overflowing with French toast and breakfast potatoes.

Until recently, a bait like that would have had Sean slinging claims about just what positions he'd had Molly in. Because until recently, they would have been completely unfounded, and while they'd have gotten the rise out of Max that Sean loved to score, it would have been fiction. So far from the truth that joking about it would be within the realm of cool.

Not now. It was bad enough he was planning to basically lie to the guy's face until Molly felt secure enough in what they were doing to share it. So instead of returning the trash talk with a hard slam, he shrugged, derailing the feeding frenzy before it began. "Pretty much. Damn, Brod, breakfast smells incredible. You put jalapeños and rosemary in the potatoes again?"

To Sean's dismay, Molly kept her distance through most of the afternoon, finding one excuse after another to avoid being caught in close quarters with him: a trip into town for more bug spray with Sarah, running down to the park office with Max to pick up a few more bundles of firewood, and the most telling of all…when she'd asked Brody if he'd give her a cooking lesson after Sean suggested they all go for another swim—knowing full well the other two couples would pass.

Cooking. Seriously, Moll?

Now the sun had set, and Sean was parked between Jase and Max while Molly and the girls huddled around Brody's prep station, sipping Moscow mules from those ridiculous copper mugs Brody swore were an essential component of the drink.

She was laughing at something Sarah said, her eyes closing as her head tipped back. He loved that laugh. Loved the length of neck she exposed when she gave it up. Loved it even more when she gave it up for him.

"So what about you, Wyse?" Max said, cutting into his thoughts and reminding him there was a conversation he was supposed to be following. "You have any cool travel lined up this fall?"

"Morocco, Barcelona maybe?" Jase asked with a wink.

Sean mentally called up his calendar, thinking about meetings and flights. What he might be able to shuffle so he didn't have so much time away from Molly. "Milan month after next but…you know, maybe Sarah would like to go instead."

She'd have a blast in Milan.

And then he'd be able to stay in Chicago with Molly who, when he looked over, was doing an impression of a teapot, if he wasn't mistaken. She'd be great with kids. The kind of mom who'd play with them and do different voices when she read stories. The kind of mom who wanted to tuck them in at night herself.

"Shit, Wyse, you trying to get Sarah to leave him already?" Jase asked.

Max leaned forward, looking Sean in the eyes. "You serious, man? Damn, she'd love that."

Jase was shaking his head, starting up about how

much he hated when Emily had to travel, while throwing in all the requisite qualifiers about understanding it was part of her job, yada yada, but he'd gotten spoiled having her in his bed, and now he couldn't sleep when she wasn't there.

What a wuss. But even as Sean thought it, a smile was creeping over his mouth. He couldn't wait to get spoiled from having Molly in his bed. He couldn't wait until he got to be the guy who caught her hand as she was walking past and pulled her into his lap.

He'd never thought about that stuff for himself before. Not with the plans he'd been making. Mutually advantageous marriages weren't exactly made of those heart-and-soul moments. But with Molly…Molly might let him walk with his hand in her pocket. Molly might catch his tie and pull *him* in for a kiss, just because she wanted one.

He hoped so.

———

It was close to one by the time everyone was ready to knock off for the night. The girls had walked up to the bathroom together to get ready, Emily and Sarah giggling about tent sex while Molly walked quietly beside them, not ready to join the conversation.

Last night had been amazing, but for whatever reason, today, she'd been nervous. The last time she and Sean had given in, she'd known exactly what the next day should look like—like every day that had come before. Normal.

Like nothing between them had changed.

But that wasn't the new plan.

This was a new day. Different from all the ones that had come before, even if she and Sean were the only ones who knew it.

She'd been a chicken, dodging him at every turn. Because what did this new normal look like? Especially when they weren't ready to share it.

"I'm sorry, Molly. You're probably ready to puke, listening to us blab." Sarah slowed by the drive to the site where she and Max were set up. "I blame it on Brody's generous pours. I've been running my mouth all night, and you're probably ready to overdose on TMI."

Molly's brows shot high, and suddenly, she felt guilty. Had she seriously tuned out the last ten minutes of conversation?

"No, I'm fine. Just a little out of it, and I'm blaming Brody's drinks too. And the raccoons last night. Just tired."

Emily raised a hand to her mouth, trying to cover the yawn they'd all been fighting. "We need to find Molly a guy."

Say what?

She craned her head, checking to see whether Sean was within earshot. Max was standing outside his tent at the next site, waiting on his wife, but Brody and Sean weren't visible from where she'd been standing.

"Seriously, Em, we do," Sarah agreed, that sleepy haze in her eyes starting to clear beneath the glow of the lantern. "You know what? We can. I mean, look at us. We're smart…connected."

Okay, this wasn't good. "That's sweet, but I'm not really into the whole setup thing."

Emily was grinning down at her, nodding a little too enthusiastically. "We get *shit done*, Moll."

Yeah, they did. These two took to projects like nobody's business. But even without Sean having just stepped into the picture, Molly wasn't sure she would want to be one. "I know you do. You guys are impressive...like whoa, but I kind of have a rule about finding my own dates."

She should totally have that rule.

Emily leaned in, probably closer than absolutely necessary, the lantern giving her a sort of ghost-story look. "You know what you need, Moll?"

This could be fun. "What's that?"

Those big, soft brown eyes that Jase had waxed poetic about for the first six months they were married bore into her. "You need to get the hell out of Sean's tent."

"Amen, sister," Sarah agreed with a hiccup.

Okay, and now Emily was really close. "Especially after that close-encounter business with his boner and then that knitting channel stuff. I know you guys are besties, but you gotta draw the line."

This was the part where she was supposed to take her drunk girlfriends' hands, look them in the eye, and share what was happening between her and Sean. But that would mean admitting to them that she believed she and Sean had a shot. It meant risking that she would look like the worst kind of fool when Sean realized there was a reason Molly had never been on his radar before.

Besides, they'd been together for, like, five seconds.

If things worked out, there would be time to tell their friends later. And if they didn't, that would be okay too. But for tonight, she had another way to handle this. "You're right. I should get out of his tent."

Both women were nodding.

"Tonight. I'm going to get out tonight."

Emily was still in full bobblehead mode, but Sarah's eyes had taken on a wary look.

"But there's a reason I never bunk with Brody. He snores like crazy."

Lies. At least as far as she knew. Brody just didn't like a roommate unless he was doing her.

"So maybe I could bunk with one of you guys. You know, if you think I should really get out of Sean's tent. Like, tonight."

And suddenly, both women were shaking their heads. "No, no. It doesn't have to be tonight."

Ha!

"Seriously, there's no rush."

"Your sleeping bag is already in there."

"Yeah."

Molly heaved a deep sigh of relief—mostly for their benefit. "You're right. It's no big deal for this trip. Okay, thanks, girls. I feel way better."

Emily agreed she did too, but Sarah was looking at Molly with a critical eye, as if something didn't smell right.

Time for a quick exit.

"Okay, hey, has Max been holding your tent flap open this whole time?"

Whatever Sarah's BS meter was picking up, she forgot about in a blink. Next thing, she was running for her tent, squawking about keeping the bugs out.

One down.

"Em? You gonna make me wait all night?" Jase called from the next site down.

Em offered a quick shrug, her grin going wide before she skipped off as well.

Crisis averted.

Molly stood where she was for a minute, the lantern dangling from her fingers not bright enough to make out their tent beyond.

What was she doing?

A part of her wanted to run, not walk, that last distance to get back to Sean. Make the most of every minute they had together.

But the other part of her couldn't stop asking why she wasn't being smarter. Why she would set herself up for the kind of heartbreak and rejection she'd spent most of her life actively working to avoid. Why she would risk her relationship with Sean, when deep down, she knew a romantic relationship couldn't last.

Knowing she wouldn't find any answers standing alone in the dark, she did the only thing she could and put one foot in front of the other until she made it back to where Sean was waiting for her outside the tent, arms crossed.

"Looked like you might be ready to turn tail and run there for a minute."

Of course, he'd been watching her, making sure she got back okay.

He was still Sean. Overprotective and caring and all-too-easy-to-fall-for Sean.

The man she could talk to, Sean.

"After everything, I feel like I suddenly don't know how to be with you," she admitted nervously. "What to do."

He nodded, reaching past her to open the flap of the tent. When they were zipped inside, he cocked his head at her and grinned. "You'll figure it out, Moll. But if it makes you feel any better, I know exactly what I want to do."

His confidence tugged at her smile and her heart. "Yeah?"

Crawling toward her until she was leaning back on her arms, he lowered his voice. "Oh yeah. I've been waiting for this kiss all damn day."

Her heart fluttered, and then in the next beat, he caught her by her hips and, in a move so swift and smooth, he *had* to have been thinking about it all day, Sean had her pj bottoms and panties cast aside and her knees flipped over his shoulders. "Sean!"

"Shh, baby. You just kick back and think about what you want. Take your time. I'm going to be at this a while."

And then he kissed her.

Chapter 16

SO VERY *NOT* THE WAY HE'D SEEN THIS MORNING GOING.

Sean ran his hands over the worn boards of the picnic table, focusing hard on keeping them from balling into fists and harder still on keeping his fucking mouth shut.

"But seriously, Sean, you have to know *somebody*. Just think about it," Sarah charged, giving Sean the serious face she used with him across the conference table at work. The one that said she meant business.

The one he didn't like very much right now, at least not in the context of her applying it to finding his girlfriend a date. Even if said girlfriend would probably flip out that he was trying to label her already, but whether she was ready to admit it or not, that's what she was. And thinking of her wearing his label was about the only thing keeping a smile on his face as Sarah kicked off her latest crusade.

"Maybe you ought to slow down here, Sarah. I know you mean well, but have you even talked to Molly about this yet?"

Molly was still asleep, and after the way he'd kept her up, the poor girl needed her rest. Especially since he had every intention of doing the same tonight. Hell, every night for as long as she'd let him. But that said, it wouldn't have been the worst thing to have her out there fending the girls off on her own.

Emily sat down on the opposite bench, swinging her long legs beneath the table and then scooting over to make room for Jase, who was carrying her coffee, since she had a spiral notebook and pen in hand.

"We talked to her last night," Emily interjected, flipping the notebook open and scribbling across the top. "She was into it."

She most definitely was *not* into it.

What she *had* been into? His mouth between her legs until she'd come not once but twice. *That* she'd been into.

This business with Sarah and Emily—Jesus, the two of them together?—working to find her a date? Not a fucking chance. She'd probably been trying to put them off, figuring they'd forget about it by the next day. But obviously, not so much.

The rapid-fire clacking of Emily's pen against the top of the page labeled WHAT DOES MOLLY WANT set his stomach on edge. Emily looked intense, focused.

"Jase, you and Sean have known her the longest. You've seen what kind of guys she goes for. Tell me about the last three."

Sarah shook her head. "Let's make it five."

The girls looked to Jase, and Jase looked to Sean, a sorry sort of helplessness in his eyes. "Five?"

Dollars to doughnuts, the guy had nothing. "Well, there was that guy…that time. You know, the hair guy," Jase said, waving his hands around his head as if he was giving them anything to go on.

And sure, Sean knew exactly who he was talking about. Hair guy also went by Eric, a clerk at a local skate shop. She'd gone out with him a couple of times but hadn't been that into him.

Emily was staring at Jase, an expectant look in her eyes. When he didn't go on, she blew out a frustrated breath and waved her hand. "And? What did she like about him? Why did she go out with him? What set him apart from the guys she didn't go out with?"

Jase blinked and again looked to Sean.

He felt bad enough that he was lying to his friends about what was going on with Molly, but he couldn't just leave Jase hanging in the wind, especially when the man's wife was looking at him like that.

After a sigh, Sean bit the bullet. "She went out with him because she said he was pretty mellow. She liked his smile and that he made her laugh. And she liked the hair. Something about wanting to put her fingers in it."

Max walked over and sat, handing Sarah a mug of coffee.

"So this is Operation Land Molly a Man in action? Do I want to be here?" he asked, having the sense to look at Jase and Sean, rather than his wife and Emily.

Jase shook his head. "Definitely not, man. Run."

Sarah took a sip of her coffee and smiled, snuggling in to her husband's side. "We're talking about Hair Guy, trying to identify what attracted Molly to him. And why it didn't work out."

"Fuck if I know what she saw in him," Max grumbled, his brows pulling together. "But it didn't work out because of his work ethic. Something about him calling in sick all the time and trying to get her to play hooky. She didn't respect him."

Emily's pen was moving in a blur across her page. "Perfect. So strong work ethic, good sense of humor, mellow, and hair appeal. I may need to go directly to the source to understand that last one better."

"And before Hair Guy?" Sarah asked. Knowing better than to bother with Jase again, she cocked her head and waited for Sean's answer.

"Bar Guy." Also known as Richy Oldsmith. "He was actually an inventor, pouring drinks to earn enough bank to launch his product." He could remember being a little jealous over the way Molly kept talking about him, telling Sean how she thought they'd get along because they were so much alike.

"His kick to the curb was courtesy of being impractical," Max added, with a grin.

———

"What's up?" Molly asked, rubbing the sleep from her eyes as she half stumbled over to the picnic table where most of the group was congregating. Brody was probably chatting up the group of girls camped down by the bathrooms. Everybody was laughing, smiling—everyone except for Sean, that was. He had a pee-in-his-cornflakes kind of dour going on, and after the night they'd had, whatever was bothering him had to be pretty big to wipe the smile from his face.

Sean sat back, shifting over on the bench to make room for her. "The girls decided to get a jump on finding a new guy for you. So we've been going over your previous boyfriends, making lists of what you liked and didn't like. They want to make sure this next one's a winner."

And like that, she was awake. No wonder Sean looked miserable.

"Um… You guys don't have to do this. It's nice that you want to, but I think it's better if I find my own dates."

"We tried that," Sarah said with a laugh. "So now you get to just kick back and let Emily and me do our work."

Sean was still watching her, his eyes dark, frustrated.

There was no question what he wanted. Her to come forward with the truth, but she just wasn't ready.

And he must've seen it in her eyes, because his cut away, and the muscle in his jaw started to tick.

She didn't want him to be mad at her. She didn't want to hurt him or cause him any suffering. But they hadn't even had a full day alone to see how they actually felt about trying out this couple thing. It was too soon, and he had to understand that.

Maybe he did. Because after a long breath, he smoothed his hand back through his hair, returning the rumpled mess she'd spent hours perfecting the night before into a semi-neat state. And then he was looking back at her, the smile she hated from all those society shots front and center on his face. It wasn't real, but he was willing to play along.

She let out the breath she hadn't realized she'd been holding.

"Okay, this will be way better now that you're here," Emily said, her eyes glittering with excitement. "We've already been through Hair Guy, Bar Guy, Inventor Guy, and Sean was just about to tell us about Homeless Guy."

Molly let out a snort, turning to Sean, who didn't seem the slightest bit apologetic. "Homeless Guy? This again?"

Sean sat back, cocking that strong jaw to the side.

"Did he or did he not try to take you to his friend's couch on not one, not two, but three separate occasions?"

"And in case there was any question, that right there is why she dumped him," Max said with a shrug.

"Yeah, yeah, thanks for the hot tip, Max." Emily looked to Molly. "But let's get back to the original attraction. What made you say yes?"

Welcome to the hot seat. Molly could feel the heat creeping up her chest and neck. She knew the answer, and prior to this weekend, nothing on earth would have made her own up to it. She would have been too worried about someone connecting the right dots.

But now…

"His eyes," she admitted, remembering the way they'd held hers that first time, the familiarity of them. "He had these gorgeous brown eyes that reminded me of a crush I never quite got over."

She couldn't meet Sean's eyes now. Not with that smug smile planted on his lips. The one that more than anything, she wanted to kiss right off.

Finally, Sean turned back to the girls. "All right, enough about Molly. How about me? You want to hear about my ideal woman?"

Molly coughed on her sip of coffee, choking for a second before she regained her composure.

Laughing, Sarah started gathering the empty mugs from around the table while Emily shook her head and closed her notebook. "Pretty sure we're all familiar with that, mister."

Oh no.

"If we're talking marriage material," Sarah chimed in, walking over to the wash bin to start the mugs. "I've got this in three… Ivy League, last name found on the *Fortune* 500 list, summa cum laude graduate from the Stepford School of Social Graces."

Jase grinned, climbing out from his side of the picnic table. "She's got your number, Wyse."

Max stood as well, leaning over to clap him on one shoulder. "And if we're *not* talking marriage, then the exact opposite of that."

Molly tried to push the air through her throat, but it was too tight. They'd said exactly what she would have just two days ago. And even if she *wanted* to believe that somehow things had changed that much, she didn't know if she could.

"Whoa, Em. Hold up, will you?" Sean called after her, jogging a few steps to catch up. "Just remembered something important I don't want to forget. Mind if I bum a sheet of that paper and your pen a minute?"

Needing a moment to get her emotions back in check, Molly went up to the bathrooms to brush her hair and teeth. When she came back to get changed and start packing up, that's when she saw it. The neatly folded sheet of ripped-out spiral paper on her pillow.

What Sean wants in a woman…

She unfolded the page and let out a soft laugh, chased by too much emotion. There were two words on the page, surrounded by a heart.

Molly Brandt.

The morning went by too fast. They hiked the four-mile trail, stopping along the way to picnic with the sandwiches she and Max had made that morning. Jase and Emily had been the trailblazers, while she and Sarah compared notes on Max's quirks, with the rest of the guys bringing up the rear.

Every now and then, she and Sean found a moment to hang back, slipping off for a second alone, during which Sean would do his damnedest to convince her to tell their friends what was going on.

Molly's back pressed into the bark of the tree as her fingers slid through the silk of Sean's sun-kissed hair. His mouth moved over her neck as he pulled her in to him.

"Sean, we're going to get caught," she chided when he pulled her knee up his side and then splayed his hand wide over the back of her thigh, squeezing the muscle as he groaned into her neck.

"Ooh, naughty stuff, Moll. Thrill of discovery."

"No!" she gasped, refusing to acknowledge said thrill snaking through her at the idea that they might have minutes or maybe only seconds.

What they were doing was asking for trouble, but she couldn't resist the stolen moment.

His laugh rumbled against her sensitive skin, and her arms tightened around his neck.

"Sean, they're going to notice we're gone. Again."

Sliding his hands up and down her hips, he stepped back and grinned at her. "Probably."

"What?" she squeaked, batting his hand away when he hooked his finger in the hem of her tank and started pulling it up.

He gave her a stern look and caught her by the wrists,

holding them in one hand above her head. Again, he reached for the hem of her shirt. "Struggle all you like, Moll, but I want my mouth on these perfect tits. Just for a second. Then I promise to be good."

She stilled, gaping at him. Because no way had he just—

Her tank was up, and with a flick of his finger, the right cup of her bra was down, the tight peak of her breast exposed to the afternoon air. Molly's eyes darted around, making sure they were alone as that unwelcome spear of exhilaration shot through her center.

"Sean." She sighed again as he just stood there, his eyes hungry and fixed on her exposed breast. Her ears straining for any sound to warn her of her friends' approach, she urged him on. "Please."

He wet his lips and leaned down close enough to her breast that she could feel his breath, then looking back up into her eyes, he said, "Did you want something, Molly?"

Oh God, he was playing with her. Teasing her when he knew they might be caught at any second. She should be pissed. Railing at him.

Instead, she gave another half-hearted tug at her wrist, bit her lip, and nearly moaned when all it earned her was Sean's raised brow and tightening hold.

Her hips moved forward in a restless shift, a fact that did not escape Sean. His eyes darkened, and his nostrils flared. "Eh, eh, Molly. We can play more of this game later, baby, but for now…just say it."

She shuddered at the sound of his voice and the pushy directive that shouldn't be making her ache the way it was. "In your mouth, Sean. *Please*."

"Fuck, that's hot," he growled a second before

covering her breast and swirling the warm, wet tip of his tongue over her nipple. After a deep suck that had her breath fracturing above his head, he switched to her other breast and did the same.

So good. And over way too soon. Because then Sean was releasing her wrists with a gentle kiss on each one before carefully straightening her bra and fixing her shirt for her.

Ever the gentleman…just when he'd shown her how much she liked his darker side.

Sean stepped back, and she caught him by the belt.

"Not so fast, Wyse."

Again with that arched golden brow, only this time, the look on his face was surprised rather than smug. She liked it almost as much.

"My turn." Rather than even try to hold his wrists, she pointed to his chest and leveled him with a look. "Stay."

The corner of Sean's mouth twitched, his eyes burning hot as she let her fingers drift down the center of his chest to his fly.

She tugged at his belt, earning her a look of pure alarm.

The brat in her couldn't resist. "Just for a second," she promised, easing his zipper down as she dropped into a low crouch.

"Molly," he warned, his voice gone satisfyingly hoarse.

But she already had her hands on him, pulling his rapidly growing shaft from the confines of his boxer briefs.

A shudder ran through him as she waited, his cock a bare inch from her lips. Looking up from beneath her lashes, she definitely understood the appeal of this game.

"Say it."

He groaned, sliding his fingers into her hair, sifting through and then gently gripping again. "Your mouth. *Please*."

Heat surged though her center. Parting her lips, she took him in, sliding down his shaft as far as she could go. A string of hoarse expletives sounded over her head, and she smiled, easing back until she left him with one final lick of the tip.

Standing up, she dusted her hands on her thighs and grinned as though she weren't every bit as affected as he was. More so.

"You ready to get back?" she asked cheekily.

Before she could react, Sean reached out and, catching her by the back of the neck, dragged her into a kiss that turned her knees to jelly and her brain to mush. When he let her go, he shook his head.

"Not really, but I don't think I'm going to be able to exact the kind of revenge that deserves here in the state park."

⁓

They'd taken the tents down and packed up most of their supplies before the hike, so things moved quickly once they got back to the campground. The cars were loaded, Brody's grill and umpteen coolers secured in the truck. Molly started walking over to Emily and Sarah's car for the ride home.

"We're stopping at the outlets on the way back. You game?" Sarah asked.

Molly stopped where she was, dread cementing her feet in place. "The outlets." She hated shopping, but

Emily and Sarah loved it almost as much as they loved their husbands. "For how long?"

Then Sean was there, one hand on her shoulder as he pulled her back into his side. "Molly can ride with us. You girls have fun."

She turned in to him, finding it harder and harder not to just lean in to his chest and rest her head there. "My hero."

"You know it, baby."

―᷾᷾―

The ride home after camping was always quieter than the ride up. Jase and Sean sat up front, listening to a game on the satellite radio, while Molly sat in the back, surrounded by the coolers and extra camping gear cleared out of the girls' car to leave trunk space for shopping.

Jase dropped Molly first. The gear was mostly Sean's, so she didn't need anyone to help her get up to her place, which meant she wouldn't get a chance to see Sean alone. No kiss goodbye. No plans. Just an all-too-convincing wave from the far side of the passenger seat. Nothing to tip Jase off. Nothing to reassure her about what came next.

Upstairs, she dumped her dirty clothes into her laundry bag and checked her phone. Nothing, but why would there be? They'd said goodbye less than ten minutes before. He and Max probably hadn't even gotten to the storage place.

This was ridiculous. She'd see Sean at work tomorrow night or the next day. He'd call or text like he always did. Because them being *together* together didn't change anything except that in addition to hanging out in their spare time the way they already did, they'd be having sex on the regular too.

Only somehow, she didn't believe that.

From where she was sitting, everything felt different.

Maybe she should just text him. Or call. See if hearing his voice would reassure her some.

This was pathetic. She plugged in her phone to charge beside the bed and left it there while she went to shower. When the last of the dirt and sand had been scrubbed clean, she pulled on a pair of clean, soft sweats, rolled at the cuffs, and a Wyse Hotels T-shirt.

One glance at her phone was all she gave herself. No missed calls or texts. She rubbed a hand over her anxious belly, feeling stupid for not just calling. For being this undone over a guy.

Except this wasn't just any guy. This was Sean. The guy she'd loved for more years than she wanted to admit. The guy she'd finally gotten over. The guy who in one weekend had managed to undo all her hard work and break down the walls around her heart, turning her into a giant, steaming pile of squish.

Three days, and she was back where she'd been at sixteen, at twenty. She was in love with him, staring at the phone, willing it to ring. Praying he would feel the same way she did.

Only this time, it was worse. Because this time, Sean was telling her he wanted her too. This time, he was letting her believe there was a chance. This time, he'd given her just enough to tear down the walls around her heart and leave her vulnerable and exposed. Breakable.

The worst thing about it was that she knew better.

Sean wanted her, for now. There was no questioning

that fact. Yet a part of her couldn't help feeling as though, despite his assurances that it wasn't the case, maybe what was happening between them had more to do with his family than it did with her.

What if he was reacting to his parents' betrayal? What if it really was some not-quite-midlife rebellion… because, yeah, she could understand how learning that his perfect family had been a farce might make a guy feel like he wanted to run as far and fast from the footsteps he'd been following as he could get. But eventually, Sean was going to slow down and catch his breath. Eventually, he was going to stop running altogether and take a hard look at what he wanted his future to look like. And Molly just couldn't believe it was her.

The front door to her apartment swung open, and she dropped her phone on the couch as she jerked to her feet. Sean stalked in, throwing the door closed behind him as he crossed to her and, in one swift motion, caught her in his arms to deliver a crushing kiss. Her arms flew around his neck, her fingers finding their way into his hair as she melted into him.

"Molly, this has to end," he growled against her neck, tightening his hold and lifting so her feet dangled as he carried her back to the bedroom.

End? Her heart stopped. "What?"

"You've gotta let me tell them." He tossed her back on the bed, following her down and covering her with his body. "Do you have any idea how fucking hard it was not to touch you? Not to just tell Jase to drop us together at my place?"

Her breath rushed out, and her heart started to beat again.

He caught her face in his hands, those gorgeous eyes of his searching hers. "Tell me you're okay with them knowing. Tell me—"

"I missed you," she gasped, arching up for his kiss, a desperation she'd never felt before rising within her, making her hands shake and her breath fracture. She pulled at his clothes, rolling over so she was on top, begging him to touch her, groaning when he did and his urgency surpassed even her own. And then he was inside her, filling her with one powerful thrust after another, telling her how beautiful she was, how much he wanted her, how fucking good she felt around him, and how he was never going to let her go.

It was too much. Everything she needed to hear. And for that moment, she even let herself believe.

After, when they were lying together, the sweat drying on their bodies, she lifted her head from Sean's chest and met his eyes. "I really missed you," she whispered, hating how true it was almost as much as she needed to say it. "I was standing in here, aching because I didn't know when I'd get to see you again. Wishing I'd been able to kiss you goodbye." She swallowed. "But I'm not ready to tell anyone about us."

Sean nodded, the corner of his mouth that always seemed to be hauling the rest of his face around angled down. "I get it. You need time."

"I need some time with you. Alone."

Brushing a bit of her hair back from her face, he added, "So you have a chance to see how we are separate from everyone else."

She nodded, praying he could understand.

Snaking his arms around her, he dragged her up and

over him. "I've been waiting a long time to feel like this about a woman. And the fact that it's you, Molly... I can't even tell you how amazing that is. Sure, I want to be able to touch you or kiss you without having to check whether there's anyone watching, but you better believe I want time for us alone too." He rested his hands on her hips. "It's not just about the sex though. Don't get me wrong, being inside you is off the charts. But I want us to be alone, because I've always liked it being just the two of us maybe a little more than I should have. And most of all, I want you to feel as right about us as I do."

"Does it feel different to you?" she asked, not sure what she wanted the answer to be. "I mean, hanging out now. Does it feel as comfortable...as natural, as it did before?"

His brows furrowed as he considered. But then he shrugged. "It's different, I guess. But in a good way. Moll, I know you're nervous, but we're not losing us, okay?"

When they were together like this, she wanted so much to believe.

He brushed a thumb over her bottom lip. "Just give it a chance. That's all I'm asking."

She looked down at this man she loved and nodded. She'd give him anything he asked for.

Chapter 17

SEAN'S DART SAILED THROUGH THE AIR, NEATLY CLOSING OUT 20s when it hit.

Brody jumped off his chair, pumping his fist in the air a few times. "That's what I'm talkin' about, Wysc. This is why I love your ass."

Sean grinned, bumping knuckles with his teammate and taking the grudging congrats from Emily and Jase for the victories they were. Sarah and Max hadn't bothered looking up from the paint samples they'd been discussing since they arrived, which meant the timing was perfect. Sean signaled their waitress for another round and then headed up to the front of the bar where Molly was just finishing helping one of the girls.

Her head came up and, damn, that smile. Had she always looked at him that way and he'd just been too blind to see it, or was the smile that caught him right in the center of his chest something new? Something the guys—or more likely the girls—might notice?

"Nice toss. Way to close out the game."

"Saw that, did you?" he asked, leaning against the bar instead of wrapping his hand around her waist and pulling her into his arms like he wanted.

"I did. Emily looked like someone shot her puppy."

Sean leaned a little closer, pitching his words for her ears only. "You look like someone who needs to be kissed."

He'd been careful, checking first to make sure Jill or one of the other Belfast staff weren't within earshot. He wanted their relationship to be out in the open, but more than that, he wanted Molly to be good with it first. He wanted her to be confident and feel secure.

Much as he'd like to pretend he didn't, he knew exactly what was holding her back. It was him. Everything he'd been saying, planning, working toward for the past ten years. She didn't completely trust that his change of heart was going to stick. That he'd realized what a fool he'd been, trying to emulate the behavior and choices of a man who had betrayed everything he'd claimed to have valued. And Sean couldn't blame her.

Molly blushed, ducking her head so that fall of silky blond and hot pink shielded her face.

"You need some help bringing up another case of longnecks or anything?" Sean asked.

Her lips pressed together in a tight line as she nodded once.

"Cool, I'll meet you in back."

Cutting through the crowd, he headed around the corner to the back hall that led to the bathrooms, offices, and storeroom. None of them visible from the main seating area.

The seconds ticked past, and he propped a shoulder against the wall. Totally casual. Sure, his heart rate might have kicked up a notch or two once she'd agreed to meet him. But he was chill.

He checked his watch, as if it was going to tell him how long he'd been waiting, even though he hadn't checked it before he set up shop like some junior high chump trying to play it cool waiting for the chick he liked at her locker.

Just then, Molly rounded the corner, that sweet blush still hot on her cheeks as she cast a furtive glance behind her.

Sean caught her arm and pulled her in to him, turning them around so she was against the wall and he was standing over her, one arm braced above her head.

"You're killing me, Molly," he ground out before taking the kiss he'd been thinking about since he woke up hard as a spike, fucking alone in his bed that morning. She was so sweet that the single taste he'd been promising himself suddenly wasn't even close to enough. "Making me blow every bit of game I ever had straight to hell."

She bit the tender pad of her bottom lip and peered up at him, one brow raised like she thought this was funny or something. "Me? Really? And this loss of game—alleged loss of game—is my fault?"

Damn, when she looked at him like that, he couldn't think. Rocking into the space between them, he nodded. "Hell yes, it is. You keep walking past our table, stopping next to me and asking if there's anything I want, lingering just long enough for me to get a hit of that coconut, and then leaving me stuck at a table across from your brother, ready to bust through my fly."

Her brows pulled together, and she bit her lip again, looking significantly more amused than he felt. "Did I really make you hard?"

The whole breathless thing when she said *hard*—damn, that worked for him.

"When do you get out of here?" he asked, forcing himself to take a step back and check around the corner. No one was coming, so he took her hand in his and pulled it against his chest.

"Past your bedtime, I'm afraid." Then, snaking her hand into his jeans pocket, she pulled out his phone and checked the time. "But I've got a break coming up in about twenty minutes."

"Is that so?" He did the math. "Shit, not enough time for me to get my car."

"Your car?"

"You know, the one with the tinted windows and spacious second-row seating. I was thinking I could park in the alley—"

"Another alley?" She shoved off his chest with a teasing laugh. "Wow, Sean, you take me to the nicest places."

Uh-oh. Grabbing her wrist, he reeled her back in. She'd been joking…but he didn't like the idea that there might be any hint of truth there. Looking down into her eyes so there was no way she could miss his meaning, he spelled out just exactly what he thought.

"Baby, just say the word, and I'll take you any place you can imagine. There is nothing I want more in this world than to show you off to everyone as my girl. But since you won't even let me hold your hand on the street because someone we know might see it, yeah, I'm looking for any way, any place that I'll be able to get you alone for a few minutes. I want to be able to put my arms around you. I want to feel your head on my shoulder and your smile against my chest.

"I want to do that thing where our fingers are all

tangled up when we talk like they were Monday night. I want a few minutes where you can be my girlfriend and not just my buddy." And because this was Molly and she knew him better than anyone, he added, "Plus, there are about a million dirty things I want to do *to* you too, and FYI, you *really* would have liked where my head was at tonight—feel free to read into the wording as much as you like on that."

Molly smiled up at him, her eyes suspiciously shiny. "I liked that finger-tangly thing too."

His heart turned over, thudding hard enough that it would have hurt if it didn't feel so good. He pressed his brow to hers. "All we have to do is tell them, and we can hold hands like that any time we want."

The silence stretched, and for a minute, Sean thought she might be considering it. Hell, maybe she had been. Then she cleared her throat and, smoothing her hand over his chest, sidestepped his hold. Heading back toward the bar, she cast him a quick glance over her shoulder. "I'm pushing my break back to start in thirty. Get your car."

—◆◆◆—

The next week was brutal. It wasn't that her workload was any worse than normal; it was more that her mind was on other things. Fine, her mind was on Sean and how badly she wanted to see him.

"Molly, do you want to check the bathroom?" Cecilia asked, setting a caddy of cleaning supplies down beside the granite-topped island where Molly was checking off her list for the Paulaski house.

"Let's have a look," she said, following her newest

employee back to the white marble master bath, confident she'd find as thorough a job there as she had everywhere else. Cecilia was a keeper for sure with a stellar work ethic Molly had witnessed up close and personally when they'd met on a catering gig a few summers ago. This was the second house they'd cleaned together, basically working side by side so Molly could make sure Cecelia was as thorough as Molly needed her employees to be. Cecelia would do the next job on her own, with Molly just stopping in for a quick check at the end, and then the week after, she'd be taking the Paulaski and Delfey jobs on herself. And not a second too soon, because while Molly appreciated all the new business she could get, she'd been pushing herself and her crew to the limit.

Good for the down-payment account, but she couldn't help but feel like she was living on borrowed time when it came to her relationship with Sean…and she didn't want to miss out on seeing him.

As if that quiet, betraying thought had somehow summoned him, her phone pinged with a text.

> **Sean:** I miss my girlfriend. Let's get out of town and do the tangled fingers thing the whole weekend.

Molly stumbled, smacking her hip into the corner of the island. She fumbled the phone, juggling it a few times before she grasped it tightly between her hands and pulled it close to her chest.

Cecelia popped her head back out of the bathroom with a questioning look. "Wow, I don't think I've seen a smile that bright out of you…maybe ever. What's his name?"

"Sean," Molly replied without thinking. Popping her head up in horror, she saw Cecelia was ducking back into the bathroom.

"For a second there, you got my hopes up, but if it's just Sean, least that explains the grin. What a goof. Tell him I said hi, will you?"

Heart racing over the close call, Molly nodded and followed Cecelia back to check her work. But her mind was on the weekend and the finger tangling goodness she couldn't wait to get her hands into.

———~~~———

"Not exactly what I was expecting when you said you wanted to stop and pick up some beer," Molly remarked, leaning back on her arms and stretching her legs out along the bench.

Damn, she was gorgeous wearing that contented smile with her face tilted up to the sun.

"But worth the detour, right?" He snapped a photo and then thumbed through the others he'd taken during the New Glarus brewery tour. The one he'd gotten of Molly examining a huge copper brewing unit, her white hard hat tilted at a jaunty angle, was going on his computer's screen saver. Or it would once she let him tell her brother about them being together. This one though, this one was going on his phone along with a lock code.

No way was he going to be able to keep things under wraps much longer.

Not when having a damned picnic table between them was making him itch.

Molly drew a deep breath. "Brody's going to be fuming if he finds out we came up here without him."

If. Hmm. "Brody can bring his own date up here any time he likes."

Her eyes cut away, but not before another pretty pink warmed her cheeks. "It's kind of weird, isn't it?" she asked, staring out to the surrounding fields. "I mean, calling this a date."

"That's what it is."

She nodded, a pretty curve touching her lips. "But still, being here...alone. It's never just you and me. I mean, not out of town like this."

She was right. They'd been on countless trips together, but always as part of a bigger group. Even after their friendship had begun to set them apart, they'd never taken a weekend just the two of them. Right then, he couldn't help but wonder why.

Maybe the answer was in front of him...in the way he couldn't take his eyes off her, in how even these few feet of distance between them were too much, in how fucking good it felt to have her alone.

He'd been working his ass off not to think about Molly like that from about when she turned twenty. But now that he'd let himself? There was no going back.

"Worried we're going to run out of things to talk about?" he teased. Then he grinned when she shook her head and laughed. Because even in this new territory, that was one thing neither of them would ever have to fear. Since that first day he'd gotten her to smile, conversation between them had always come easily.

"I wouldn't say *worried*." Pushing a few streaks of pink from her brow, she met his eyes. "I mean, I'm sure we can find *something* to fill the time...even if we did run out of conversation."

Sean swallowed hard. He knew that look she was giving him. He loved that look.

Pushing up from the bench, he grabbed her hand. "Time to get back on the road, babe."

———

"Oh dear," Molly muttered, frowning deeply as she sorted through her cards early Saturday evening. "This can't be right."

Sean rubbed a hand across his bare chest and scowled at her from where he was leaning against the side of the couch, a sheet the only thing keeping him decent.

"Again?" He laughed. "You've got to be kidding me."

She clucked her tongue. "I keep counting and… yeah, looks like gin. *Again*." Letting the bedding she was draped in droop a bit more, Molly laid out one set of cards after another before peering up at Sean from beneath her lashes. "It's almost like you're *distracted* or something."

"Or something," he conceded, his eyes going dark as his focus got lost in the vicinity of her modest cleavage.

It was crazy. They'd played cards like this probably a hundred times. Kicked back on the floor, a bottle of wine or handful of beers between them, talking the hours away. But it had never been *quite like this*. She'd never sat nearly naked across from him, her body still singing from the hours of attention he'd paid it, her heart still racing from the way he was looking at her. She'd never known that, no matter when they finished playing, she'd sleep in Sean's arms and wake in his bed.

Sean bent one knee and sat a little straighter…which made *his* sheet fall a little lower. And wow. Even with him sitting on the floor, his stomach was a work of art. Bands of muscles stacked one above the next, bisected by that fine line of golden hair that ended just beneath the hard slabs of his pecs. He'd always had a beautiful body, cut with a natural athlete's definition…and at last, she could sit and look her fill.

Touch.

Taste.

Gathering the cards, he shot her a knowing look. "Pretty sure I'm not the only one distracted."

"Maybe not." Going to her knees, she crossed the small space between them.

Sean set the cards aside and pulled her into his lap.

"What are you thinking?" he asked, running the tip of one finger across her collarbone.

Such a small touch, and yet it set off a chain reaction within her. Made her ache for more.

"That I could get used to this," she admitted quietly, knowing deep down that, no matter how right this weekend felt, she shouldn't.

Looking out the picture window to the woods and the bay beyond, Sean nodded. "It's nice up here. The private lane, the house tucked deep enough into the woods so it's not visible from the road or the water. I can see the appeal."

She hadn't been thinking about the Door County cabin his friend had offered them for the weekend, but it was probably better that Sean was. Sifting her fingers through the golden-blond strands falling in her favorite kind of sexy disarray, she asked, "What did you tell the guys about this weekend?"

His brows furrowed, a frown threatening at the

corners of his mouth. "That I had some business to take care of with one of the other hotels."

Which explained why when she'd woken that morning, it had been to Sean working on his laptop beside her in bed. She'd told him he didn't need to stop on her account, but he'd practically tossed the thing aside, assuring her he'd gotten all the work he needed done already. In other words, enough so he hadn't actually lied to his friends. Not about work anyway.

Drawing her hands out of his hair, he dropped light kisses across each finger. "What about you?"

"Weekend up north with a friend," she whispered, her words breaking when Sean licked between her knuckles.

"A friend." He seemed to be weighing the word in his mind. His mouth pulled to the side in that cocky smile. "I am feeling pretty *friendly* all of the sudden."

Lowering his head, he caught her mouth with his kiss. Teasing, taking more and more until he was on top of her, the sheets tugged free. Her knees slid up his thighs, the contact of skin against bare skin driving her as wild as the promises he was making with his mouth.

"Mmm." He braced above her, rocking into the cradle of her hips. "You feel pretty friendly too."

She laughed and then caught her breath when he rocked into her again, the steely length of him sliding against her most sensitive part. "Very friendly," she agreed.

Tipping her hips into the contact, she moaned when on the next slow rock, Sean pushed inside her. "*Sean.*"

Braced on one arm, he cupped her hip, drawing her into each slow, sinking thrust, taking her deep and deeper, hard and harder, all the while keeping those dark eyes locked with hers. This was what she'd dreamed of…only the reality was so much more.

And God, the way he was looking at her.

What if she could really have this? What if she could keep him?

What if—

He sank deep, hitting that spot inside her just right, and her mind blanked of anything beyond what he was doing to her in that moment.

"Baby, not yet," he groaned, shafting into her one last time before pulling out. She wanted to grab him by the hair and pull him back, beg him to take her again—but they weren't protected. And when he backed down her body, burning a path with his mouth as he went, she really couldn't complain.

"Your mouth…is…so… Oh yes, *Sean*!" she gasped after he'd hooked her knees over his shoulders and sank into devouring her like a starving man. And when she'd barely finished, he pulled her from the floor and carried her through the bedroom and into the master bath.

"Like this, baby," he growled against her ear as he positioned her hands on the counter in front of the mirror. He rolled on a condom and then, watching their reflection, took her from behind.

He was slow. Thorough.

The possessive look in his eyes and rough scrape of his jaw at the back of her neck were as powerfully sexy as watching his fingers playing between her legs and his big hand kneading her breast. She was already there, pressing back into his every stroke, rocking into his touch, begging and moaning and promising everything and anything to the man shaking her world to its very foundation.

When she tipped over the edge, tumbling into her
release, Sean held her in his arms, telling her how perfect
she was for him, how beautiful, how sexy. Telling her
all the things she could only ever truly believe in that
flawless moment.

Chapter 18

THEY'D HAD A FINGER-TANGLY SUNDAY MORNING, EATING breakfast down by the dock before making love in the boathouse. *Making love.* The words made Molly want to giggle almost as much as she wanted to wrap herself up in them forever.

She'd had sex. Done it. Screwed and fucked.

But not until Sean had laid her out beneath the pale moonlight the night before had she made love. And it was something different. Special. Addictive.

The afternoon had come way too soon. Sean had driven them back to the city, and despite his attempts to convince her to let him stay at her place or have her come back to his, Molly remained strong. She never knew when she was going to wake up to her brother in her living room—though that didn't seem to happen much now that he was with Sarah—or Brody riding by after spending the night with his current flame. Besides, she was supposed to meet the girls for breakfast the next morning, and the rest of the week was going to be nuts as she made up for the days she'd taken off from three jobs. She'd need the sleep.

But more than that, there was the whole not-letting-herself-get-too-comfortable thing. She couldn't get used to spending every night in Sean's arms if she *didn't* spend every night there, right?

So, hard as it was, Molly had said goodbye to Sean

in her apartment, agreed to another getaway the next weekend, and then watched from her front window as he'd driven off.

When things ended and Sean realized that as much fun as they'd been having, he really did want a different life than he could have with her, no one would know how deeply that hurt cut. No one would know what a fool she'd been.

Except, what if she wasn't a fool? What if Sean wasn't going to realize he wanted something else? What if this was it?

It was a hope too terrifying to let herself have. And yet…each time he looked into her eyes, it was getting harder and harder to keep that hope at bay.

———

The next days passed in a blur of extended shifts and made-up hours. Molly wouldn't have given up her time with Sean for anything, but there was a price to pay, and by the time Wednesday night at Belfast rolled around, she was feeling the toll.

"How late you working tonight, Moll?" Max asked, sliding onto his seat at their usual table. Tonight, it was just Max, Brody, and Sean. Jase and Emily had her parents visiting, and Sarah was caught up in some project back at Wyse.

Setting the last of the drink orders down, Molly tried not to grimace when she answered. "Closing. Few hours left."

"Baby sister's making bank," Max sang, the pride in his eyes something she could feel.

Exactly. She was so close to having the down

payment for the building. Another few months, if she stayed on track with her budget and maintained her current income.

Sean shifted in his chair, a furrow digging between his brows. "But, uhh, Molly, weren't you cleaning houses from eight until two? And working on the web stuff until you started your shift here at four?"

For a minute, she didn't know what to do beyond blink at him. Because not only was that a lot of information about her schedule for a *just friend* to have, but also what the heck was he doing, offering up something to say about it? Someone was going to notice. Someone was going to figure out what was going on with them and—

Max looked from her to Sean.

He knew.

"Sean, you want some nachos? I'm fucking hungry."

Molly's breath leaked out as Sean shrugged his agreement. Okay, so he didn't know.

"Great, nachos." Molly entered the order, stifling a yawn. "Max, you want the peppers this time or not?" Sarah didn't like them, but since she was working late, it was worth checking.

"Nah, skip 'em. Sarah said she'd try to stop by."

Molly nodded and checked on a few other tables. When she circled back to her order station, Sean was there. Leaning against the bar, resting back on his elbows as he watched her fill her tray with drinks.

"Moll, you gotta be dead on your feet. The crowd's pretty light tonight. Let me take you home."

Home sounded so good. And Sean taking her there even better. But she'd known what taking the weekend off would mean. "It's only a couple more hours. I'll be fine."

"Yeah, but you'd be better getting some sleep. You know Brody would let you go. Or I could talk to him."

She shot him a look, a smile creeping across her lips. "You could talk to him? That wouldn't be suspicious at all. Going to do that after you have a chat with Max about how creaky my bed is?"

He pushed a hand back through his hair, looking out over the crowd. "Okay, you could talk to him."

She wanted to snuggle into his side. Rest her head on his shoulder and just soak up his sweet intentions. But more than that, she wanted to clock the hours and make the tips that staying until close would get her. "Don't worry about me. I'll be good. Now go back to your table."

The guys stayed for another hour, but then Sarah texted Max to let him know she was wiped and going straight home, so it was time to call it a night. Molly had wanted to steal a moment in the back hall with Sean before he left, but a couple of big groups came in, and all she'd been able to manage was a wave from across the bar as he was leaving.

No big deal. Not really.

Three and a half hours later, Molly's brain and body were completely fried. And apparently, she looked it too, because Brody insisted on giving her a lift. Standing at the bottom of the stairs, she thought about what she'd meet at the top.

An empty apartment.

A lonely bed.

Brody had already pulled away. She could get an

Uber and go over to Wyse. But as incredibly tempting as the idea of crawling into bed with Sean was, she couldn't do it without waking him up. Heck, she'd have to have them call up from the front desk—not exactly discreet. And then once she was there, the poor guy wouldn't even be able to go back to sleep.

Giving in to a heavy, sulky sigh, she started up the stairs, resigned to a night alone.

She let herself into the apartment but stalled in her steps before the door closed behind her.

"Sean?" she asked, stunned to see him sitting on her couch, his laptop open in front of him, papers and files spread on the cushions and table. Closing the laptop with a weary smile, he stood.

"Hey, beautiful. You made it, huh?"

Dropping her bag, she walked into his arms, something powerful welling in her chest.

"Barely. What are you doing here?"

"I felt crappy about you having to work so hard to make up for our weekend. Wanted to do something nice for you."

She peered past his shoulder to the makeshift office he'd set up. "A show of solidarity?"

"Figured I'd get some work done tonight and sleep in a little tomorrow. And I didn't want to fall asleep and then wake up when you got here."

"I know I said I didn't want you to stay over, but you can't even imagine how glad I am you're here."

"Yeah?" he asked against the top of her head.

"Yeah."

Sean tipped her head back to meet her eyes. "Don't get me wrong. I'd love nothing more than to fall asleep with you in my arms. And no way will I turn it down. But my plan was more about you falling asleep *beneath my hands*." He led her back to her bedroom and waved her inside.

"What is all this?" she asked, taking in the assortment of bottles, candles, and small tubs laid out on the nightstand beside her bed. He'd taken the comforter off and spread out an enormous bath sheet for her to lie on.

"I figured your muscles could use a break and maybe a little attention too. It just so happens, I've got an in with the spa at Wyse."

It was quite possibly the most thoughtful thing anyone had ever done for her. And Molly found herself blinking back tears.

Then Sean was helping her out of her jacket and stripping off her T-shirt and denim skirt.

When she was in nothing but her panties, she crawled onto the bed and stretched out facedown.

From a basket next to the bed, Sean pulled out a hot towel, which he pressed into her back, letting the wet heat soak into her skin. The mattress dipped, and she heard him rustling through containers on the bedside table. A moment later, he removed the towel, and those strong, capable hands were rubbing some kind of lavender-scented oil or cream into her tired muscles.

It was pure bliss. A kind of luxury she never indulged in, couldn't justify.

"You'll tell me if this is too hard," he said, his voice low, close to her ear.

"No," she moaned. "It's perfect. So good."

He worked her shoulders and arms, her neck and

lower back. Every muscle getting spoiled by his thorough attention.

"Just fall asleep, baby. I'll be here when you wake up, if you want me to be."

Molly rolled over and reached for her favorite gap between the buttons of his shirt.

"Molly, this is for you. I just want make you feel good."

God, she loved him. And tonight, she didn't even care what a mistake that might be.

Tugging him closer, she whispered against his lips, "Then make me feel good."

—⁓—

There was something to be said for sleeping in. Sean didn't do it often, but having planned for it this morning, he couldn't even feel guilty about lying there with Molly's perfect body cuddling in close to him, the minutes ticking past as he watched her sleep.

He could get used to this.

He *wanted* to get used to this if she would just let him.

Burrowing deeper into his side, she let out a soft moan. It wasn't the same as the ones he'd wrung from her the night before—but the sleepy, contented quality might be even better.

Her head lifted, and she squinted up at him through a fall of white blond and hot pink.

"Morning, beautiful," he greeted her, gently brushing her hair from her eyes.

She crawled over him and collapsed across his chest, dropping a single groggy kiss at his nipple. "What time is it?"

"Eight thirty."

Her head popped up, brows high. "Wow, you really did sleep in."

"Mmm. How about I buy you some breakfast at S&G?"

Pushing up from his chest, she backed off the bed. "Can't. I've got a two-bedroom I need to start in an hour and a three-bedroom after that."

Sean sat up and reached for her hand. Tugging her back down on the bed, he leaned over her. "You're working too hard, Molly. You can't keep this up."

He was all for hard work. He respected the hell out of it, and no one worked harder than he did. But Molly wasn't just running desk duty. She was physically laboring, sometimes for sixteen hours a day.

"*Spoiler alert*, I can." She laughed, palming his chest to give him a little shove.

He didn't budge. "I'm serious."

That pretty laugh died on her lips, and suddenly, he was staring down at the stubborn mule his best friend could be. "So am I, Sean. I've got a couple of long days ahead, and sure, I was beat last night, but I can handle it. I have before, and I will again."

Shaking his head, he backed off, giving her room to get up. "Okay, I know you *can* handle it. But Molly... if this is what catching up after a weekend away looks like, are you even sure you want to go away again next weekend?"

Molly looked back over her shoulder, doubt digging a tiny line between her brows. "Don't you?"

Shit. He was off the bed and turning her around in a blink. "You know I want every minute I can get with you. And since you aren't ready to go public yet, next weekend is pretty much all I've been thinking about since we got back *last* weekend. I just don't like seeing what you have to do to make it work."

Pushing to her toes, she kissed his chin. "Just the cost of quality time these days."

He wagged his head to the side. "I guess what I'm saying is maybe it shouldn't be."

"What does that even mean?" she asked, pulling on a pair of his old sweats and a Wyse T-shirt.

Jesus, she was wearing his old sweats—he gulped— with no panties underneath. That was *so hot.* "It means tell me what you're making cleaning condos and managing Belfast, and I'll get you a job at Wyse that pays more, with half the hours."

The air changed, a tension-filled silence suddenly accumulating between them. *Uh-oh.* Mentally backtracking through his words, he came up empty. "What?"

"Just going to hand me a job, Sean? Stick me in some made-up position? I have zero experience or education in the hospitality industry, so it would have to be. Cut me a check every two weeks for services rendered?"

Ahh. Right. Yeah, now he got it. "Molly, it's not like that."

"No, it's not. Look, I've got a tidy little business going with this housekeeping thing."

"Exactly. Hire more staff, and then you can step back from the hands-on work."

"I don't need to step back. I don't want to. I want the income. Because every dollar I earn brings me closer to getting my name on the mortgage for this building."

The building.

He knew she was slowly getting closer to having the down payment for the place. And he knew with the way she'd grown up—with the day-to-day uncertainty of whether she'd have a place to sleep that night— ownership and having a steady stream, or even better, *multiple* streams of income was important to her. He got it.

But she didn't need to break her back to make it happen.

"So why not take a job at Wyse and keep building your website and housekeeping businesses on the side? You don't have to be the one actually down on your knees scrubbing the baseboards."

Molly threw up her hands and stalked into the bathroom.

Fluent in Molly-speak, he recognized the nonanswer for what it was: end of discussion.

Only that was bullshit. He had a legitimate suggestion. One he was smart enough to know he'd have to wait a couple of days before bringing up again.

He pulled on his jeans and followed Molly into her bathroom. "You have time for a lunch break at least? I could meet you somewhere."

She spit out her toothpaste and wiped her mouth before turning so her hip was propped against the counter. "I could do lunch. But won't you be busy making up for your morning off?"

Normally, he would. But after going from having Molly all to himself for the whole weekend to barely seeing her once they got back, the work could wait.

He'd have plenty of hours to get caught up while she worked the closing shift at Belfast that night too.

"I'll work when you work." And damn, what a difference saying the right thing instead of the wrong made. Because then Molly was looking at him with those eyes that had gotten him into the best kind of trouble. She stepped into his space and let her fingers trail along his still half-open denim fly.

"That's kind of hot," she murmured softly.

Not as hot as she was, swimming in his clothes. Or better still, him peeling her out of them.

Taking her by the waist, he popped her up on the counter and went for the Wyse T-shirt first. "I'll show you hot."

Chapter 19

SATURDAY, MOLLY WOKE TO THE SOFT PRESS AND GENTLE scrape of Sean's lips and day-old stubble working a path down the length of her spine.

"You're spoiling me," she murmured, lifting her head enough to peer over her shoulder at another spectacular mess of bedhead.

They hadn't arrived in New Hampshire until close to two in the morning, and when they finally got checked into their hotel—not a Wyse hotel—Sean had wrapped his arms around her, and they'd gone straight to sleep. It had been heaven in its own way, but after a few hours of rest, there was more she wanted Sean to do to her in this bed than sleep.

"I'm worshiping you," he corrected, swirling his tongue at the center of her back and sending an overload of pleasure rushing through her body.

She arched into the sensation, whispering Sean's name. A growl sounded from above her, and then he flipped her over and kneed her legs apart to make a space for himself between.

She hooked a lazy leg over his hip, basking in the feel of his body over hers. "I'll never get used to this," she whispered, her hands stroking lightly over his chest. "Waking up to you making my dreams look like nothing compared to my reality."

The corner of his mouth kicked up, and he rocked slowly into her hips. "Is that what I'm doing?"

He rocked again, finding that perfect point of contact that made her needy and hot, and turned her mindless. Then again, and this time, she met him halfway, her breath hitching as she answered, "As if you don't know."

That cocky shrug said he most definitely did. "What I know, Molly, is that you've been letting me do every dirty, depraved thing I can think of to you for a month now—and baby, there are not words for how much I love that about you—but you still won't spend the night at my place, and I can't park overnight in front of yours because you're afraid someone is going to see my car and figure out that we're together. It's starting to feel like I'm disrespecting the relationship I've got with your brother and the rest of our friends by sneaking around this way."

She'd known this was coming. He'd been quiet about telling everyone for more than a week, but clearly, he'd been thinking about it.

His brows pulled together, and he shook his head. "No biting that pretty bottom lip, Molly. I'm the only one who gets to bite it, and then I get to kiss it better."

She laughed, turning her head away as she released the abused lip in question. But Sean wasn't ready to let her off. Cupping her cheek in his palm, he brought her eyes back to his. "I'm serious, Moll. I know you were nervous, but you've got to see by now that there isn't any reason to be."

Her laughter stopped. Because she knew he was right. She couldn't keep lying to everyone about what they were doing. She didn't want to.

Only days ago, she'd been on the brink of confiding in Emily and Sarah, but she hadn't quite been able to take the leap.

Now Sean's eyes closed above her, his breath leaking out in a slow stream. "You aren't ready."

Before she could agree or disagree or make any more excuses to put off something they should have done weeks ago, he was rolling off the bed. "It's okay, Moll. I told you I'd give you all the time you needed, and I meant it." He sat at the edge of the bed and looked at her from over one broad shoulder. "One of these days though, you're going to realize you can trust me. I figured out what I wanted that night at the campground. It's you and me, and I swear, if you can find the faith in us, you'll never regret it."

"Sean," she said, sitting up and reaching for his shoulder, her heart aching, knowing that her delay was causing him pain. "I do trust you."

He kissed the top of her hand and then headed for the bathroom. "We should get ready."

"Damn, you look spectacular," Sean growled, using the hand interwoven with hers to pull her in close. "Let's blow off the wedding and go back to the suite so I can do my favorite dirty things to you."

Molly laughed, her shoulder coming up against the tickle of Sean's jaw. "Right, after you surprised me with this dress and those girls spent all that time on my hair and makeup? It would be a crime not to show it all off."

"The dress reminded me of your eyes. I needed to see it on you. But believe me when I tell you, it will be worth every penny just to take it off. Or maybe you don't take it off at all. Maybe you let me unzip it just a little," he murmured close to her ear, trailing a finger halfway down her spine before dropping a kiss at the back of her neck. "So the straps slide down…and then when I bend you over in front of the mirror, I can see those perfect—"

"Sean," she gasped, her eyes darting around to check the surrounding lobby for anyone who might hear. But there was no one within earshot, and even if there had been, they were in New Hampshire at a wedding for people Sean only distantly knew.

His hands were on her hips. "I'd push this pretty blue dress up over your sweet ass…rip that scrap of lace from between your legs, and get you so hot and wet, you'd be running down my fingers, Molly."

She'd stopped walking, her light laughter from Sean's first suggestion completely evaporated under the scorching description.

His grip firmed. "I want to tell you I'd make you beg me, but it would be a lie. I'd be on my knees behind you, using my mouth, my teeth…my tongue to show you how badly I wanted inside that hot-as-fuck body of yours."

Her breath was coming in shallow pants, the body in question aching in response to his words.

"And then, after I make you come…*twice*," he hummed against the shell of her ear. "When your body is slick and sensitive from having me inside you… When I can finally breathe again, because I'll know, no matter how many guys like that douche with his tongue hanging out over by the concierge look like they want to fight me to take you for themselves, *you're mine…* Then I'd straighten your skirt and zip up your back and see if we could get any farther than the hotel lobby before I started trying to talk you into going back upstairs again."

Trembling, she turned and met the dark wells of his eyes. "You're serious."

He looked at her like he couldn't believe she still didn't get it. "Always with you."

Molly nodded, not trusting her voice to form words. Because, God, more than anything, in that moment, she wanted to believe this was real. That she could have this man forever.

So they missed the ceremony itself. Sean should probably have felt some guilt about it, but this wedding had been more about getting Molly out of town with him than anything else. And while the bride's family would be happy to see a representative from Wyse there because of the business they did together, the handshake and congratulations he'd offered upon arrival was probably more than they'd expected.

Hell, once he'd seen Molly in the dress he spotted in the boutique window when he'd walked into work the week before, he hadn't been sure they'd make it to the festivities at all.

But Molly's will had been shockingly strong during that third trip down to the lobby. So they'd made it after all.

Now halfway through dessert, with Molly's fingers interwoven with his own *on top of the table*, Sean was enjoying being surrounded by strangers for the night and getting to be the couple they privately were in a public setting. Call it practice, call it a dry run—whatever, it was one step closer to Molly being his girlfriend back in Chicago around all the people they loved best.

It was coming. He could see it in her eyes. Feel it in the way she leaned into his hold, pulling his arms around her just before they arrived. Something had changed in the hours since they'd woken that morning. He knew it.

———

"I don't think I can dance anymore." Molly laughed as Sean pulled her flush against him, swaying back and forth to the big band music.

"I should've told you to bring your motorcycle boots. You'd be going all night."

Molly laughed, letting her head fall back. "Can you even imagine my boots with this gown?"

A low growl rumbled from Sean's chest. Then he leaned close to her ear. "I can imagine those boots with a lot of things. But right now, I'm imagining those boots with a whole lot of nothing."

God, she loved him. Maybe it was time to just give in and let this thing between them out into the light of day. Then, even if it fell apart and everyone saw how naive she'd been, she'd at least know they'd had a fair shot.

"Sean?" came a singsong voice that had Molly freezing where she stood.

Sean groaned under his breath, cutting an apologetic look her way. "Sorry, Moll."

"I thought that was you," exclaimed Paula Stratton, the client whose Gold Coast condo Molly had been cleaning every Tuesday morning for the past several years. She hadn't recognized Molly yet, but that was sure to change once she paused long enough to take a breath. "Darling, your mother said they had other commitments. Tell me they've managed to make it." Then shifting her focus past Sean, she waved someone over. "Adelynn, join us."

Adelynn was draped in couture with penciled-in brows and appeared to be about the same age as her friend, both women most likely in their midforties. She stepped around them, her drink sloshing past the rim of her glass as she fell in line with Mrs. Stratton. The corner of Adelynn's red-lacquered mouth twitched as she took in Sean and then, more critically, Molly. "Oh dear, Paula, from the looks of things, it's safe to say Beverly and Warren didn't arrive with their son."

Sean's hand flexed at Molly's back, his body going tense beside her.

One look at her, and this Adelynn woman knew Molly didn't belong. That if Sean's parents were there, she wouldn't have been.

Molly tried not to fidget or touch her hair or pull at her clothes as though she was attempting to figure out what exactly had given her away. Chances were it was the streak of pink in her hair, which was still visible even blown out and styled as it was.

"Paula, Adelynn, what an unexpected pleasure to see you here," Sean began with that plastic smile Molly hated from the papers, his tone devoid of all warmth or sincerity. "Allow me to introduce you to my *date*, Molly Brandt. Molly, this is Paula Stratton and Adelynn Wakefield."

He didn't realize she and Mrs. Stratton went

back several years. Although it appeared neither did Mrs. Stratton, whose brow was pinched as she looked from Sean to Molly and back again, a disconnect there in her eyes as she struggled to place *Sean's date*.

Molly straightened her shoulders and smiled, about to remind her client, when a surprised breath escaped the woman, accompanied by a flash of something that looked like distaste in her eyes. Or maybe not, because just as quickly, the socialite returned to her usual friendly self. "Molly! I didn't recognize... I didn't realize..."

Maybe it had only been Molly's own insecurities making her imagine things that weren't there.

"Hello, Mrs. Stratton. Nice to see you."

"And you too, dear." Mrs. Stratton raised a brow and turned to her friend to continue the introductions. "Adelynn, Molly's the girl who cleans for us."

There was nothing wrong with what Mrs. Stratton had said, but suddenly, the air changed. Adelynn's eyes sharpened, her mouth pursing into something that wasn't quite a smile but made Molly feel a bit like the butt of someone's joke, despite the fact that the only words exchanged had been to finish the introductions.

Still, she was there with Sean, and she wasn't going to let him down.

"Beautiful reception, isn't it?" she offered to both women.

"Why yes, Molly." Mrs. Stratton nodded enthusiastically. "It's lovely. Though this venue doesn't hold a candle to our Wyse."

Molly waited for Sean to acknowledge the compliment, but he just stood there watching the other woman with something Molly didn't recognize in his eyes. Something cold and untouchable.

He looked…upset.

Jumping in before Sean's silence became uncomfortable, Molly smiled widely. "I couldn't agree with you more, Mrs. Stratton. If you ask me, the Chicago Wyse Grand Ballroom stands alone."

"Oh, Molly, you're familiar with the Wyse? Do you clean there as well?"

She shook her head. Something about the question—the delivery more than the words themselves—rubbed. No. It was nothing. Or at least, nothing she was going to let get to her.

"Yes," Mrs. Wakefield chimed in, sounding delighted. "Is that how you came to be acquainted with Sean? Or perhaps Sean's hired you for some *other* purpose?"

There was no mistaking the pointed inflection in her words, and Molly's mouth sagged open in disbelief as humiliation burned up her neck and cheeks.

Sean went rigid beside her, and when she looked up at him, he was openly glaring, the muscle in his jaw clenching and unclenching as though he was barely restraining himself.

"Adelynn," he warned between gritted teeth, pulling Molly closer to his side. "That was a *mistake*. Apologize to Ms. Brandt."

"Sean," Molly whispered, grabbing his hand. "Let's just go."

Mrs. Stratton turned away, covering her mouth as she quickly excused herself, leaving Adelynn standing there all too amused by her hurtful, disgusting implications. "What did I say?"

"Something, I assure you, you will regret," Sean snapped back.

The other woman blinked, looking back and forth between them again, suddenly seeming to rethink her approach. "Sean, I didn't mean—"

"Of course you did," he answered in a cutting voice that sent chills down Molly's spine.

Then he was pulling her through the crowd. They didn't stop to say goodbye as Sean ushered her out of the reception, avoiding her eyes as they went.

Not that she could blame him.

When they reached the drive where Sean let the valet know they needed a car, Molly kept walking to the edge of the pavement. The temperature had dropped, but even gulping the brisk night air, she couldn't cool the burn of humiliation.

Sean stepped in silently beside her.

"I've never been so embarrassed in my life," she whispered. "Is that what it would be like every time we ran into someone from your other life?" They weren't touching, but she could feel him tense just the same.

He didn't answer, but he didn't really need to. She knew. It wouldn't be every time, because regardless of social status, most people weren't built that way. But some were. Which meant every time they did go out, she'd wonder whether it would be *that* time.

Her stomach tensed at the miserable thought.

Sean shrugged out of his jacket and wrapped it around her. Still not meeting her eyes. Still not saying a word.

The look on his face was tortured. Guilty.

"They know your parents," Molly stated, searching his reaction, finding only the muscle in his jaw clenching and releasing. "Your mother is going to hear what happened. I'll never be able to look her in the eyes again."

He looked up at the night, his breath straining as he wiped a hand over his face.

"My mother doesn't care about those two social-climbing harpies. But she does care about you. She loves you."

"Trying to convince me…or yourself?" Molly wasn't entirely certain Beverly Wyse was capable of love.

When he finally met her eyes, she saw defeat in them.

This was the reality check she'd known was coming.

This was where Sean realized what being with her would actually mean. That for as much fun and feel-good as they had alone, she was never going to fit into his world the way one of those women his parents were always picking for him would.

She swallowed, steeling herself against the stab of pain in her chest. "Your parents know what good friends we are, Sean. If you tell them that's all this was, they'll believe you. No one has to know."

That brought Sean's head around in a snap. He searched her eyes, the easy smile he always had for her nowhere to be found. "Is that what you want?"

No. Never. She wanted Sean. She wanted a life together where the only thing that mattered was them. But she'd learned early on, you couldn't always have what you wanted. No matter how long or hard you wished for it. "Can we just go back to the hotel? Deal with the real world tomorrow."

Sean nodded, looking away. "Yeah, we can do that."

Chapter 20

TUESDAY MORNING, MOLLY WAITED OUTSIDE THE GATE-house for security to let her through. She wasn't looking forward to seeing Paula Stratton. Especially after the way things had ended over the weekend.

She and Sean had barely spoken after the wedding. His phone had started blowing up before they'd even made it back to their room. Some crisis with the international end of the business that had kept him on the phone through most of the night. Desperate for her own distraction, she'd pulled out her laptop and gotten in a couple of hours adding a web store to a client's site, but when Sean walked back into the bedroom, it wasn't to pull her into his lap or kiss her and tell her everything was going to be fine. That he wanted her.

It was to start throwing his clothes in his bag. They were flying back to Chicago in two hours.

Sunday, she'd gotten a bouquet of flowers from him, along with a text apologizing for cutting their plans short and letting her know he was going to be in New York for the next few days.

It wasn't like this was the first time Sean had dropped off the face of the earth to take care of a work emergency. But it was the first time it had happened since they'd been together. And with his absence following so closely on the heels of that disaster of a reception, it was the first time she'd really considered that everything might not be okay between them.

Monday had been a complete bust. Literally. She'd broken four glasses and dropped a tray with five entrees. Brody had finally sent her in back to keep her from burning the place down. Hopefully, today would be better.

"Ma'am, you can go back," the security guard at the gate offered, cutting into her thoughts as he let her into the private gated community. She breathed deeply and braced for what she anticipated would be a suddenly very interested client.

She hadn't even made it inside before she realized how mistaken she'd been.

Beverly Wyse opened the door, a smile very different from the one she'd been greeting Molly with for over ten years on her lips.

"Beverly, this is a surprise. I wasn't expecting to see you here." Understatement of the century. "Is Mrs. Stratton home?" *Please, please, please let her be.* Because as much as Molly didn't care for how she'd felt seeing the woman socially, this was business. And business would be about a million times easier to handle than some quality alone time with Sean's mom.

"Paula had a few errands to attend to, but she was gracious enough to invite us to stay. We need to talk, Molly." Then, waving her toward the kitchen, Beverly added, "There's some fresh coffee on the counter. Why don't you pour yourself a cup and come sit a moment?"

Molly's stomach twisted in on itself. "I'm sorry, but I have another appointment after this one, so I should get started. If you'd like to talk this afternoon, I've got a few hours before I'll be going over to Belfast."

Because there was no way she was going to have Sean's mother—whom she could only presume had flown out to Chicago for the sole purpose of having a *chat* with Molly—follow her around this house discussing Molly's suitability for her son while she scrubbed toilets on her knees.

"You're such a responsible girl, Molly. I've always respected that about you. But Paula isn't expecting you to clean today. Though I believe she's left you a check."

Molly stepped over to the counter where a check for three times what she charged sat atop a folded piece of stationery with her name penned in neat script across it.

Fingers trembling, she read the few concise lines terminating her employment.

This woman who had been smiling sweetly at her for years, calling her every kind of adorable each week, and ensuring that she'd been telling all her friends about what an excellent business Molly ran…had just fired her.

"You had to have known she couldn't keep you on," Beverly offered, gently twisting the knife. "How would it look?"

Molly couldn't even think that far. She was too busy wondering what this would mean for Brandt Housekeeping. One customer she could live without, but in a business based so heavily on word of mouth, what if Mrs. Stratton was just the first domino to fall? What if Mrs. Stratton told her friends—Molly's other clients—that she was Sean's mistress?

So maybe she *could* imagine how it would look after all.

Nausea rose within her. If she lost enough clients because of this, she'd be forced to start letting employees go. Hard workers who were relying on those paychecks.

God, *she* relied on those paychecks. If she lost the building…

Shaking her head, Molly tucked the check in her pocket with numb fingers and forced any emotion from her face.

When she turned back to Beverly, the other woman had taken a seat in the living area and was waiting for Molly to join her.

More than anything right then, she wished she could call up Sean—her best friend, not the man whose kisses she'd become a slave to this last month. She needed the guy who was always there for her, no matter what. The one she knew down to her soul. She needed him to tell her what to do. Whether she should come clean about their relationship to his mother or tell Beverly that nothing had changed and she and Sean were just friends and anything else she'd heard was a simple misunderstanding.

Another sick feeling washed over her at the thought of looking Sean's mother in the eyes and lying to her.

Like she'd essentially been asking Sean to do with all their friends and everyone he cared about for a month straight.

She'd been so selfish. So unfair. So scared.

Maybe it wouldn't come to that.

She sat, trying to ignore the way her rolled-up sweatpants, ankle socks, and Brandt Housekeeping T-shirt contrasted with Beverly's designer suit and jewels. Trying to remind herself that all she needed to say was that she and Sean were friends. Anything Beverly wanted to know beyond that, she'd need to discuss with her son.

Beverly took a sip of her coffee and set the neat little cup on the low table between them. Then, meeting Molly's eyes, she announced, "I'm disappointed in you."

Molly's eyes went wide, and she felt the room spin. Because that was so not the way she'd seen this conversation kicking off.

"Beverly," she said quietly, undone by how deeply that single sentence affected her. She didn't care what most anyone thought about her...except apparently, she did. "Sean and I—"

"Have been seeing each other for a little over a month now. I know." She pushed the coffee away, as if suddenly finding it unpleasant.

Molly couldn't breathe. She didn't understand. "How... When..." She shook her head, trying to clear it to make sense of what she was hearing. There was only one explanation. "He told you?"

Beverly waved her conclusion away. "Hardly. After the unfortunate family business earlier this year, Sean was upset. Understandably. He started behaving rashly. His father and I simply wanted to keep an eye on him. Make sure he didn't get into any trouble he couldn't get himself out of."

No way this was happening. No way Beverly Wyse was telling her they'd had Sean *followed*.

"At first, we assumed this was just an indiscretion between friends, a one-time thing. We'd hoped so for both your sakes. But apparently not. Then we accepted that so long as it remained quiet, who were we to judge? But this past weekend was simply too close." Beverly met Molly's bewildered stare, understanding in those brown eyes so much like her son's. "Frankly, I thought you cared more for him than this. Can't you see the impact this relationship would have on Sean?"

Molly's throat was bone dry, the only sound escaping a single crack before she turned her face away.

"Adelynn's family has business ties with Wyse that go back generations, and Sean has severed them… because *she slighted you*."

"What are you talking about?" Molly choked, pushing farther back into her seat. He hadn't said a thing to her. Or maybe he had. Saturday night, he'd told Adelynn she would regret her words. Molly just hadn't understood what he'd meant. If she had, she would have asked him not to do anything. Because that choice to sever ties would have a trickle-down effect, and what if it meant jobs? "Can you stop him, change his mind?"

Beverly stared at her for a long moment before answering. "Believe me, we tried. When Sean feels… *passionately* about something, it is next to impossible to sway him."

Something told her Sean's mother wasn't just talking about the repercussions from Saturday night.

"Molly, this isn't your world, so no one could expect you to fully understand the extent to which Sean's personal and professional lives are intertwined. But this business with Adelynn will be just the beginning. Warren and I have invested a lifetime in building the Wyse brand into what it is today. It was and is our deepest wish that Sean will continue that tradition." Beverly sighed, sending another wave of her disappointment to wash over Molly. "However, we have sacrificed too much to allow him to diminish what we've built every time someone disrespects *you*. And mark my words, Molly, it will continue to happen. You don't have the education or, forgive me for being blunt, the sophistication to avoid it. You have no understanding of the circles he travels in. Of the business that makes up his whole world. You won't know the right names, and you won't understand the dynamics at work professionally or the social intricacies needed to navigate his world. Molly, you won't even understand when someone is slighting you. And Sean won't stand for it."

Molly could barely breathe, but Beverly wasn't done.

"He needs a woman by his side who will be an asset, Molly, but if he stays with you, he will alienate himself from his family, his peers, his *legacy*. Can you even imagine what that would do to him?"

No, she couldn't. She *wouldn't*, because it meant thinking of the man she loved with her whole heart giving up all the things that had filled his heart for as long as she'd known him. It meant considering how he would feel when he realized what being with her had cost him.

And even if it wasn't as dramatic as all that, after Saturday night and now this, there was no way she could pretend there wouldn't be some new degree of strife and conflict in Sean's previously peaceful life. What would it do to their relationship? What would it do to their friendship?

Pushing out of her chair on legs she wasn't sure would support her, Molly pressed a hand to her unsettled stomach and walked to the window overlooking the community courtyard. Children played merrily in the immaculately kept, ornately patterned brick roads surrounded by twelve-foot walls topped with a spiked metal fencing that would give anyone considering trying to climb in second thoughts.

This wasn't her world.

333

Beverly was right. Molly would never fit in, and if she tried to, she might cost Sean his place in it as well.

There was some rustling behind her. Cabinets opening and closing. The tap running. And then Beverly was pressing a glass of water into her hand.

"I know you care for him. You always have."

Molly turned to Beverly, a question in her eyes.

Beverly offered the most reserved of shrugs. "A mother knows these things. I also know with the way Sean feels about you and your brother—even if he realized he'd made a mistake, which I don't believe he has yet—his sense of responsibility and obligation to the two of you won't allow him to walk away."

Molly felt the cool trail of tears on her cheeks and wiped at them with the backs of her hand. Beverly had seen enough of her weakness already. "You're saying I need to be the one to end things with Sean."

A nod.

"For what it's worth, Molly, I've always liked you. I'm just sorry Sean didn't have better sense when he decided to act out over this business with the family. It was rash, and I'm certain he would never have allowed it to begin if he'd thought you would be hurt."

Molly was the one who should have known better. She wasn't the right woman for Sean. It wasn't news to her. She'd known it from the start. It was just that some small part of her had been holding out hope that he'd be able to prove her wrong.

∽∽∽

It was Thursday night before Sean made it back to Chicago, and he only made it back that quickly because he'd practically worked through the night Wednesday to do it. He didn't want to spend another night away from Molly. Leaving the way he had was a fuckup he'd been paying for for days and one his ego hadn't let him fix.

What happened at the wedding with Paula and Adelynn had been utter bullshit. Paula was on a first-name basis with everyone but hadn't even offered Molly the option. And then that business with Adelynn essentially suggesting Molly was on Sean's payroll for sex?

Fuck Adelynn Wakefield and anyone else who dared to talk down to Molly. It made him sick.

Sean's fists balled.

They'd been so close. He could see it in Molly's eyes, feel it in the way she leaned in to him... She'd been about to take the leap. And he'd been making all the best plans about what came next. They were going to go home and tell everyone about their relationship. And he was going to get down on one knee in front of the friends and family they loved most and ask her to marry him. She was going to say yes because she was Molly and he was Sean, and there wasn't one fucking thing better than when they were together, and they both knew it.

But then reality had come crashing down in the form of two stuck-up snobs.

He'd been worried from the start Molly wouldn't put up with the superficial bullshit that made up half his life. And what happened the very first time she even dipped a toe in that shallow pool? Paula Stratton and Adelynn Wakefield.

It was a small wonder Molly hadn't turned around from that encounter and broken things off with him on the spot. For a minute, he'd thought that's what was happening, and then he'd gotten the call from his dad, and he'd grabbed hold of the hotel emergency with both hands.

Oh, it was legit. Wyse was about to break ground in Switzerland, and the deal was on the brink of falling through. His father was flying out to handle negotiations in person, which meant Sean was needed in New York. He'd had to leave, but he could've handled the departure differently. He could've talked to Molly more before he left, only he'd been afraid if he gave her time to talk, she'd tell him it was over. That she didn't want his life. So instead, he'd thrown himself into the work, letting day after day go by with little more than a text. And each night, before he finally gave in to fatigue, he told himself she was still his.

Now here he was, with more than twenty-four hours since her last response, a text telling him they'd talk when he got back.

It didn't take a genius to figure out that wasn't code for "Can't wait to see you, lover!"

The lights in her apartment windows were burning bright when the driver dropped him off. He trudged up the stairs, all the things he needed to tell her getting jumbled up with all the reasons she might not want to hear them.

He let himself into Molly's apartment and tossed his keys on the table by the door as he called out to let her know he was there. A second later, she was standing in her bedroom doorway, dressed in the denim skirt that drove him crazy and a long-sleeved T-shirt with a T. rex on the front. Classic, gorgeous, perfect Molly.

One look and it was like suddenly everything was right in the world again. Whatever the resolution with the hotel in Switzerland, it didn't matter. All the Paulas and Adelynns in the world didn't matter.

The only thing that did matter was making things right with this girl so he could get his ring on her finger. Hopefully, she'd be willing to tell her brother about them before they did...but hell, he'd take her any way he could get her.

"I love you," he announced, knowing what a jackass he had to sound like but not caring so long as he got to say the words and she got to hear them.

"Sean." She sighed, her focus suddenly dropping to the floor, and the express train to his happily ever after ground to a screeching halt. Because that one word, those four little letters, reminded him that just being back might not be enough. Not after this week.

"I'm sorry I didn't call," he began, cutting off whatever she'd intended to follow his name.

Her hand was already up, waving his apology away.

"It's okay. But we need to talk."

She still wasn't meeting his eyes, but hers were blinking in quick repetition, gutting him as he realized it was because of tears.

"Molly," he pleaded, not even knowing what he was asking for, except for whatever was happening in that moment to stop.

"This isn't working." Her words were a whisper, but they met him like a wrecking ball.

"What do you mean, it isn't working?" he asked, forcing a calm into his voice he didn't feel. He knew what she was saying. Of course, he fucking knew. And he knew why. But still, he couldn't accept it.

"I mean, I don't think we should be together like this, like a couple, anymore."

The bag in his hand dropped to the floor, and he

walked over to the couch where once upon a time, Molly had crawled across his lap, where they'd watched hours of yarn porn, where she'd fallen asleep against his chest and made him feel, for the first time in his life, like there was only one path. One thing that mattered.

Her.

He looked down at that couch and then sat in the single chair instead.

Christ, he felt like he was drowning. Like water was lapping at his chin, too close to his mouth. That any second, he would go under.

Running his hand through his hair, he pulled himself together. Straightened his tie and looked at the woman he loved looking back at him like he was a regret. She was still standing where she'd been when he'd walked in, still looking like everything he wanted. But it felt like she was getting farther away by the second.

He had to remain cool. If there was any chance of salvaging his relationship with her—his friendship— then he was going to have to keep his shit together. Be reasonable. Rational.

"Is this because of that Wakefield woman? Because Molly, if it is, I swear I already—"

"It's not. Not entirely." Then she wrapped her arms around her middle and shook her head, letting her hair fall like a veil in front of her eyes. He remembered how she used to do the same thing when she was fifteen because she didn't want him—anyone—to see her.

Molly.

He cleared his throat. Took a measured breath.

She sighed and walked over to him, sitting at the edge of the coffee table. "Sean, these weeks we shared were like a fairy tale." She swallowed, blinking quickly. "It's time I'll always cherish. But the kind of future we'd have together in the real world isn't the kind of future I want. Not for myself. Not for either of us."

He wanted to bolt out of his seat and tell her that was garbage. Pull her hard against him and kiss her until she realized how wrong she was. He wanted to demand to know how she could have looked at him the way she did, made him feel all the fucking things he did, and not see that what they had was real. It was *everything*.

Only maybe that was the problem. Maybe it had never been all that for Molly. And maybe that's why she'd been so hesitant to tell anyone about them. Yes, they had chemistry between them. That part was irrefutable, but beyond the physical, beyond the friendship that had been between them for over ten years, maybe that certain something he'd been looking for in all the women he'd dated over the years and had only found with Molly…maybe it just wasn't there for her.

She'd tried. Given them a chance. But ultimately, Molly didn't want the kind of life Sean had to offer.

"So that's it?" he asked quietly. Resigned. "We're over?"

Was the flash of pain in her eyes his imagination?

"We'll always be friends," she whispered. "But the part that was *more than* friends has to be done."

Sean nodded. The only thing he could do now was let her go.

Chapter 21

IT USED TO BE THAT WEDNESDAYS WERE THE NIGHTS MOLLY looked forward to all week. Whether she was working or not, she'd be able to see all the people she loved most, gathered together in her favorite place. But here she was, two weeks since she and Sean had ended their relationship, and her stomach was roiling over the evening ahead.

Last week, she'd had a reprieve when Sean was called out of town again. But now he was back. He'd even texted on Monday to let her know he'd be there. So for days, she'd been making herself sick, anticipating what it would be like to sit across from him and know that thing between them was broken. That he wouldn't be shooting her the smiles meant just for her, that it wouldn't be a matter of time until he found a way to get her alone, to back her up against some wall and—

She cleared her throat and tried to hide beneath a bar menu she'd memorized before it went to print, hoping that no one showed up until she'd fought back the stupid tears that seemed to reside only a single thought away these days.

Not surprisingly, Brody showed up first, dropping into the seat at her right. He was wearing jeans and a long-sleeved charcoal-gray T-shirt that looked like it was at max capacity handling the brawn beneath. One wrist was sporting a wide leather bracelet and the other a watch that probably cost more than what she made in a year. His hair was pulled back in a tie she'd bet he put in and took out six times over the course of the day.

"How's it going, boss man?" she asked, going for the kind of casual and easy she hadn't felt in any part of her life since before she and Sean said goodbye.

"Not bad, Moll. Lucky for you Jill didn't want to give up that shift tonight. New bartender had some kind of bug, showed up, and hurked—like, full-on projectile—five minutes after walking in the door. Jill was scrambling for an hour to get someone to fill in."

Her hopes soared. "Are you short? You know I can cover the bar." Maybe she wouldn't have to just sit there all night. At least she wouldn't be stuck sitting five feet away from the lap she desperately missed crawling into.

"Nah, she's got it covered. Besides, you look like you could use a break."

"Good to know it shows," she said with a laugh. "Wonder if I've got some mild version of what the new guy has." Whether the persistent stomach upset was viral or not, she'd be able to use it as an excuse to cut out early. Not that she'd catch up on any rest even if she did. She was exhausted all the time, but no matter when she went to bed, all she did was toss and turn, thinking about Sean and what it had been like for a little while. What it had been like at the end, when she'd told him it was over and he'd sat there looking completely impassive. No denial. No demand. Just nodding along until finally, there had been nothing more to say and he'd left.

Shoot. She didn't want to start crying again, especially with Em and Jase and Sarah and Max all headed toward the table.

Sarah's brows pulled together as she neatly tucked herself into the chair between Brody and Max. "Molly, you okay?"

Brody had a hand up, signaling Jill to come over. "Bug going around. Don't let her share your beer."

Sarah frowned at her. "Again?"

She could have kissed Brody right then, but since the guy had been warning everyone off an exchange of germs, she figured better not to.

They were all laughing and joking around when Sean showed up a half hour later. Molly knew the second he walked through the door. She could feel the pressure change in the room around them. That queasy sort of nervous tension accumulating deep in her belly.

Their eyes met from across the bar, and he stopped. Just stood there for a second like maybe he wasn't going to stay.

That pause nearly killed her. Because this was Sean. *Her Sean.* And after almost two weeks of not seeing each other, instead of running up to him for the giant bear hug that she'd always considered her due, she sat glued to her chair, willing her eyes away from the clean lines of his chiseled face and that half-cocked smile she knew wasn't coming.

"Hey, guys," he said, settling into the open chair across the table.

The way his eyes drifted past her without stopping had her stomach kicking up another revolt. Pressing a hand to it, she looked away, blowing a slow breath through her nose.

She could get through this.

In time, maybe she'd even be able to look at Sean

without thinking about how close she'd been to having him forever. Without wondering how very bad it would have been to pretend she didn't know what being with her might cost him.

No. She never could have done that to him. And the very fact that Sean hadn't put up more than a cursory argument when she'd told him it was over was all the evidence she needed to confirm she'd done the right thing. No matter how much it hurt.

When Molly had it together, she returned her attention to the table and found Emily drumming her fingers, watching her intently. Oh no. She knew that look.

"Enough's enough, Molly. Who's the guy?"

Max's face lit up. "You dating someone, Little Sis?"

She was going to have to tell them something. But right then, all she could think was that she could feel Sean's eyes on her, waiting for her answer.

Time to tug up the big-girl panties.

"No guy. Not anymore," she answered as casually as she could manage. Molly reached for the beer Jill had brought over and then, on second thought, put it back.

"It's over already?" Sarah asked, her pretty smile melting into a pout. "That stinks."

Emily was nodding in agreement, but she wasn't through. "So what happened? Two weeks ago, you thought this might be the one."

Molly was shaking her head, that sick feeling growing by the minute as heat spilled into her cheeks. From the corner of her eye, she could see Sean leaning forward in his chair.

"No. That's not what I meant," she lied, wondering why she hadn't just kept her mouth shut.

Emily sighed, her eyes filling with compassion. "You were all breathless and whispery, like you could barely keep from telling us his name. Molly, you were so excited. What happened?"

"Yeah, Molly," came the voice she couldn't stop remembering, midnight gruff at her ear. "What happened?"

She turned, meeting Sean's dark stare. Her walls were starting to crumble. This was too much.

Finally, she managed the truth. "We were just too different."

"Jesus, Molly," Brody muttered from beside her, but he was looking at Sean. Of course he knew.

Max grunted. "Sounds like a douche. Fuck 'em, Moll. You can do better."

She smiled, knowing her brother was just trying to be on her side. But she couldn't let it go. "Nah, he's a good guy. I want him to be happy, and I'm really hoping we can stay friends."

This was where Sean was supposed to assure her they would. Where he gave her the smile the two of them—and maybe Brody—would understand. But when she met his eyes, all she found was that same closed-off stare from two weeks ago. No words. No smile.

Nothing.

She was going to lose it. Jumping off her stool, she started cutting around Brody. "Give me a minute, guys, I'm not—"

Her stomach lurched, and the edges of her vision went dim.

"Whoa, Molly," Jase said, jumping up from where he'd been sitting at her other side. His big hand caught her beneath the elbow, the other circling around her back. "You okay? Looked like you were going down. Here, sit a sec."

Sean was standing now, a deep furrow between his brows as he watched her. "Molly?"

Brody caught a passing server and grabbed a water off her tray. "Drink some."

"I'm fine," she grumbled, taking a small sip. "I just… I think I've been fighting a bug, and it's starting to get the upper hand."

"Fighting for how long? Because you've been kind of pukey for the past few weeks." Sarah's brows furrowed, and she looked as if she might be counting on her fingers before adding quietly, "Maybe even longer."

It was the counting that snared her attention, made Molly's throat go Sahara dry as she ticked off weekends in her mind.

Too many weekends, only that couldn't be it. Her heart started to race. No way was *that* it. She missed months all the time. Had from as far back as she could remember. It's why she never bothered keeping track. Only this time…

All the clues had been there: the relentless fatigue, the tears, the loss of appetite, the achiness she'd thought meant her period was finally coming…and then figured was stress or a bug when it didn't. But for every obvious sign, there'd been another equally compelling explanation: a broken heart.

She looked across the table at where Sean had gone deadly still.

"Oh my God, Molly." Emily's eyes went wide, her palms flattening over the table as she leaned in, the action pulling along the rest of their friends at the table as well. "Could you… I mean, is it possible you might be pregnant?"

The reactions around the table ran the gamut.

Max shot back in his chair with a dismissive grunt. "Fuck, Emily, come on."

Jase raised a brow, looking from Molly to his wife and then back again.

Sarah's eyes bugged as she took in Molly's face and then turned to her husband, resting a hand gently on his arm.

Brody muttered a quiet "fuck," running a wide hand down his face.

But it was Sean who Molly couldn't look away from, the way his head came up in slow motion, his eyes demanding answers to a question she hadn't even considered until only seconds before.

She opened her mouth to tell him, *No. Not to worry*. That they'd been careful, but they both knew they hadn't been quite as careful as they could have. Sure, he'd always *finished* with a condom, but they'd almost never started that way. Which meant it most definitely *was* possible.

And that's the moment the queasiness took it to the next level.

Molly pushed back from the table and darted to the bathroom, barely making it in time.

The door opened behind her, and then strong hands were there helping her to her feet as the only voice that mattered sounded at her ear.

"Come here, Molly," Sean said, pulling her against his chest and wrapping his arms around her. "I've got you."

Tears rushed past her lids as the reality of it hit her. It couldn't be.

Pushing back from his arms, she wiped her face and walked over to the sink to rinse her mouth. Meeting Sean's eyes in the mirror, she gave him a watery smile. "We don't know anything yet."

The look he gave her suggested otherwise. "How long?"

Long enough that she should have thought about it. "Since before we went camping."

He blinked, those deep-brown eyes dropping to her belly as he nodded, no doubt remembering the same things she was. How reckless they'd been, and not just that first time.

She was always so careful. About everything, especially sex. But with Sean, she'd just felt so safe. So right. So caught up and carried away. And when she should have cared enough about him—about herself and her plans, God, *his plans*—to just *stop and think*, she hadn't thought at all.

"Sean," Molly whispered, her voice breaking. "What are we… How are we…?"

"Together, like always. Whatever the results, whatever you decide…I'll be there," he answered, meeting her eyes with the kind of conviction powerful enough that for one perfect second, she actually believed.

The bathroom door flew open, and she jumped, instinctively stepping away from Sean as Max stalked in. "Who the fuck is the guy?" he demanded. "Jesus Christ, Molly, I didn't even know you were dating."

Sean straightened, and Molly sent him a pleading look. She wasn't ready to see him laid out on the ladies' room floor by her brother.

Max turned to Sean. "Did you know?"

"Yeah," he said, looking Max in the eye. "I—"

"Max," Molly cut in, desperately pulling at his sleeve as she ducked into his line of sight. "I'm sorry I didn't want to tell you. It was new, and I was nervous…and then we broke up."

Sean's hand landed on Max's shoulder, bringing his attention back around. This wasn't good. "Look, Max, I need you to give Molly and me a couple minutes. I know you want answers, and you'll get them, but just let me talk to her first. Then I'll talk to you."

She closed her eyes as another layer of guilt landed squarely on her shoulders. Sean hated to lie—to anyone—but for her, he'd done it. Now the truth was coming out, and her refusal to let Sean be honest with Max was going to seriously damage their friendship.

"*You'll* talk to me?" Max rubbed the back of his head and let out a humorless laugh. "Okay, I see where this is going. But take it easy, Sean. The girls aren't even back from the place on the corner with the pee-stick thing."

Molly nodded. "Okay, but umm, maybe we should take it out of the ladies' room for now. In case any customers need to use it. Sean, could you let me talk to my brother a minute in Brody's office?"

Both guys seemed to register that they were in the ladies' room for the first time and followed her out to the hall. But when Molly and a bristling Max started for the office, Sean kept pace. She stopped at the door, meeting the intensity of his eyes. She could see Sean was already at his limit and didn't want to risk what might happen if he were the one to tell Max about them. Her brother needed to understand why his best friend hadn't been straight with him from the start—that it had been because of her—*before* he went ballistic. "Sean, please."

Max shouldered past, too spun up to register the silent exchange happening between them. "Sean, I get that you two have probably cooked up some sort of secret pact about this shit, but this is Molly's fuckup and— *Jesus, man?*" he demanded as Sean grabbed him by the front of his shirt and shoved him into Brody's office.

"This is no one's *fuckup*," Sean grated out, vibrating with anger. "Do you understand me?"

So much for wanting to explain. Turned out that having Sean get in his face was all the explanation Max needed. That sharp intellect of his kicked back in, and his cold gray stare narrowed, threatening like a storm. "No. No way you did this. *To. My. Little. Sister!*"

Molly tried to get between them, but in the blink of an eye, they'd taken it to the floor. One man rolled on top of the other and then back again, fists flying as she begged them to stop.

The door burst open, and Brody came plowing in with Jase on his heels. Within seconds, they had the men separated. Brody stood between them at the ready, but it was clear they were done.

"Molly, you okay?" Brody asked, and all eyes landed on her.

"I'm fine," she promised, looking from Max to Sean. Needing each to hear her. To believe it.

"The girls are waiting for you in the ladies' room. They've got a test, if you want to take it."

Minutes later, it was official.

"So I guess maybe you didn't want to get out of Sean's tent after all?" Emily murmured as she, Sarah, and Molly all stared at the test window reading "Pregnant."

Molly laughed quietly as more tears spilled down her cheeks.

She was going to be a mother. And Sean was going to be a father.

Sarah was shaking her head, her concern split between Molly and her husband, who, according to Jill, would be good as new after ten minutes with a bag of ice on his eye.

"So Sean was the guy you thought might be the one?" she asked gently.

"I'm sorry I didn't tell you guys. I wanted to. I was just…"

"Don't worry about any of that." Emily sighed. "We always thought that maybe… I mean, there was always something a little deeper with you two. And after the weekends away at the same time… But then you were back and he wasn't."

"And you seemed so upset," Sarah added, leaning in. "I don't think either of us believed if you guys ever got together, it wouldn't last. So we assumed we'd been wrong the whole time. Chalking it up to wishful thinking, you know?"

Wishful thinking. Nodding tightly, Molly fought back another bout of tears. Yes, she knew exactly.

"It shouldn't have happened. Neither one of us was thinking clearly." Molly covered her face with her hands and whispered the truth she couldn't deny. "I was so stupid."

"What? No way," Emily countered firmly. "You were following your heart, and no one's going to judge you."

Molly peeked between her fingers, catching Sarah's raised brow and twitching lip. They started to laugh, really laugh, because that just wasn't true.

Emily's head dropped forward, and she held up her hands. "Okay, Max will."

Sarah bit her lip. "But that said, if you want to talk about it, we're here."

Molly nodded. "I will. I want to. But right now, I need to talk to Sean. And probably Max too."

Sarah started toward the door but stopped before opening it. "Molly, I know what a big part of your life Max is. He loves you like crazy and only wants to make things better, but sometimes he forgets you aren't his responsibility anymore. It's okay to remind him. This... What you're dealing with tonight? It isn't really about Max. It's about you and Sean. So that's what you focus on. I'll take care of Max, and you can talk to him tomorrow."

Molly pulled Sarah in for a tight hug, trying to blink past the tears that wouldn't stop falling. "Thanks, Sarah," she whispered, thinking for the millionth time how lucky she was to have her for a sister-in-law.

"How the fuck long do those things take?" Max demanded, pushing up from the couch, only to have Jase plant a hand on his shoulder and push him back down.

Just as well. There was only room for one of them to be pacing, and all things considered, Sean considered it his due.

"One minute," Jase replied with the kind of certainty that had all of them turning his way. "I only know because I got the tests, just in case Emily decided she was ready to try. The front of the box says the results are ready in one minute."

"It's been ten," Max groused, returning the bag of ice to the side of his face and shooting Sean a scowl as he passed.

It had been twelve and a half minutes. Not that it mattered. Molly would come talk to him when she was ready. But the very fact that she hadn't already rushed in and collapsed on the couch in relief or sent some emissary to report the false alarm was telling enough.

A baby.

He rubbed at the spot at the center of his chest that felt like it was bursting and breaking all at once.

Two weeks ago, the news that Molly was pregnant would have been the best he'd ever gotten. But now, damn it, why couldn't things be different? Why didn't Molly want him?

Except, he knew why.

From his spot on the couch, Max pointed a finger at him. "I don't care how this started. What you thought you were getting into. You're going to marry her," Max stated flatly. As if it were as simple as that. As if it hadn't been Sean's first thought.

As if it weren't everything he wanted.

Max rubbed his hand over his face and winced.

Sean would feel bad about that bruise later, but for now, it served the asshole right for starting it.

Letting out a frustrated breath, he met Max's stare. "I couldn't even convince her to let me tell you we were together." He hadn't even been able to convince her to keep dating him.

Brody looked over from where the bear of a guy was holding up the wall. "Like *together* together? Not just a *thing*?"

"*Together* together." He still couldn't believe he'd thought for even a single minute that he could live with anything less than Molly's forever. But then he couldn't believe he'd managed to ignore what she meant to him for more than a decade either.

"She didn't want you to tell me *what*?" Max demanded. "This is the time to start talking. You're my best friend."

Throwing his hand out to the side, he fired back, "And *she's* mine! What do you want me to tell you, Max? That I thought this was a *forever thing*, that I wanted her like I've never wanted anyone in my life? That I'm fucking *in love with her*, but she doesn't want to be with me?" His breath was ripping though his lungs. "That even standing here knowing I'm about to have the best news of my life confirmed, something I hoped for but thought I'd never have, I still feel like I've lost everything?"

The room around him went silent, the three guys he loved like brothers staring at him without a clue of what to say.

Finally, Max pushed off the couch and walked over. Clapping him on the back, he bowed his head. "It's going to be okay, man."

Jase and Brody echoed the sentiments, and Sean let out a heavy breath. "Sorry about your face, Max."

Wincing again, Max nodded. "I get it. *Now* I get it. And hell, you know how I am about Molly. But I should have known I didn't need to be that way with you about her."

The office door creaked open, and Molly stood in the doorway. Her eyes and nose were red, but it looked like she'd stopped crying.

Brody went to the door and ushered her in before directing Jase and Max to follow him out.

When they were alone, Sean crossed to Molly and pulled her in to his chest. It didn't matter that they'd barely spoken in weeks or that she was breaking his heart. She was Molly and he was Sean, and when the chips were down, they were there for each other.

She buried her face against his chest, and her shoulders quaked as she gave in to the tears.

Gathering her closer, he brought her over to the couch and pulled her into his lap. For a perfect moment, she rested her head against his chest, and he could almost pretend everything was going to be fine. That he was holding the woman he loved and the smallest spark of life they'd created between them. That he'd never have to let them go.

"I know you. I know you want to do the 'right thing,'" she whispered, her voice shaky. Fragile. Her fingers tucked into the gap between the buttons of his shirt. "But trust me on this, Sean. Letting you marry me because I'm pregnant wouldn't be it."

Letting him. Christ.

Did she have any idea how much it tore him up to hear that?

"All I want is for you to be happy, Moll. To know you aren't alone. That I'll be here to support you in every way." Even if it was killing him to know he couldn't make her happy the way he wanted to…with them together. How could he blame her? He understood.

Molly sniffed, pressing herself closer to him. As if on some level, she still felt like that's where she wanted to be.

Maybe there really was a chance for them to be friends again. Not like they had been before, where the boundaries were so few and far between, it had been all but inevitable they'd stumble past them at some point. But still good friends with a shared life between them, who could be a comfort to each other from time to time.

"Sean, I can take care of myself," she said gently. Then, after a pause, "And our baby."

Tears blurred his eyes. It was real now. *Our baby.*

Easing one hand between them, he covered the flat of her belly with his hand. It would be so small. So precious. Maybe even a little girl.

He cleared his throat. "I know you can, but you'll never have to." He should have stopped there, but then all he could think about was the way she'd been looking at him that last morning in the hotel. That look couldn't be faked. "Molly, we could make it work. If you—"

Molly stiffened, then began to extract herself from his hold. "Sean," she warned, getting to her feet. "Don't."

He stood too. Reached for her, but she turned away. "I can make you happy, Molly."

She spun back, tears flooding past her lashes. "You can't!"

"Since when?" he challenged, taking a deliberate step into her space and then another. She didn't move, didn't wipe at her tears or tell him to stop or back away. Those tragic pools of blue just watched as he reached for her, as he brushed a bit of silky blond from her brow and then curved his fingers around the back of her neck. "Since when haven't I been able to make you feel good, Molly?"

He ducked his head, catching her with the kiss he hadn't tried to hide, the kiss she'd seen coming but hadn't stopped. Their lips touched, and for one gut-wrenching moment, Molly tensed. Every muscle in her body on lockdown. Even her breath refusing to budge.

This wasn't how it was between them. From the first kiss, contact alone had been enough to spark an inferno. How could everything have changed within one damn night?

Only then he felt it, that warm rush of breath against his lips and the slow clutch of her fingers into his shirt as she pressed herself *closer*. It was the invitation he hadn't waited for, the one he wouldn't ignore. He kissed her hard, needing her to feel how badly he wanted her. How much he missed her. How wrong it was that they were apart.

One hand was fisted in that silky short shag, the other running the length of her back, kneading the firm muscles of her ass.

He couldn't let her go, couldn't get enough.

She moaned around the thrust of his tongue, winding her fingers into his hair that way he loved, even though it always made him look like he'd just been pulled out of the dryer. So good.

He was seducing her right there, taking advantage of every weak spot and sensual vulnerability she had. It wasn't the right time, the right place. But if he didn't stop, maybe she wouldn't either. Maybe if she just let him love her—

"Sean, what are you doing?" she gasped when his mouth found that sweet spot beneath her ear.

Simple. "Reminding you how good I can make you feel."

She pushed him away, heartbreak he couldn't understand in her eyes. Heartbreak that mirrored his own. "How good you make me feel has never been the problem."

Shaking his head, he leaned in to her. "I know there are elements about my life you don't want to be a part of. I understand. But we could work around it, Molly. If there was even a chance you thought I could make you happy...*we could find a way*. If it meant I could—"

Fresh tears filled her eyes, and quietly, she answered, "I can't spend the rest of my life being grateful to you for sacrificing yours."

The answer stunned him. Because that answer wasn't about Molly not wanting to put up with the politics of his life. That answer was about something else altogether.

"Is that what you think I would be doing?" he asked carefully.

Tears were streaming down her face, each new path slicing through his heart.

"I know you, Sean. I've known you for almost half of my life and, long term, I won't be able to give you what you need."

"I need *you*."

"Right now, you think you do, but if you take a step back, give yourself some perspective...you'll see I am right." Her eyes lowered to where she was wringing her hands in front of her. "I was there, Sean. Available, for years. But in all that time, you never looked at me and saw the kind of woman you wanted for your future. There was a reason for that."

"Because I was an idiot," he shot back.

"Because you were *realistic*. You were waiting for someone I could never be. Someone like Valerie." She turned away. "Someone who understands the social intricacies of your world. Someone with the sophistication, education, and poise to be an asset to you."

An asset? Social intricacies?

There was no way... She wouldn't have. Only in that moment, he knew. She had.

"My mother came to see you."

Molly walked across the office, stopping at the chair in front of Brody's desk. "I'd already started to figure it out on my own. She just clarified a few of the finer points."

Drawing on every reserve of calm he could muster, he took a deep breath and met her eyes. "Figured what out, Moll?"

"That I'll never belong in your world."

His jaw clenched, and it took everything he had to keep his voice level as he asked the only question that mattered. "Because *you* wouldn't be happy there?"

She shook her head, rubbing her arms. "Because neither one of us would be. Sean, being with me would cost you in ways I couldn't live with. It would impact the parts of your life that, up until now, you have never invited me into. It has already."

"Molly, that's nuts," he coughed out, frustration building fast. "What are you even talking about?"

"Adelynn Wakefield and your business relationship with her husband."

The Wakefield name alone was enough to have his fists clenching.

Molly blinked, looking away. "You don't need to protect me, Sean."

"The hell I don't," he challenged, wondering how she could not understand. "I love you."

"I know you do. You have since I was fifteen. Which is why I *know* you would do anything, say anything to make things right for me. Like bribe student housing to look the other way about me living in your dorm. Fly back from Italy to come rescue me in Texas when that jerk dumped me on vacation there. Move into my apartment so I could unload a roommate who wasn't paying his way. End a successful working relationship with a long-time business partner because his wife insulted me." She sighed, shaking her head. "Or just refuse to see reason on this because now I'm pregnant, which adds a whole new level of obligation to the mix."

She was so fucking wrong, it made him sick. Made him angry all over again.

"Molly, you aren't seeing this clearly."

Wiping her eyes with the back of her sleeve, she shook her head. "I think I am."

Chapter 22

SEAN HAD WANTED TO GIVE HER A RIDE HOME HIMSELF, BUT Molly hadn't thought she could handle any more emotional heartbreak, so she'd asked Max instead. It might have been a mistake.

"Whoa, go easy, Molly!" Max barked as she used her hip to bump open the Belfast door on their way out. "You've got a passenger in there now."

Her eyes bugged as she stared at her brother in disbelief. "It was a door. I just opened it."

"Yeah, but you bumped it with your hip. Not hard, I don't think, but…is that okay?" he asked, scrubbing a hand over the top of his head as he gave her a nervous look that was equal parts adorable and terrifying.

She was probably looking at a solid eight more months of Max in extreme overprotective mode. "I'm sure it's fine, Max."

Only then she was thinking about it, and the truth was, she didn't actually know that many people with babies—and the ones she did, she hadn't been paying attention to how they handled doors.

She looked at her brother as a fresh wave of panic started to well within her. "I have no idea what I'm supposed to do," she whispered, and oh man, the tears were kicking in too.

Max's normally steely eyes bugged wide, filling with a panic very similar to her own. He looked back into the bar, no doubt thinking about going for reinforcements. Sean and Brody were both still in there. But then he turned back to her and straightened into that big, strong superhero of a guy she'd been looking up to her entire life. The one who would never let her down.

"We're going to the bookstore, and I'm going to get you that giant instruction manual on having babies everyone uses. Then you'll know exactly what you need to do. And not do. Right?"

She nodded, tears streaming down her cheeks as she stood in the middle of the sidewalk in front of Belfast. Max wrapped her in a hug and patted her head in a way she knew he meant to be soothing but really just made her laugh and pull away. Wiping at her cheeks, she squared her shoulders and took a deep breath. "That sounds perfect, Max."

The bookstore had an entire section dedicated to pregnancy, and one look at all those titles had Molly's head spinning and her legs working an involuntary retreat—until she bumped into Max and he ushered her back toward the shelves.

"So the lady at the help desk said this is the one to start with. She gave me a list of books we can get in addition, so if you don't like it, I can bring you back tomorrow."

She held up the book and chuckled to herself. "You planning on becoming my full-time driver and personal assistant, Max?"

A touch of red tinted his cheeks, and he scowled down at the floor. "No, but I figure it's the least I can do with the way I reacted. With what I said."

Molly shook her head. "It wasn't an easy way to find out. You were blindsided."

"So were you. And even if you hadn't been, what I said was shitty." He sighed and then met her eyes. "I'm sorry, Moll. Really sorry."

Deep emotional stuff wasn't Molly's thing. Especially with her brother. It made her uncomfortable and squirmy, like there was probably some "right thing" to say that everyone else would know without having to think about it. But for Molly, the only words she could manage were the ones that came straight from her heart. "Thank you, Max."

He raised a brow. "Forgive me?"

Like there was any question. "I forgive you."

But Max wasn't the only one who needed to ask for forgiveness. She blew out a long breath, and a look of pure panic flashed across his face.

"Are you okay? Should I take you to the hospital?"

Cripes. "Max, I'm fine. I just... I need to apologize too. Sean wanted to tell you about us. From the first minute we realized there actually might be an us, he wanted you to know." She laughed, thinking about that night at the campground. About the way it had felt when he had climbed into her sleeping bag and how much she'd wanted to believe everything he'd said.

She hadn't been able to resist.

Max reached for the pregnancy book and started flipping through the pages. She had a feeling he wasn't seeing a single word, just avoiding the awkward eye contact—then he winced, looking horrified as he shoved the book back at her. So maybe he'd seen a few words after all.

"Why didn't you want me to know?" he asked, nodding them toward the front of the store to check out.

They passed the aisles for self-help and diet and nutrition before she could answer him. "Part of it was I didn't want you to hurt him." She dared a glance at her brother, who was staring at the floor as they bypassed the magazines. His brow was furrowed, his jaw tensed. "I know how protective you can be about me, and even when I tell you you don't need to be, you don't always listen. I was worried you wouldn't give him enough credit."

There were six people in line and one girl checking them out. It felt like a conversation they ought to save for the privacy of Max's car, but they'd already started it, and besides, she didn't recognize anyone. So when Max asked her, "Why not?" she answered.

"Maybe because I was having a hard time giving it to him myself."

"*Molly*."

And then because she'd given him that much, she gave him the rest. "And I think maybe I was embarrassed to admit *I thought* we might have a chance. I mean, we all know what Sean wanted for his life…and I'm not exactly it."

She could see her brother struggling for something to say. He wanted to tell her she was wrong, just like she wanted to hear it. But they both knew better, and in the end, he just pulled her in for a hug.

———✳———

Six days later, Sean was wearing a hole through the hardwood in Max's living room, while Sarah spent the evening at Molly's place. Max pulled a couple of beers from the fridge and handed one to Sean.

"You ask her again?"

Sean nodded, taking a long draw. He'd been over to see Molly every day since finding out about the baby, trying to get through to her on—well, anything, but it wasn't happening. Not yet.

"She said no to marrying me. No to living together. No to dating casually and just letting things happen—and after that one, she asked me if I thought she was an idiot." At this point, he was pretty sure they were all in agreement that *he* was. "I asked her if she'd thought about slowing down with her workload."

Looking up, Max asked, "How'd that go over?"

"About as well as when I brought up child support."

Max grimaced, shaking his head. "Anything you didn't ask her this time?"

He hadn't asked if she thought about him. If she missed being in his arms the way he missed having them around her, because it had made her cry the last time, and her tears were more than he could handle.

"Why can't she see that she's all I want?" he demanded, looking at her brother because he was the closest thing to Molly Sean could get. "That this has nothing to do with circumstances or obligations or anything other than the fact that I love her. That I'm *in love with her*."

Because there was a difference.

"Maybe because she knows you?"

Sean stopped where he was, wondering if Max was looking for a matching set of shiners. "That's exactly what she said. Only it's total bullshit, because if she knew me so very well, she'd know that leaving me to save me from my good intentions was breaking my heart and making us both miserable."

That was the worst of it. Knowing they were both suffering.

Molly hadn't left him because she didn't want him—but because she didn't believe he could really want her. It was killing him to think of her lying there in bed at night, feeling alone.

Worse, feeling like he found her lacking in any way.

"Look at it from her side a minute, will you?" Max suggested, moving into the living room and taking the seat next to the fireplace.

After all the pre-Sarah years of lawn chairs and milk crates, it was still fucking weird seeing Max's place fully furnished.

"Her side how?" And maybe that was part of his problem. Sean still didn't entirely get her side.

"She's a maid who manages a bar part time." Max shrugged. "You really gonna stand there and tell me that's what you had in mind when you started looking for the future Mrs. Wyse?"

"How the hell can you keep selling her short like that?" Sean demanded, willfully ignoring what he didn't want to face. "She's a hard-working, self-taught entrepreneur balancing two businesses with an eye on breaking into a third. While working a fourth. She might not have a degree, but she's one of the sharpest, most intelligent people I know, and if I could get her to take one, I'd give her any damn job in my hotel she wanted, because I know without a fucking doubt that she'd be able to learn it."

Max squinted at him, scrubbing the back of his head. "She's my sister. I know she's smart. It's the rest. The pedigreed shit you've been so focused on until"—he drew a slow breath—"until you started screwing my sister. For years, any time you began seeing one of these women your parents shoved in front of you, the first thing you'd give us was the criteria she met. The right name, the right school, and all the bullshit that went along with them. The polish and grace and sophistication. How the hell do you think Molly's ever going to feel like she belongs in your world—like *you think* she belongs there—when she's had your 'ideal' shoved down her throat at every turn since she was old enough to make the comparisons?"

Sean stopped his pacing and looked at Max, a sinking feeling in his gut. It had never been his ideal, but all Molly had ever seen was him going along with it. "How the fuck am I going to convince her?"

Max met his eyes. "You know how stubborn Molly can be."

Sean gave Max a look. "Seriously, man?"

"I know you know. And I think I've got an idea. But you're going to have to follow two rules."

"Anything," Sean said.

"Okay, rule number one: Back off. I know it's going to be hard, but you gotta give Molly some space."

Sean's molars locked down. He didn't like the sound of that one bit. But if Max thought he had a plan, Sean was willing to keep an open mind. "Give her a chance to get her head together. Do some clear thinking."

"Exactly. Too much has been happening too fast. Our girl can handle a lot thrown at her at once, but even Molly has her limits." Max walked over and clapped Sean on one shoulder. "And right now, you're just another source of pressure. Let her breathe a little, and she'll remember you're her biggest source of comfort. More than Brody. Shit, even more than me."

"Really?" The grin he couldn't fight made Sean feel like a grade-A ass, but damned if that wasn't what he'd needed to hear. Then he thought about what it was like when he didn't get to see her, and the smile dropped from his mouth. "How long?"

"That's going to depend on you. And following rule number two: Figure out what she wants most, and give it to her."

Sean's lungs deflated. "She wants me to let her go, Max. And not just for some time to breathe."

Max crossed his arms and met Sean with a level stare. "If that's what she *really* wants, then you're going to have to do it. But I've seen Molly when you haven't been around for a while. And I'm telling you, it's not pretty."

———

"Come on, Moll," Brody chided, easily taking the drink-laden tray off her hands and carrying it through the bar himself. "We talked about this. You were going to call it a day by six. No exceptions."

Molly followed him to the table and started handing out pints, while her boss stood flashing that teddy bear grin around as he waited for her to finish.

Then tucking her under his arm, he led her back to his office and sat her down. "What are you still doing here?"

Slumping back in the couch, she sighed and started picking at her thumbnail. "I'm going crazy at home. I've got work I can do, but every time I sit down, I can't concentrate."

Brody pulled a chair over. Resting his elbows on his widespread knees, he nodded his head to the side. "Give yourself a break. It's a lot to adjust to in only a few weeks."

She nodded. He was right, but it was more than that, and they both knew it.

Brody rolled his shoulder. "You seen him?"

"Not for a few days." More like a week. After they found out about the baby, Sean had been dropping in to see her every day. Every day, asking her to marry him. Every day, breaking her heart a little more by making her say no.

But the last time, it had been different. She'd sensed it from the moment he stepped into her apartment. Seen it in the way he searched her eyes. Heard it in that last plea.

"Molly, I'm asking you to really think about this. We could have it all. Just give me a chance to show you."

She wanted to. God knew she did.

But she couldn't do it. Not to herself, not to her baby. Not to the man she loved.

She couldn't spend the rest of her life feeling like the burden that never went away. The charitable sacrifice filed under "the right thing."

She wouldn't.

So she'd said no. And right there before her eyes, something had changed in him. He had stopped being *her Sean* and, within the span of a handful of breaths, had become the Sean she recognized from those few times his professional and personal lives overlapped.

He'd told her he would be in touch and kissed her cheek when he said goodbye.

That had been five days ago.

She knew what it meant. Sean was giving her what she'd asked for.

"He's going to be there for you, Moll. You can't

doubt that," Brody assured her, those compassionate green eyes holding hers.

She nodded. "I know." They just needed to get through all this first. And once things were back the way they were supposed to be, they could be there for each other as friends. As family. Just not quite together.

Brody wasn't satisfied until he'd fed her dinner, warned her against taking anything from the Baby Readiness Binder Jase had put together for Janice without checking for a more current study, and shared the latest article he'd come across regarding infant sleeping habits. She gave the big guy a hug and then headed out into the cool, dusky evening.

She hadn't even made it to the corner when her phone rang.

It was Sean's lawyer, asking if Molly would be free the next morning.

—␣␣␣—

Molly stepped off the bus twenty minutes before her appointment and stared up at the sleek new building that had only wedged itself into the Chicago skyline the year before. The cost of office space in the glass-and-steel mammoth was supposed to be through the roof, but she imagined any lawyer a Wyse retained would be more than able to cover it.

Wide curved steps led up to an open, gleaming entry where businessmen and businesswomen streamed in and out in what seemed to be an endless supply. Slowly walking up, Molly scanned the seating areas by the fountains and potted trees for Sean, certain he would be waiting for her. They hadn't communicated about the appointment, but there was no chance he wasn't aware of it.

Another five minutes passed. She tucked her coat around herself a little tighter and followed the crowd through the doors, her sense of unease growing with every step. Where was he? She knew she'd been unreasonable the last time Sean had brought up the subject of child support and figured he'd set this appointment up to ensure she understood there were laws in place to protect her and their child. They needed to come to an understanding about it. She was prepared, or at least she would be when she found Sean. The bank of elevators for Derschel, Willis & Gray was located on the second level, so she took the escalator and looked out over the airy atrium, searching again.

She chewed her cheek and pulled out her phone. No texts. No missed calls.

Reaching the Chicago offices of the country's top law firm on the seventy-sixth floor, Molly was greeted by name by a man she'd never met before, offered something to drink, and then ushered into an expansive dark-wood conference room that was every kind of intimidating. A team of lawyers lined one side of the table, and an even bigger team lined the other side. Her side. Apparently, Sean had retained Derschel, Willis & Gray on her behalf, and the other guys were there to represent him. Though he would not be present.

Molly thought about the crackers tucked in her canvas bag and wondered if she was going to need them.

A handsome man a few years older than she was made the introductions around the table before giving her his own name. Derek Greggory. Sean's half brother and boarding-school rival. Turned out Sean thought he'd have an extra incentive to make sure Molly's interests were being served. Before she'd even had a chance to process that she was meeting *Derek*, the lawyers started to explain why she'd been asked there. The words were coming—her lawyers periodically jumping in to clarify a point regarding child support during pregnancy and after or offer an opinion—but all Molly could focus on was that Sean wasn't there.

She wasn't going to see him.

And then they handed her a document with a letter from Sean clipped to the top, and her world crumbled.

Molly,

You were right. I hadn't been honest with myself about the kind of future I wanted. But I see things clearly now. I will forever be grateful to you for helping me to reevaluate my priorities before I made a mistake that might have cost us both the future we deserve.

In light of recent events, I believe I have found a woman uniquely qualified to be my partner through life. Before she is willing to commit, she requires some assurances and security. She needs to know that I will put her and the child we will someday have above all others. To do this, I need to make a clean break.

In time, I hope you will understand.

SEAN

Tears spilled down her cheeks, nearly blinding her as the lawyer spelled out the terms of the one-time cash payout for the care and support of their child. The nondisclosure agreement, with penalties severe enough to ensure it would never be violated by either party.

Sean was leaving her. She'd told him he needed a woman like Valerie, and *he'd found one*. He'd found one, and now he was throwing the other side of his life away?

Because that's what this agreement was about. Sean, her best friend in the world, the father of her child and constant in her life, was offering her a check so that he could walk away and never look back. Ever. There wouldn't be any changing his mind after this. The penalty for Sean violating the NDA was a price greater than he would ever be able to pay. And he'd put it in a legal, binding contract and asked her to sign it.

What had happened to the man she'd fallen in love with not once, but twice? The lonely boy who'd ached for a family capable of emotional connection so much that he'd build one for himself. He'd made her his family. He'd made Max and Brody and Jase his family. And now he was not only prepared to walk away from all of them—because that's what this agreement meant—but also from this tiny life that was the two of them together in the most precious, incomprehensible way.

"This isn't real," she sniffed, looking from one member of her legal team to the next. "You don't know him. He would never want this."

Choking back a sob, she covered her face.

Raised voices sounded from beyond the door in the back of the conference room. It opened a crack and then slammed shut as more yelling followed and then a thud that shook the walls.

Molly stared as Derek walked over and opened the door just enough to speak through it. Nodded tightly and then walked back. "I'm sorry. Nothing to be alarmed about. Just a…scheduling dispute. It's been sorted out."

Another partner slid a document in front of her. "The amount on offer is…exceptionally generous. That said, you are under no obligation to take it. We can begin working out a schedule of child support immediately."

Molly held up a hand. God, she didn't want anything at all, or at least she didn't want Sean's money. What she wanted—to be the right woman for him—she couldn't have. "Just wait. Please. I need a minute."

She pulled out her phone and called Sean, walking over to the windows overlooking Grant Park far below.

He answered on the first ring.

"What are you doing?" she whispered, clutching the phone tight. "This can't be what you want."

The sharp pull of Sean's breath sounded through the line, followed by a muffled exchange in the background. Then—"Molly, you don't have to sign it," he said, his voice raw and worn. "But I'm asking you to do it for me."

She closed her eyes and bowed her head. Listened to the silence stretch between them.

Then, returning to the table where eight lawyers sat politely waiting, she picked up a pen and, half blind with tears, signed her name across from Sean's.

"It's done," she stated dully, a cold numbness creeping through her chest.

Another rush of breath from his end, and just before he disconnected the call, he promised, "Baby, you won't regret this."

Molly blinked. A stitch pulling between her brows.

Because that didn't sound like a man who'd just put his *hotel* on the line to ensure that he would never be tied to the life he'd created. It sounded like a man who had just scored the victory of his life. It sounded like—

The back door to the conference room swung wide, and *her Sean* shouldered through, those deep-brown eyes locked with hers as he crossed the space with purposeful strides.

"Those documents set?" he asked, not bothering to look at the team of lawyers scrambling from their seats.

"Yes, Mr. Wyse."

"W-what are you doing here?" she stammered shakily, too broken and confused to make sense of the half-cocked smile on his face. He should be *dying inside*. The way she was.

"Being honest about the future I want." His hand slid around her waist, and then he was pulling her along with him out of the conference room. Like somehow he believed that was all the explanation she required.

Across the hall, there was another, smaller conference room. Through the windows, she saw two reporters with their cameras set up behind them, and an icy chill settled in the pit of her stomach.

No.

Sean reached for the door and pulled her closer. "I'm showing the woman I want as my partner through life that I put her and the child we'll be having in just over seven months above all else."

Molly's throat clenched, and fresh tears flooded past her lids. "Sean, don't. You can't."

Because suddenly, she understood what this relentless, insane man had just done. What she'd driven him to do.

His eyes went to her lips, and his mouth followed. He kissed her like she was his next breath. As if he wasn't on the brink of tossing away the thing he loved best in this world.

Then he was opening the door and pulling Molly along with him to the front of the room.

Ignoring the press, she tugged at his shirt. "Sean, please."

But he was a man on a mission and wouldn't be stopped.

"Thank you for coming today. I have an introduction and a brief statement to make. First, I would like to introduce Molly Elizabeth Brandt. Ms. Brandt is the new owner of the Chicago Wyse Hotel. In addition to the Wyse, Ms. Brandt currently runs two other successful Chicago businesses and is expecting her first child— *our child*—early next year.

"And if she ever agrees to do me the honor, I will make her my wife as soon as humanly possible. If she doesn't, well, we'll be together either way. I'm not going anywhere." He flashed her the smile her heart couldn't resist.

She was shaking her head, beyond the ability to protest verbally. There had to be a catch. A loophole. Something.

But Sean was already wrapping things up. "Any questions regarding whether I will continue to run the

Chicago location should be directed to my boss, the
Maybe-Future-Mrs.-Wyse. Thank you for coming."

The short press conference at a close, the reporters
quickly cleared out, offering their thanks and congrats as
they went. And then it was just the two of them.

Sean grinned at her. "So, Moll, should I drop my
résumé on your desk?"

"How could you do this?" she asked, her voice
unsteady. He'd given up everything.

"Easy. I already owned the Chicago Wyse. It just
took a few extra signatures to free it up, so I went to
my parents and explained that I didn't want their life.
I want you, I want our baby, and I want their support.
Apparently, I must have been fairly compelling, because
it went smoothly from there."

Her jaw went slack. "They're going to think I was
after—"

"They know what you were after, Molly. The right
thing. Setting me free. A life where you didn't have
to feel like you did growing up. And now they have a
better understanding of my priorities too."

She could only imagine what that had looked like.

"Molly, I'm sorry about my mother coming to you.
I'm sorry about what she said, what she assumed. And
most of all, I'm sorry for not doing a better job of
showing you, myself, that our life together wouldn't be
about you *fitting into* my world. You *are* my world. And
whether you're my wife or my best friend with a baby
but without benefits, what matters most is that we're
together. Because you are the only thing I don't think I
could survive without."

Her heart was pounding, her fingers trembling. "But,

Sean, this is crazy. How could you be so casual with the Wyse? You love that hotel."

He shook his head and smiled at her with all the confidence in the world. "I love you. I care about the Wyse deeply," he added with a teasing wink before turning serious again. "And there was nothing casual about what I did here today. I entrusted my business to the woman I love and believe in more than anything or anyone in this world." Taking her hand, he pulled it to his mouth for a soft kiss before pressing it to that spot she loved best above his heart. "I had to show you how important you are to me…and show you that I understand what's important to you too. I know with the way you grew up, you didn't feel wanted the way you should have, and you didn't feel secure."

She choked out a breath, suddenly seeing what Sean had done.

"I want you more than I've ever wanted anything in my life, Molly. I want our baby. But even if you decide us being a family isn't what you want, I need you to know that you and our baby are secure. Neither of you will ever want for anything…but especially not a roof over your head. You have 623 of them now. Actually more than that, because I bought your building for you too. But that's just a present, not part of the NDA or anything."

Her eyes closed as fresh tears filled with too many emotions to count spilled down her cheeks.

"Molly, say something," he begged, his voice devoid of all teasing.

"You're crazy," she whispered as her fingers caught between the buttons of his shirt and she pulled him in close.

"And you're stubborn," he growled, a breath from her lips.

She shook her head, peering up into the eyes she'd loved since she was sixteen. "I love you, Sean. I can't believe you did this... I'm sorry I—"

"Shh, let's just go back to that first part, can we?" That half-cocked smile went even wider. "So you *love* love me?"

She laughed, her heart so full, it hurt. "Yes, I do. Kind of desperately and hopelessly, and I'm pretty sure for the rest of my life."

Sean let out a slow breath, nodding once as his eyes filled with so much hope and relief and love that she wondered how she had ever doubted him.

"Then this time, Molly, I'm begging you."

Stepping back, Sean bent slowly to one knee and pulled a medium-size black velvet box from his pocket. Holding it up, he opened the lid, revealing a tiny, misshapen pair of soft, knit, green baby booties with uneven stitches and a breathtaking diamond ring tucked between them. "Please, Molly, be my wife."

It took her three tries before she could fight past the emotion and find her voice, but when she was able, she stroked her finger over one booty and asked, "Did you knit these yourself?"

Sean laughed and nodded. "They aren't perfect. But I figure by the time she gets here, I'll have mastered it."

She. He wanted a girl.

"They *are* perfect." Every single stitch was made with love.

Taking Sean by the tie, Molly tugged him to his feet and stared up into his eyes.

"I love you."

"I love you too. So *say it*. Give me the happily ever after. I want the fairy tale, baby."

She laughed, because only Sean. "Yes! I'll marry you."

Epilogue

Brody

THE SUN WAS SETTING OVER THE OCEAN, CASTING THE BEACH in a warm, golden glow. White sand sifted through Brody's toes as he stood between Jase and Max, the three of them decked out in white tuxedos with their pant legs rolled up. Emily, Sarah, and Janice stood for Molly, each of them wearing a dress of their own choosing but in matching shades of cream. The girls looked gorgeous, their smiles almost as bright as the bride's. But not a one of them could compete with the grin on Sean's face.

Jesus, that guy.

Two weeks was all it had taken to coordinate the schedules and set up the sunset beach wedding of Molly's dreams. And at least three times that Brody knew of, the guy had tried to talk Molly into flying to Vegas to elope early. Not because the planning of where to put the tiki bar or the seating chart for eight was just too much to handle—no, the guy just couldn't fucking wait to get his ring on her finger.

It wasn't like Brody hadn't seen it before. Max and Jase had been just as nuts. But watching his previously sane buddies go off the deep end never ceased to surprise him.

Now Sean had finally made it to his day. He and

Molly were exchanging rings, speaking the kind of heartfelt vows that hit Brody deep in the chest and had the couples stealing meaningful looks at each other from across the sand. The kind of vows that made him wonder what it would be like to love like that.

Brody'd had his share of relationships over the years, several that had even been serious. But never like this. And now watching as Sean pulled Molly in for the kiss that finally made her his wife, Brody rubbed at that hollow-feeling spot inside his chest, bothered by it for the first time. Not that he was about to run out in search of some girl to help him fulfill his happily ever after. First, he wasn't really built that way. And second, the only girl he'd been even remotely interested in as of late was crushing hard on someone else.

No way was he getting near that.

Everyone was jumping around cheering and whooping into the ocean air. Brody threw his arms around the newest Mr. and Mrs. Wyse, pulling them in to his bear hug. For now, watching two of his best friends in the world find their fairy-tale ending was everything he could ask for.

"Congrats, guys. I love you."

About the Author

Hard-core romantic, stress baker, and housekeeper non-extraordinaire, Mira Lyn Kelly is the *USA Today* bestselling author of more than a dozen sizzly love stories with over a million readers worldwide. Growing up in the Chicago area, she earned her degree in fine arts from Loyola University and met the love of her life while studying abroad in Rome, Italy...only to discover he'd been living right around the corner from her back home. Having spent her twenties working and playing in the Windy City, she's now settled with her husband in rural Minnesota, where their four amazing children and two ridiculous dogs provide an excess of action and entertainment. When she isn't reading, writing, or running the kids around, she loves watching the Chicago Blackhawks and action/adventure movies, blabbing with the girls, and cooking with her husband and friends.